SILVER LIGHTNING

Sasha S. Abraham

BLUEROSE PUBLISHERS
India | U.K.

Copyright © Sasha S Abraham 2024

All rights reserved by author. No part of this publication may be reproduced, stored in a retrieval system or transmitted in any form or by any means, electronic, mechanical, photocopying, recording or otherwise, without the prior permission of the author. Although every precaution has been taken to verify the accuracy of the information contained herein, the publisher assumes no responsibility for any errors or omissions. No liability is assumed for damages that may result from the use of information contained within.

BlueRose Publishers takes no responsibility for any damages, losses, or liabilities that may arise from the use or misuse of the information, products, or services provided in this publication.

For permissions requests or inquiries regarding this publication, please contact:

BLUEROSE PUBLISHERS
www.BlueRoseONE.com
info@bluerosepublishers.com
+91 8882 898 898
+4407342408967

ISBN: 978-93-5989-794-3

Cover design: Rishav
Typesetting: Rohit

First Edition: January 2024

*This book is dedicated to my family.
Your unwavering support means the world to me.*

Chapter 1

My earphones blasted with music, blocking out the shouts and the chatter of all the others in the school bus. It did its job perfectly. I didn't care whether I was missing out on the latest school gossip; about what Timmy Foster said to the teacher or whether Maria was going to be expelled or just suspended for supergluing and cutting off her arch-enemy's hair with a Crayola Safety Scissors Set.

The bus rumbled past houses, occasionally stopping to pick some kids up. My bus was the liveliest as well as the most crowded. Clearly, too many kids live in my neighborhood. Almost fifteen have to stand up throughout the twenty-minute ride and three children are squeezed in two-seaters, to make enough space for those who are left standing.

My stop being one of the first, I never had to worry about finding a seat. But sometimes, I wondered what it felt like to stand in a moving, ugly yellow-colored metal contraption.

Someone tapped my shoulder and I swung my head from the window.

'What?' I asked, as I took off one earphone.

Camilla raised her voice slightly, 'I *said*, did you do the homework Mr. Parker gave us? I really need to copy it down.'

I frowned. 'I already told you. No. Take it from someone else.'

She nodded and twisted her head to the seat behind us.

Camilla Rayson was my friend. And by friend, I mean someone whom I'm forced to pair up with in labs and projects. We didn't know each other that well, even though we'd been in the same class since first grade.

She always had a tired and exhausted face and today was no exception. She had dark circles as if she hadn't been sleeping well for a long time. Her marble gray eyes looked bleary and she kept blinking as if someone had thrown salt into them. It was as if she had literally rolled out of bed and climbed onto the bus.

The bus screeched to a halt and the jabbering subsided. There was a scramble for the door as Aheart School entered everyone's view. I got up and smoothed down my uniform skirt and slung my bag, contemplating the perfect moment to cut the line and get to the aisle.

I never did. Everyone rushed past without so much as glancing at me. Even Camilla was gone. Only a kindly-looking older girl stopped for me. I murmured a thank you and climbed down the steps. I walked slowly towards the gate of the most famous private school of my county.

But unlike the others, I snuck off to the gardener's shed. Phones weren't allowed in Aheart for sixth and seventh graders, but we brought them along for the bus rides. When we entered the school, I hid it in the gardener's shed. Whether he notices or not, he hasn't told anyone.

I walked over to a small cubbyhole and stashed it beneath a grubby bag which hadn't been moved for years.

As I made my way over to the building, I suddenly stopped dead in my tracks. The ground was shaking. My heartbeat thundered as it went on for two minutes. I looked around to see if anyone else noticed.

No one did. They kept walking indifferently.

My shoulders relaxed. I concluded that this earthquake was one of mine. *It was one of those which only I could feel.*

In class, I was forced to sit next to Camilla as usual. No one was sitting with her and I can't really blame anyone. Who would want to sit next to the girl who takes way too many leaves and appears only once in a blue moon?

'Where's your cousin?' I asked her, trying to strike a conversation.

Camilla twisted a strand of her wavy, chocolate-colored hair around her finger. 'Josh broke his left arm, the one he writes with. So there was no point for him to come.'

'What happened?'

'He fell off the roof.'

I frowned. I had seen their house before and their roof had no railings or protection. 'Why was he on the roof in the first place?'

Camilla stifled a yawn and looked as though she was too tired and sleepy to answer that with a convincing story. Luckily for her, Mr. Parker swept into the room, the bad-tempered glint in his eyes assuring everyone that whoever did not do homework was not going to get off lightly.

The lesson went on in a monotonous rhythm. Camilla continued to act tired and uninterested in everything, but that was to be expected. All the days she *does* decide to come to school, she either acts sleepy or worried. And the same is the case with Josh.

'Kendra!' Mr. Parker snapped.

I looked up with a start. 'Um, yes?'

'Are you paying attention?' He glowered.

'Of course.'

'Then tell me what I just said right now.'

My cheeks heated up in embarrassment as my eyes scanned the board and twenty others stared at me.

'Uh, you asked to find the value of y in $12y = (100 \times 8)$.'

Mr. Parker's scowl deepened. '*No*. I asked you to hand over your homework, which I assigned for you to do. And let me guess:

you were very busy due to unavoidable circumstances, so you didn't get time.'

I sat down, my face flushed red, making a mental note to find another convincing reason for missing homework.

I tried to pay attention but another tremor knocked a pen off my table.

This one had way more force than the others. I had actually gripped the sides of the desk, and the lightbulb started swinging back and forth. I thought this was a real earthquake, in the real world, but again, no one noticed.

No one except . . . Camilla.

She gripped the sides of her chair as she gave the ground an accusing glare. She snatched her pencil case that had fallen off and slammed it back on the table, and she tried to make sense of the Algebraic expressions in the textbook.

I stared, blankly. Camilla . . . *feels* the earthquakes. I wondered why I hadn't noticed this before but realized that I rarely see her, so I couldn't tell.

From the corner of her eye, she caught me looking at her. She pulled out her secret weapon of staring back at me until it was unnerving.

She kept her distance from me for the rest of the day. The tremors occurred twice again, each slightly stronger than the last, leaving me uneasy.

I decided to ask her on the bus.

I ran to get a seat and tapped my fingers impatiently as I waited for Camilla. Normally, I'm not this fidgety but this time, it was a big deal. Someone possibly knew an answer to these weird happenings.

I saw a familiar mane of shoulder length brown hair. She made her way to my seat and sat down, smiling in a friendly but uncertain way.

'Hi.'

'Hi,' I smiled. 'Didn't see you in History class today.'

'I was not feeling well,' Camilla said. 'I was in the nurse's office.'

'Do you feel the earthquakes too?' Subtle.

Camilla stared at me, baffled, but I noticed her posture become tense and on guard. 'What earthquakes?'

'You know, those tiny ones which keep happening every now and then, but no one else notices.'

Her face broke into an amused smile. 'Kendra, the last time this place was struck by an earthquake was like five years ago...'

'Not even a feather moved, yeah I know,' I grumbled. I had heard this too many times and wasn't keen on hearing it again from someone whom I knew was probably lying. I don't know what made me certain, but it did.

'Just forget I said anything,' I sighed.

'Okay,' she replied. We were quiet for some time, and she got up and gave up her seat for a sixth grader, and purposely stood as far from me as possible.

I looked away towards the window, frustrated at not getting answers. That was when I realized I had forgotten my phone in the gardener's shed.

Out of the corner of my eye, I saw Camilla take out her phone and talk to someone, not tearing her eyes off of me. I wanted to march up to her and tell her to stop lying to me.

But then, doubt started to nag. I began to wonder, "Maybe *I'm* the one going insane. Keep Camilla out of this. I can be wrong after all."

I took a deep breath and decided that the next day I would keep my eyes peeled for anything suspicious. If nothing was amiss, then maybe everything would be fine.

After reaching home, my day went normal enough. My older brother, David, came home alone. His twin, Cole reached later, looking nervous and he jumped each time the phone rang.

Before dinner was when my suspicions were confirmed. Cole had skipped school and a teacher had spotted him. And he had been doing this for a long time now.

Mom and Dad both lectured him, while David and I tried to watch TV. We couldn't help but snicker every once in a while. We both knew what he had been up to and David had long been trying to warn him about the trouble Cole was walking into.

Now, his smug and snarky proclamations of being careful were pretty amusing, listening to Mom and Dad ground him for two weeks.

But, as I said, everything was normal.

Chapter 2

A piercing headache greeted me the next day. My temples started to throb the second I opened my eyes and I winced in pain. My cat, Cottonball, completely oblivious, meowed and shifted positions from my stomach to her pillow.

I quickly got ready, put on my uniform, and went downstairs to tell my mom about the headache while I ate my cereal. She wasted no time in feeling my forehead and jabbing a thermometer in my mouth.

'Your temperature is normal, so you couldn't be having a fever,' she said, frowning. I must have looked miserable enough because she added gently, 'If you don't want to go to school today and just rest, you can.'

I thought for a while. Usually, I would take up the offer without hesitation, but my final assessment tests were coming up and I wasn't too keen on failing. So I said 'I'll be fine' but truthfully I wasn't feeling too confident.

Mom still didn't look convinced but she handed over some medicine for me to take.

'Good morning,' my dad greeted everyone as he entered the kitchen.

'Arthur, Kendra's having a headache,' Mom said.

'Is it bad?' Dad asked me, eyeing me in concern.

'Yes,' I replied. 'No temperature, though.'

'Do you want to stay home for today?' he offered.

My response wasn't much different than the one I gave Mom. So, to be on the 'safe side', he made Cole drop me off at school in his car. Dad's expression and tone assured me that argument would not be welcomed.

Cole wasn't too happy about the turn of events either. Ever since he had gotten his drivers' license, everyone had been asking him to drive them some place or the other. The fact that I kept trying to talk to him throughout didn't help his cranky morning mood.

'Why are you talking to us so much?' asked David, who was in the passenger seat. 'Oh wait, let me guess. You lost your phone?'

'It's in the gardener's shed,' I said, glumly.

When we reached, I saw that my bus was already there. I decided to stay and wait for Camilla, but not-so-surprisingly, she was absent. So was Josh.

The classes weren't all that bad. By the fifth period my headache had decreased drastically.

But just when things seemed to go back to their natural order, that's when it also went terribly sideways.

I was making my way to science class, when I heard voices from the Forbidden Room. The room which always remained locked and no one was allowed to enter.

A streak of curiosity got the better of me. I crept closer to the door, to hear two *very* familiar voices.

'Are you sure no one will find it here? If it falls into the wrong hands, it's going to be a disaster.'

'Well, she said that no one uses this room. I can't believe I'm saying this, but we're going to have to trust Kendra on this.'

On hearing my name, I instinctively pushed open the door. It stopped abruptly after opening a fraction, as if something was blocking it. I gave it a shove and it flew open.

My mind couldn't comprehend the two people, before the person blocking the door pulled me in and someone shut the door.

'Here's the deal,' Sean started. 'You don't say a word about this to anyone, and Cole will give you half his allowance.'

'Wait, what?' Cole exclaimed. 'Sean -'

'Do you want her to go around telling everyone about this?'

'Fine,' Cole sighed. 'Take my allowance which I worked for all summer at Burger King.'

My mouth hung open, my mind not quite past the fact that Cole and his best friend Sean were at my school, much less snooping around.

'What are you *doing* here?' I demanded.

'Not important,' said Cole, who I just noticed was standing on a chair adjacent to a mahogany wardrobe. 'But you *cannot* tell anyone we were here.'

My eyes drifted up to the top of the wardrobe. 'What's up there?'

'Nothing's up there,' Sean replied, sharply. 'Focus Kendra. Promise you won't tell anyone about this.'

I couldn't tear my eyes away from the top of the wardrobe, but I nodded slowly. I didn't want to get sucked into any unnecessary drama, but definitely wanted to know what on earth was going on.

The bell suddenly rang and Sean ducked out the open window. Cole gave me one last warning look before he jumped out. I heard a car engine start.

I wish I could say that Cole's death stare knocked sense into me to not poke around.

It didn't.

I scrambled up the chair Cole had been standing on and peered over. My breath hitched when I saw what was there on the top.

It was the size and shape of a basketball, except it was made of glass. It looked so fragile, I was afraid that if I touched it, it would shatter to a million pieces. A thick mist of some sort was trapped inside. Half of its color was a deep, earthy brown, while the other was a bright, electric blue, both sides slowly merging with each other almost magically.

It reminded me of my eyes. I had heterochromia, or whatever it is you call it when your right eye is brown and left eye is blue.

I reached out for it.

Suddenly, my headache struck again without warning, the pain almost making me black out. Red spots danced in front of my eyes as I clung to the wardrobe and winced. I had to get out of there before the pain got any worse.

I jogged to my Science class and made no effort to pay attention in class.

For one, the headache was trying to split my brain in half, and I was too busy dishing out theories as to why Cole and Sean were in my school.

They came with that glass orb, and if I had to guess, I'd say that they were trying to hide it. But why? And why would my headache reappear at the exact moment that I reached out to touch it?

The earth trembled. But that was not what surprised me.

A loud *BOOM* went up in the distance, as if a bomb just exploded. I jumped out of my skin and clutched the sides of the table. Another explosion went up in the distance.

I looked around wildly, my heart hammering in my ribcage. I wondered why on earth an alarm or something hadn't gone off. But again, no one noticed.

A twinge of fear crawled up inside me. I was starting to think that there was more to these earthquakes than I thought.

'Why don't you go see what it is?', said a tiny voice in my head.

I looked up. Mrs. Johnson was facing the board, and everyone else's heads were bent down to their work. Without thinking, I got up and ran out of the class. I hoped no one saw me, but after hearing Mrs. Johnson call out my name in protest, I knew that that was out of the window.

I didn't stop. Instead, I tried to outrun her in case she was following.

I was now out on the football field. This was where I had heard it come from. I was determined to find out what was going on and put an end to it. I wasn't going to allow myself to be pulled into a situation I didn't ask for.

'Kendra?'

I turned round sharply and came face-to-face with Camilla. A very concerned and suspicious Camilla. There was a crazy light in her eyes, which I did not like at all. A light which seemed . . . unearthly.

Camilla raised her eyebrows and pursed her lips. 'Where are you going?'

I felt like screaming but I controlled my voice as I said, 'I'm skipping class.' With that, I turned around and got the fright of my life to see Josh standing there and staring at me.

Josh looked much like his cousin. His hair was a shade darker, but their gray eyes were identical. Meaning even he had the glint of a madman.

Seeing him looking at me as if I were a dangerous zoo animal who has escaped from its enclosure, I took it as my cue to run.

They followed me, power-walking and yelling things like 'Come back!'

If they thought I was going to look back, they were delusional beyond belief.

I just wanted to get as far away from them as possible. Something about them and their behavior had my brain screaming alarm bells.

The chase was going pretty well for me, until I conveniently tripped. I scraped my knee against a rock, and my shrieking headache refused to go anywhere. I scrambled to get up, but it was useless. Camilla and Josh had run when I fell and now they had caught up with me.

'Sit down, Kendra,' Josh ordered.

'I'm not going to –'

'Sit.'

I admitted defeat and sat on the ground. I looked around and found no one to be nearby. It was just me and them.

Camilla froze. 'Hold on. Your blood . . . it's red.'

'Yes,' I said, slowly. 'Yes, it's red.'

Camilla turned to Josh and said, *'Maybe we made a mistake. Maybe she's not the one we're looking for.'*

Something about her voice had changed, about her accent and the way she formed her words, but I understood completely.

Josh frowned. *'But it can't be a mistake. The description matches her perfectly. We've been all over this region and she's the only one we've found who fits the description. Besides, there is no way I'm going to search another country twenty four-seven. Either she's the one, or someone else will have to take the job.'*

'I'm going to stop you right there,' I interrupted, *'What do you mean by description? What are you guys* talking *about?'*

Both froze. They wore such shocked expressions that you'd think that I had just confessed a crime.

Camilla spoke, *'You can understand what we're saying?'*

'Of course, I can understand what you're saying . . .wait a minute,' I said, finally realizing that all this time I had been speaking in a foreign language.

My mind was spinning circles, and I badly wanted to run away again. But my bleeding knee and petrified body had other ideas.

I jumped out of my skin at the sound of another *bang* going off in the distance. I looked around to see no smoke or fires. Rather, the sounds and skies were clear as day.

Camilla's expression softened. 'I know this is scary, but you have to trust us.'

'Trust you? I barely know you!' I exclaimed. 'How am I going to trust you two if you're not giving me answers?'

'You will get them,' Josh assured. 'But can you please come with us first?'

'I'm not going anywhere!' I cried, hysterically.

Camilla sighed, like her patience was being tested. 'You know, we could very well drag you away. That's how it's supposed to happen. But if you're being unreasonable, then we have no problem being the same.'

'How am I being unreasonable?' I said, lowering my voice. 'You say you want to take me somewhere I don't know, and my day is going crazy as it is. Tell me how I'm being unreasonable.'

Josh looked at his cousin, as if to say, *She's got a point.*

Then he turned to me. 'How about this: we take you wherever we want to take you, and if it's too much for you, we will bring you back.'

I hesitated. 'You promise?'

'We promise.'

I slowly nodded.

Josh held out his hand and I stared at it. 'I don't have any gum, if that's what you want.'

He frowned. 'What? No. I want your hand.'

'Why?'

'You can't teleport, right? We'll have to lend you strength.'

The more I listened to them, the more reasons my brain gave to turn and run.

I took his hand and Camilla held the other. All I could hope was that nothing would happen and all this would be a very cruel joke. Unfortunately, it wasn't.

Our palms started growing warm. I felt drowsy, and my headache was a mere buzz in my head, like an annoying fly. I wanted to sleep, but my conscience told me to stay awake.

I felt dizzy and I closed my eyes for a minute. Camilla and Josh's hands felt like hot iron. My legs were as stable as noodles, as the ground beneath my feet trembled violently, stronger than any earthquake I had felt. I dared to open my eyes, only to find the entire world around me spinning.

Overwhelmed and exhausted, everything went black and I slipped into darkness.

Chapter 3

'Kendra?' That one voice made my eyes fly open. Through the haze, my eyes focused on a frowning Camilla and a concerned Josh.

'Are you okay?' Camilla asked, sounding genuinely confused. I groaned and sat up. The smell of the sea filled my nose and I understood why.

We were on a beach that looked quite similar to the one that was half an hour away from my house. I wondered if all that panicking was in vain when we were just going to the beach.

The sky was tinted orange, telling me that it was evening and the low tide lapped on to the shore in a rhythmic way.

'Why did you pass out?' Josh asked.

'Why did I pass out . . .?' I repeated, not sure how I was supposed to answer that.

'First time teleporters never pass out,' Josh said. 'They are exhausted, but never to the extent of fainting.'

'I don't know,' I shrugged. 'Why would you expect me to remain sane when everything is going in circles?'

'Wait, you actually *saw* that?' Camilla said.

'Yes,' I replied, feeling slightly self-conscious. 'Was I, uh, not supposed to?'

'Well, no one has *seen* –'

'Welcome!'

We jumped and turned to the direction of the voice. Josh and Camilla scrambled to their feet and helped me up.

Standing before us was a woman who was smiling warmly. Her

copper hair, which glinted in the evening sun, was thrown over one shoulder, and she had on an indigo velvet dress, complete with white fur draped across her shoulders and back.

My first thought was, *Who wears something like that to the beach?*

But something clicked when I saw a dainty tiara nestled on her head, and when Josh and Camilla bowed and curtsied.

She must be the Queen, or some sort of powerful authority around here.

I imitated Camilla and curtsied, though I imagine it resembled a frog trying to tap dance.

My second thought was, *Why is she staring at me like that?*

Her smile unsettled me, as if she was confronting an enemy, but trying to act rational and lady-like.

'Welcome to Zantoris, Kendra,' she said. 'I am Ardella, Queen of all Pixies.'

My mind point-blank refused to comprehend any of this. Zantoris? Pixies? None of it made any sense.

Camilla nudged me, as if I was expected to say something back. 'Thank you for having me . . .?'

The queen's gaze drifted to my knee, and her face fell. 'What's wrong with your knee? Is that . . . your blood?'

I suddenly remembered my bleeding knee. It was never treated. I wondered how much I had bled, and how much longer till I lost consciousness again.

'We'll explain later, My Lady,' Camilla said, hastily.

Ardella nodded, the smile wiped from her face completely. Then she realized she had dropped her guard and smiled politely again. 'Do come right this way. We will drop you to an infirmary so you can regain your strength.'

But when I stood up, I realized I had reached my peak. A wave of exhaustion washed over me as my eyes rolled back and I lost consciousness.

||||

I woke up with a gasp and sat upright. I was in bed.

I was still tired, but not so much that I couldn't walk. I felt something tight around my knee, so I guessed it was a plaster around the wound.

My surroundings resembled what I always thought a hotel suite for the rich would look like. The walls were painted a dark rustic brown, and the white floral curtains were drawn, allowing no natural light to come in. Not that there would be any. I glanced at my watch and it read 1:47 am. A chandelier filled the room with a dark golden, almost orange light, and two armchairs were present at either side of my bed. I noticed something on the one on my right side.

I heaved a sigh of relief as I grabbed my phone and switched it on. But I found that I couldn't go beyond the home screen. All apps either said I was offline, or they wouldn't activate no matter how many times I tapped on the icons.

Basically it was a useless rectangular gizmo I was carrying for no reason.

Another interesting object was kept beside the phone. A brass bell. I picked it and examined the tiny inscription at its base. It read, *Ring if in need of assistance.*

I slowly rang it. Nothing happened. I repeated, this time a bit more forcefully.

In less than a minute, the door opened. A woman in silver uniform and a tight bun entered. 'Did you ring the bell, Miss?'

'Yes,' I replied, putting down the bell on the armchair. 'Can you please help me?'

'Of course,' she replied. 'I am your nurse, and I am here to take care of you. Do tell me what you need.'

'I actually . . . is there any way I can contact Josh and Camilla? I think they brought me here.'

'Yes, there is, but they are most probably on campus, sleeping,' the nurse replied, before adding gently. 'Is it to ask about . . . all this?'

'Yes,' I said. 'Can you tell me?'

She shook her head. 'I am sorry but it is not my place to tell. The Finders have the responsibility to introduce the new Terran to Zantoris and its laws.'

'Right,' I said, adding "finders" to my list of things to ask about. 'Another thing. How long have I been out?'

'Oh, six hours,' Nurse answered. 'You were just thoroughly exhausted from teleporting for the first time.'

'Okay, thank you,' I said.

'It's late, Miss. If you want to sleep, you can, although I expect you don't feel like it?'

'No,' I said, deciding six hours of sleep was enough.

'You can stay up, then. Would you like a book?'

I nodded, and the nurse went outside to fetch me one.

This place didn't seem much like a hospital room, but I wasn't complaining. The spotless white and beeping machines always frightened me.

The nurse returned with a book. 'Since you are from Earth, I assumed you would like something from the Terran Authors Section. I hope you haven't read *Pride and Prejudice*?'

Without really waiting for an answer, Nurse handed me the book, drew back the curtains of the window and left, telling me to ring the bell if I needed anything else.

After thirty minutes of trying to read, I realized that my mind was in such a muddle that I couldn't comprehend what I was reading. I put the book down on my lap with a sigh, and looked out of the window.

Everything was pitch black. Neither the moon nor the stars were visible.

That was when I saw the lightning.

A single strip of lightning, silver in color. It flashed brightly thrice, and the third one's brilliance made my eyes close, as if I had been staring into the sun itself.

It left red spots in my eyes, and try as I might, I couldn't erase its image from my mind.

Suddenly, I saw someone standing in the far end of my room.

Chapter 4

The next morning, I had a visitor. 'Good morning,' Camilla greeted, smiling. This was the first time she smiled in front of me or wore a genuinely positive expression.

She wore a white button-up full-sleeved shirt, but the collar was perked up and the topmost button was open, exposing her throat. She had on a dark brown pleated skirt and black stockings with black sandals. Now that she didn't look like a victim of insomnia, I realized how striking she looked. I especially liked her hair, which was a mass of dark brown curls falling to her shoulders.

'Morning,' I replied, not having the heart to say "good".

Camilla drew back the curtains, the room lighting up with sunlight at once. 'You slept okay?'

'I guess,' I replied. 'Weird dream, but otherwise okay.'

Camilla nodded, and sat on an armchair. 'So . . . I guess you want an explanation?'

'You *guess?*'

'It's not that complicated, really,' she said. 'Let me start from the beginning. Um, you read books, right? You probably have read a lot about mythical creatures like elves, dwarves, vampires and stuff. Where do you think these creatures come from?'

'Imagination,' I guessed.

'Yes, but what do you think led humans to imagine them?'

I didn't answer, mostly because I wasn't sure what she was implying.

'Look, it's no accident all these ideas come to humans,' Camilla continued. 'There are more than a million species and kinds of creatures that live. Some are similar to humans—like us—while others are polar opposites.'

'You're basically saying that there are extra-terrestrial beings, besides humans?'

'Yes.'

My mouth hung open and I sat at a loss for words. I hoped for the millionth time that this would all be some prank. 'Why haven't we ever seen you guys then?'

Camilla said, 'Millions of years ago, we actually lived together. Like, on the same planet. We basically wanted to maintain harmony in our diversity. But it kind of all fell apart.'

'Because of humans?' I said. Given some of our histories, I knew our "diversity and harmony" wasn't much to talk about.

'Uh-huh. They were the last species to be created, and we thought that they would be like us. Peace-loving, generous creatures. That didn't last a decade. Man got greedy and saw in us abilities they could never have. They wanted it, but we were hesitant. We were always willing to share, sure, but giving up our powers was just a big step. Humans thought that us telling them to give us some time to think about it was us refusing. So they waged war.'

'The war was too much for some species, like pixies and fae as it was not in their natural instinct to fight. So five unnamed races came together and formed an alliance. It was to separate us from humans and let them be. They gave up all of their power and life just so that we could live in peace. They trapped us inside a black hole and wished for black holes to be deadly for humans so they could not enter. Inside the black hole, we are separated into divisions where four species live together. In those divisions, we are further divided into different countries according to which kind we belong to.'

'You were separated from each other because they feared war,' I realized. 'Which other species are in our group?'

'Well, we're pixies, so that's one,' she replied. 'Then we have vampires, dwarves and leprechauns. Leprechauns are the newest addition, as sprites went extinct a few years ago.'

'What happened to them?'

'No one knows. No one's interested in finding out either.'

'Why?' I asked. 'Are all species enemies with anyone outside their kind?'

'No, we're allowed to interact with the outside countries, just not outside our divisions. Remember, it was the humans who started the war. Separating us was just paranoia.'

'Okay . . . though I'm confused,' I said. 'What does this have to do with humans imagining you—I mean, us—as fantasy creatures?'

'The subconscious is far stronger than they think,' Camilla explained. 'So, unknowingly, they are writing about what is based on their faint memory of us. But they do get many things inaccurate, as the memory is more than a million years old. For example, pixies aren't pointy-eared, mischievous beings they believe. We were once but we've evolved.'

I closed my eyes and leaned my head against the bedpost. 'Wow . . . this is a lot to take in. Can I, uh, have a glass of water?'

'Sure,' Camilla sprang to her feet, filling a copper cup with water from the tap from the sink.

I stared at it warily. 'Is that safe to drink?'

'Nothing in Zantoris is polluted.'

'Zantoris?' I asked, as I sipped the cool water and felt it make its way down my throat.

'The Land of Pixies,' Camilla said, plopping herself on the armchair again. 'It's divided in two: Kingdom of Zantoris and

Kingdom of Devuniake.'

'Who lives in Devuniake?'

'You'll know later. But for now, if you have a will to live, stay away from there. It's impossible to enter easily, anyway, but if you find yourself there, do yourself a favor and get out.'

That raised another batch of questions, but Camilla quickly said, 'I'm not going to say anything about Devuniake right now. That's not part of the package of what the Finder is to tell the new Terran. Do you have any other questions?'

'Yes,' I promptly replied. 'Why were there so many earthquakes back home?'

'Oh *that*,' she laughed. 'It's simple, nothing to worry about. See, to find a pixie among humans, the current King or Queen gives a description to the Finders, which will help them. We are also given a fixed time, and Josh and I were running late. Two years were almost up and we still hadn't found you. So our King Alazar, who isn't exactly known for his sweet temper, sent earthquakes to West Palm Beach as a warning. It's a good thing he didn't provoke a tsunami.'

'How did he send the earthquakes?' I asked, my wariness and caution giving way to curiosity.

'Pixies who are born and raised in Zantoris are called Zantorians. They have power and dominion over any form of nature, like wind, water and land. They can even control natural disasters while Terrans—pixies from Earth—have different abilities like shapeshifting, telekinesis, things like that. Zantorians have had their power since birth, but Terrans only receive them on the day they turn eighteen.'

I smiled. 'That's . . . kind of cool.'

'I thought you wanted to go back home,' she teased.

My face went slack, and my eyes lit up in horror. 'Oh my God,

I have to go back! They've probably noticed I'm missing!'

'Don't worry!' Camilla assured. 'They don't know you're gone.'

'What do you mean?' I cried, still panicked.

'Time is weird,' she explained. 'You can stay here as long as you want but on Earth, you will only be missing for two minutes.' I calmed down. 'So when I go back, everything will keep going on as I last left it?'

'Right.'

'I have one more question,' I said.

Camilla sighed, like she seriously thought I was done. 'Go ahead.'

'Why are there pixies on Earth and why do you bring them here?'

'That's complicated. Many other races have people like them stuck down on Earth. Pixies are one of the few that take back their people, in fear that someone will find them and use their power. Now are you done?'

'Of course not. Why were you so shocked when you found my blood was red?'

'Pixie blood is dark blue, not red. But you spoke our language so fluently, there was no mistake that you had to be a pixie. Besides, everything in your description fits perfectly. Now, please. No more questions.'

Camilla got up and motioned me to do the same.

'Where are we going?' I asked, promptly forgetting the no questions request.

'You'll see,' Camilla said. 'Wow, either you ask a lot of questions or the last guy I brought didn't care so much.'

'Do you and Josh often do this?' I shoved my phone in my skirt pocket and walked with her outside the room. 'Finding random pixies from Florida?'

'Yes,' Camilla replied, coming to terms with the fact that she could not stop the questions. 'Yours was the first time we actually searched two whole countries, otherwise we'd normally just stick to state. That's why we missed so many school days. And we had literally no sleep. The only way to cover up the dark circles was aloe vera and makeup.'

'Who brought *you* here?'

She let out a sour laugh. 'Oh, you'll meet him soon. We're going to *his* house right now. His mother oversees all the newcomers and takes care of their school admissions and living facilities.'

I frowned, not liking the idea of school. Being in a foreign land, I had hoped there was nothing known as school.

'You don't like him?' I guessed.

'Let me give you a hint,' Camilla starts. 'He once sabotaged my grades from the system and I was held back an entire year. It took me so long to convince the Board that I had passed.'

I frowned. 'What's his problem with you?'

'He seems to have it in for all Terrans, probably because they were raised by "inferior" humans.'

'So that means I'm a target?'

'A very vulnerable one, yes.'

I sighed. Something told me this was going to be a long week.

Chapter 5

Zantoris reminded me so much of home, it pulled at my heartstrings.

Palm trees lined the streets in an orderly fashion and the warm breeze carried the salty smell of the sea. The air smelt fresher, and the aura of the whole place put me in a familiar mood, like the times when my family walked to the beach whenever we were free and together.

I didn't see any cars or anything like that, but there were a ton of buildings with intricate architecture, too advanced to be a man-made creation.

What confused me a little was how there was no difference in the way humans and pixies looked. Yes, outfits were definitely different, but otherwise, I counted ten fingers and toes, two hands and legs, one head and perfectly square teeth.

I noticed that I earned some looks from random people. I guessed it was because of my uniform.

'How do you get around here?' I asked, as I watched a mother trying to calm down a toddler throwing a tantrum. 'Like, do you always walk?'

'Yes, we do,' Camilla replied. 'We have more stamina than humans, but if we get tired, we simply teleport.'

'Why can't I teleport?' I wondered. 'It's something all pixies know, right?'

'Yes again. All pixies have to know how to teleport. Terrans find it difficult for one or two days, but by the end of five days, they get the hang of it.'

I caught sight of people doing activities that people back on Earth would do on a normal day. It all seemed so familiar but so alien at the same time.

Leaving the infirmary behind, we walked for ten minutes before we reached a lake. The morning sun gleamed on its brilliant bluish-green waters and cattails sprouted in its midst. I was about to ask how we were supposed to cross it, when I noticed a bridge passing over it. Camilla advanced towards it and I followed.

'What is this river called?' I asked, as I ran my hand through the railing.

'Calder, after the family who owns it,' she replied, her eyes fixating on something over the horizon. 'Ivan controls water, so this is kind of necessary for him.'

'Who's Iv – wait, the guy we hate?'

'We?' she said, looking amused. 'You haven't even met him yet.'

'Yeah, but I have a bad feeling about him.'

I bombarded her with questions till we reached the end of the bridge. My breath hitched as I took in the house. No, not house, the *mansion*.

A stone wall stood high, protecting the well-tended grounds and whitewashed four-storied house from the outside world. Three pillars stood at each side of the huge front door and right above it, a long balcony overlooked the entire property. Two gargoyles glared down at us as Camilla knocked.

'Wow, these people are *rich*,' I muttered, eyeing the two fountains in the garden and a massive waterfall which cascaded down the entire wall into a tiny moat.

'Makes sense, really,' Camilla said. 'Atticus is the senior officer of the Zantorian Congress, and Cordelia is in charge of all new Terrans. They make truckloads of money from both jobs *individually.'*

The door shuddered and groaned open. There stood a distinguished looking man wearing an authoritative expression.

He had immaculate dark hair, and piercing green eyes, which bore right through me. His serious face creased into a polite smile, and opened the door wider.

'We've been expecting you,' he said, in a sort of a formal, business-like voice. 'Come in, come in. Welcome to Zantoris, Kendra. That is your name?'

'Yes,' I replied, shrinking back at his intimidating physique. 'I'm Kendra Astor.'

'I know,' he said. 'I am Atticus Calder, Senior Officer of the Zantorian Congress.'

I was pretty sure he would have handed me a business card if that were a thing here. He wore a black velvet coat and a white shirt inside, with the same collar style as Camilla. His shoes made a booming noise every time he took a step.

He led us through a wide, dimly lit corridor. Warm light erupted from the lamps found every five feet, and the walls were painted a rich shade of maroon. The carpet failed to muffle Atticus' footsteps but erased any proof of ours.

He threw open the door at the end of the corridor. We entered an enormous room, as big as a hotel lobby. Unlike the corridor, this room was brightly lit, though all with artificial light. There were no windows whatsoever.

Camilla's sandals click-clacked against the marble floor as we made our way to the center of the room, where someone was sitting on the couch with their back turned to us.

'Son, we have guests,' Atticus announced.

The boy turned around.

Platinum blond locks framed his face, and he had hard emerald eyes, just like his father. He had a long, sophisticated nose, and his face was lost somewhere between handsome and unearthly. He was dressed more or less the same, and his expression hardened when he saw the two of us.

He gave a subtle eye-roll, and went back to doing whatever he was doing.

Atticus pursed his lips in disapproval, and cleared his throat. 'This is my son, Ivan. Ivan, please greet our guests properly. This is Kendra Astor, our newest Terran.'

'Welcome to Zantoris,' he mumbled, not bothering to get up and face me.

Atticus gave up and left the room. I heard him walk a few feet down the hall, open a door and say, 'They're here.'

After a minute, he reentered with Josh and a woman, who I guessed was Cordelia, Atticus' wife.

She brushed her fair locks out of her face and smiled warmly, telling me at once that she was much friendlier than her husband and her son. She advanced, hitching up her purple dress and said, 'Welcome! It is so good to meet you at last! I am Cordelia, and I will be overseeing your settlements and well-being for some time while you are here. And I assume you are Kendra Astor?'

I nodded.

Suddenly something crashed upstairs, and Atticus ran out.

'Excuse me,' Cordelia said, before rushing out with her husband.

'What's that?' I wondered aloud, puzzled. 'Their dog?'

'No, animals don't exist in Zantoris,' Josh said. 'It's probably their construction work. How are you feeling?'

'Physically, fine,' I answered. 'Mentally is a whole other story.'

'It's normal,' he reassured. 'When Cam and I came here, we were pretty scared. But in the end, everything just clicked into place. Why are we still standing? Let's sit.'

'How old were you?' I inquired, noticing how the two cousins consciously chose seats farthest away from Ivan.

'Eight.'

'Eight? That's way too young to be kidnapped and brought to this world.'

Josh grimaced. 'Yeah, it wasn't pretty.'

I nodded as my eyes fell onto a cabinet. It was filled with awards for things I didn't bother to read about. The only thing in the room which seemed of personal value was a photo resting on a mantle above the fireplace.

It showed Cordelia, Atticus, Ivan and another girl I didn't recognize. She had her father's looks, but her mother's cheerful aura. The photo was set at the beach, where even Atticus managed to have a genuine smile.

Only Ivan seemed to be uncomfortable. He seemed stiff as cardboard as his mother put an arm on his shoulders.

Suddenly, the picture was snatched away. Ivan had caught me staring at it and wasted absolutely no time in donning the most vicious scowl he could muster, grab the photo and stalk out of the room.

'What's *his* problem?' I commented, incredulously. All I did was glance at a family photograph, and I got a cold shoulder.

'No one can say,' Camilla shrugged. 'He's only this way to Terrans. Otherwise, wherever you go, there are always glowing, rainbow-like opinions of him.'

'Hmm-mm,' Josh nodded. 'He gets outstanding grades and manages to be considered "the best" in school by the others. He has everyone brainwashed, and people prefer to look the other way whenever he makes fun of Terrans.'

I wrinkled my nose. 'Please tell me this will be the last time I see him.'

'Oh, heavens no,' Camilla chuckled without humor. 'You will be coming with us to Aternalis Academy for Young Pixies, and since he's twelve too, you will definitely be seeing him in a lot of your classes.'

I refrained from the urge to groan loudly. I hadn't even been here a whole day, before someone told me I was to go to school.

Then Cordelia came back. Her eyes glanced briefly at the now-empty mantle, and I saw an unrecognizable emotion flicker in her eyes. Then she smiled at me.

'Now Kendra, I need you to come with me,' she said. 'Josh, Camilla, she will be staying with us till Monday so you needn't worry about anything.'

They both got up and Josh checked his watch. 'We better head back to campus, there's only five minutes left before breakfast.'

No sooner had he said that, they both disappeared with a bright flash, reminding me of the silver lightning I had seen in my dream the other night.

I looked at Cordelia with raised eyebrows. 'I'm staying with you?' I tried to remember when somebody had talked to me about this arrangement.

'Only temporarily,' she assured. 'On Monday, you will attend school, where I have already enrolled you into. Your hostel is the East Wing, Seventy-Third floor. You will be sharing the room with Camilla and another girl, Rosa. Now, mind you, you are not permitted to go to the North and South Wings, as they are the boys' hostels. Neither are they allowed to enter the East and West Wings.'

My head was spinning with all the information. 'Okay. But I just want to ask, what makes you think I'll do well here? I don't think you teach any of the subjects I'm used to, and besides I'm joining in the middle of semester.'

'You are not to worry about that,' she told me. 'Being a pixie, you will quickly adapt to the new studies. Besides, even if you don't, you will have special training arranged for you.'

Every single hope of me getting out of school shattered to a million little pieces.

Chapter 6

Over a course of two days, the only thing about pixies I had adapted to was their food. It was all one hundred percent organic, whether it was some sort of a fudgy dessert which tasted of mangoes, or a crisp, toffee-like disk, called Lemon Shards.

Girl fashion was alright, I guess. I didn't mind wearing a skirt and stockings twenty-four seven. We could wear pants, if we wished, but it was so uncommon, I didn't feel like being the odd one out. It was the heels that were the problem. Apparently, girls over the age of twelve can wear one-inch heels only on formal occasions.

After some practice and a good deal of snickering and ridicule from Ivan and his occasional bunch of friends, I finally managed to walk flawlessly without tripping. I felt like a grown-up.

Josh and Camilla visited me from time to time. I felt like I knew a lot more about them, as whenever we talked, they seemed to be themselves, rather than tired slugs who talked to each other in a weird language.

Josh, I gathered, was a very calm person. He refused to take sides in any fights happening in the school which Camilla mentions but he was more than willing to resolve them. He was also a book nerd. So that makes two of us, although I'm more interested in fiction.

Camilla, on the other hand, was the feistiest girl I had ever met. Every time Ivan made snarky remarks about her or Josh, she did not hesitate to yell back something ten times as insulting. She had strong opinions, and somehow always knew what she wanted.

Meanwhile, I take fifteen minutes to decide what ice cream flavor I want.

Then there came school.

I woke up on Monday morning and was treated to a very nice breakfast (compliments of Cordelia) and a decent amount of glaring and sulking (compliments of Ivan).

About an hour later, Josh and Camilla came and Camilla handed me the uniform to wear.

The uniform wasn't as bad as I feared. I was expecting something like robes and capes and pointy hats.

Instead, I got a full sleeved, diamond collar white shirt, a dark brown tweed skirt, white socks and black shoes. I tied up my hair into a hasty ponytail and put on a brown coat.

When I went down, I noticed that Josh and Ivan's uniform was not all that similar to mine and Camilla's. They had the same white shirt, but they had black trousers and a brown coat which had a logo of a hand holding a blazing torch and four animals, which I couldn't make out clearly, surrounding it.

Since I still hadn't gotten the hang of teleporting, Camilla, Josh and Ivan had to lend their strength to me so I could get to school unharmed.

I didn't get the concept all that well. It was basically me holding their hands as they started to glow. In a second I found myself standing before Aternalis Academy.

The school was a huge fragile-looking building made of glass. It was like the Louvre Museum but in the shape of a dome and about fifty times bigger. In the distance I saw a cluster of buildings that were similar to typical apartments.

'Those are just a few of the hostels,' Josh said.

I looked around. Ivan had ditched us to join a couple of friends of his. I was taken to the principal's office since he had to meet all the newbies first.

The school was *enormous*. When you step through the glass doors, you come to a lobby where there is a reception desk and a few sofas. As you look up, you can see the sky through the glass ceiling. There were two flights of staircases which both led to the same floor where I assumed all the classes were held. The air had a cold nip and the place smelt of lemongrass.

I went to the principal's office. Josh knocked on the door and a deep voice said, 'Come in.'

I went in. A man was sitting behind a polished desk. Bookshelves adorned the whole room, being careful as to not expose a single piece of wall.

As soon as the man saw me, he put down the papers he was so carefully scrutinizing, and his worried face creased into a smile.

'You must be our new student,' he said, reaching across his desk to get another file. 'Kendra Astor, is it?'

'That's me.'

'Welcome to Aternalis Academy for young pixies,' he said. 'I am Principal Fridolph, the Head of this school. I will assign you to all your classes, and I expect that your room is ready for you in your hostel. You will be staying in the East Wing. Here is your key for your room.'

He handed me a key, from which a gold chain with a bronze eagle at the end, hung.

'Classes start at eight-thirty am,' he went on, 'so make sure you reach school on time. Since you are new to teleporting, I have made arrangements for you to practice with Madam Felicity after all the regular classes are done.'

'Yes, Mr. Fridolph,' I said, not really knowing what else to say.

'Since there is a little more time left for classes to start, your friends can give you a short tour of the school,' he said, nodding towards Josh and Camilla, who were standing at the back of the room.

'Of course,' Josh said.

'Thank you, Principal Fridolph,' I said politely. He nodded.

All three of us went back outside.

Josh and Camilla took me on a mini tour. They showed me where all the classes were. Then they took me to the hostel area. The wings were, up close, skyscrapers. The North Wing faced north, the South Wing, south, the West Wing . . . you get the point. In the middle of the four hostels was a huge field with well-trimmed grass and daisies sprouting from the edges.

'This is where we go to our teleporting class, which by the way is your third lesson,' Camilla said, handing me a piece of paper. 'This is your timetable. Too bad we are not going to be in many of your classes.'

'You're not?' I asked.

Josh shook his head. 'We already passed many of the classes you got. We're still in your grade, but we go to slightly more advanced versions. That's why, to find you, they needed someone who was well experienced in teleporting.'

A loud gong was heard, almost deafening me. Camilla and Josh seemed perfectly fine though.

'That's the bell,' Josh said. 'Come on, we'll drop you to your first class.'

My first class was Zanarian, the pixie language I knew. It was taken by Miss Everly, a perky young teacher who never stopped smiling.

She entered the room, her bright eyes looking at everyone. Her smile widened when she saw me.

'I see that we have a new student today with us,' she said. 'I assume you are Kendra Astor?'

I nodded.

'*Welcome to Zantoris, my dear,*' she said. '*I assume you are already familiar with our language?*'

'*Yes, I am,*' I replied. Then realized that I, yet again, had spoken Zanarian subconsciously.

'Wonderful!' she said, brightly. Then, she handed me two books. The cover of one read: "*A Student's Guide: Learn to Speak Zanarian Fluently!*"

As we proceeded with the lesson, I felt movement going on behind me. I turned round and groaned inwardly.

Ivan was in this class with me. He was discreetly passing notes to his friend, who read the note and gave him a thumbs-up.

I discovered that Ivan was one of those guys who are pretty much worshiped all over the school. Everyone whispers in awe when he walks by and most girls peep at him with a soppy expression. It made my insides want to come out.

He missed no opportunity to make school life frustrating for me. He spread rumors, and the most ridiculous ones too, and did petty things like deliberately tripping me. He and his friends rigged my locker with an awful stench and no scent was strong enough to erase that pungent smell of dead and decaying frogs off of me.

As if that wasn't bad enough, my schoolwork wasn't going all that great. It was tough for me to catch up with the rest of my class, since I joined in the middle of the term.

In short, my first week was torture.

My only comfort was Josh, Camilla and a few of the friends I made.

Camilla and Rosa always lent an ear to my endless rants. I was convinced that I would fail the term, my workload was increasing ridiculously by the day and Ivan was a class act bully to everyone.

Norman and Favonius, who were Josh's roommates, also took

me under their wing. They helped me out whenever they could and bailed me out of detention when they found a reasonable loophole.

I was grateful to everyone who was nice to me. It was comforting to have an upside to being a clueless and inexperienced newbie in the massive school.

The weekend came. Naturally, the students welcomed it with open arms. Zantorians returned home to their families on Friday afternoon, after classes were over, while others teleported to Earth to visit home and still others decided to stay at school. Those who stayed back made plans that included having a sleepover with friends or going to the beach. Rosa went to the beach with a few of her friends. Before going she invited me, Camilla and Josh.

I declined. I told her that I had an extra Teleporting lesson with Madam Felicity, and an extra coaching class of History with Master Hemmingworth. Camilla and Josh said they had made other plans. With that, they disappeared without telling me where they were going.

Teleportation class was exhausting. Madam Felicity was a good teacher and she was patient with me from the beginning, though I could tell that her patience was wearing thin.

'Alright, Ms. Astor,' she said, after my sixth epic fail. 'Maybe you should sit down for a while. You might be able to do better after a break.'

I flopped down on the grass. After five minutes or so, we tried again.

'Just concentrate on where you want to reach,' She instructed. 'And calm down, you've got this.'

I hadn't.

'I can't do it,' I exclaimed in annoyance, as I remained fixated on the spot I was always on. Noticing a few pixies staring, I gave them a look. 'And what are *you* looking at?'

'Clear off, kids,' said Madam Felicity.

After several tries and miserable failures, we decided to call it a day and try again tomorrow.

'Remember what I said,' Madam Felicity told me gently. 'I know it has been days, but you will get the hang of it.'

'Thanks but . . .,' I trailed off, not having the heart to tell her that I probably won't.

My next extra lesson, History, made no attempt to lift my spirit.

Master Hemmingworth was grumpy, to say the least. He would clutch his eyebrows, shake his head exaggeratedly and throw a big fuss at the *tiniest* mistake.

'No, no, no!' he would exclaim. 'Absolutely not, Ms. Astor! Isla Andilet was not our fifth, but *sixth* princess to ever enter into the rank of queen without marrying. The fifth one was Shaylah Mirose. And . . . What is this monstrosity?!? Have you even revised any of the material we do in class? What makes you think that the most noble king to ever grace our history was born in the land of Luscinia? No, no. He came from the land of Lavreenia, my very own hometown.'

He puffed out his chest with pride while my brain sorted the information that Luscinia and Lavreenia are two different cities.

I was stuck there the whole day, trying to fathom the family tree of the Zantorian Monarchy.

I wasn't allowed to go to the dining hall for lunch. I had to settle for a juice box and a cold grilled cheese sandwich while doing my exercise book questions.

By the time it was evening, I had managed to get fifteen out of fifty questions right.

I dragged myself out of school and trudged towards the dining hall. The dining hall was near the hostels, and since I could not teleport, I had to walk all the way there.

I reached the skyscrapers. Each one had a mascot of its own. The North Wing had an arctic fox, the East Wing–mine–had a bronze eagle, the South Wing had a snake and the West Wing's mascot was a wolf. The dining hall was located between these four buildings, with a statue of each animal standing proudly at the entrance.

The dining hall had the build and structure of a typical mall. But instead of shops and restaurants, there are tables and chairs as far as the eye can see. The atrium had goodness knows how many floors which one can reach by using the built-in escalators. The fragrance of lemongrass was always aloft, the chatter of students, never ending.

As soon as I entered, my legs automatically started to make their way towards the table which was nearly hidden in the shadows in the corner of the magnificent atrium. That was where me, Josh, Camilla and Rosa sat, along with Norman and Favonius. Over the week, I had been readily accepted into this friend group. We mostly kept to ourselves, an insignificant speck of dust in the ocean of pixies at Aternalis.

For now, Favonius was the only one absent since he was visiting his family. He was to return on Sunday evening.

I advanced towards the table and everyone greeted me with a 'Hi' or 'Hey' or 'Why are you late?' or 'I didn't see you at lunch.'

As I sat down, I explained that I was held back for extra coaching of History.

Norman winced. 'Extra coaching is not uncommon for pixies who join mid-term. I went through it too, and boy, Master Hemmingworth was *harsh* back then. He is better now, but his punishments used to be pretty cruel!'

I raised my eyebrows as I took a bite of the green beans (these were compulsory for all students to eat). 'No way. He's better *now?* He must have been a nightmare in your time.'

While dinner was going on, I noticed Josh looked slightly pale, and Camilla kept her eyes on her food, refusing to look anywhere else.

After dinner, Camilla, Rosa and I said goodnight to the boys and made our way into the East Wing. We got on to the elevator which was designed to reach any floor within ten seconds, no matter how high it is.

When we reached the seventy-third floor, we walked to our room in silence. Rosa opened the door with her key and we walked in.

When Rosa went to use the bathroom, I turned to Camilla and said, 'Cam, is anything wrong?'

My friend stiffened. 'Why?'

I noted that she didn't try to deny that something was wrong. 'I don't know. You and Josh just went somewhere and came back looking like you've seen a ghost.'

'And?'

'And I'm worried. At least tell me where you've been going.'

Camilla sighed. 'I was strictly warned not to tell anyone, but since you're going to be dragged into this sooner or later, maybe it's fair that you know too.'

If I was going to be dragged into this, then it meant that it was related to me. She looked like she was going to volunteer an explanation, but then Rosa came into the room. Camilla glanced at me with a look which said, *'I'll tell you later.'*

Just then, the school's signature deafening gong sounded, which meant it was time for bed. I quickly cleaned up and went under the covers.

||||

The next day was pretty much the same, except Josh and

Camilla didn't have to go to wherever they had sneaked off to.

As a result, they were much more relaxed. Josh spent his whole day playing some kind of pixie sport which seems to be a favorite among many students, while Camilla went shopping. She bought me a ton of clothes, most of which I liked. For others, I'm pretty sure she bought them to annoy me.

The day went pretty much the same for me. I went to teleporting class which did not go much better than yesterday.

I didn't have History that day, but I had Arithmetic instead, where I did much better than last time. Miss Faye was so happy she treated me to a vegan ice cream. That was when I knew what my old school on Earth was missing.

I had a lot of free time in the evening. And this was my opportunity to actually sit down and think.

It was beginning to hit me now. I realized how much I missed my parents and my brothers. A knot in my chest tightened. I hadn't seen them in such a long time now, their faces were slowly becoming a blur.

I took a deep breath. Once I get a hang of the whole teleporting thing, maybe I can go back to Earth for some time, make up some story to Miss Johnson about suddenly running out without permission, spend the weekend with my family and then come back. I would go and visit them every weekend and just pick up where I left off from the last I saw of them.

I was on the field which filled the space between the four hostels. It was a vast and lush, green panoramic haven. It was big enough for one party to play that pixie sport and another group to just lie around and laze undisturbed. The air smelt of fresh grass and roses.

In the distance, I saw Josh. His face was red and he was sweating but he looked ecstatic. I think his team was winning. He caught me looking at him and gave a friendly smile and a wave. I returned it likewise.

Just before dinner, most of the pixies who went away for the weekend started to return. The dining hall was full again, overflowing with chatter and laughter.

In the evening, as I got into bed, I thought that perhaps all this may not be that bad after all. Maybe everything will go smoothly now.

That's where I was wrong.

My dreamless sleep was interrupted by a violent shaking. I knew at once it was an earthquake. As a lightbulb crashed to the floor, I ducked under the bed. From there, I saw Rosa wake up with a leap, and Camilla being thrown off the bed because of the powerful tremor.

A bookshelf crashed to the floor, and I heard a loud thud which seemed to come from outside, like a tree falling. I clung on to the leg of the bed, terrified.

I looked with a sigh of relief that both Rosa and Camilla had taken cover, underneath their bed and table, respectively, but in the darkness, I could see a line on Rosa's cheek. She had hurt herself, possibly from the fallen chandelier.

The earthquake continued for one more minute before everything went deadly still.

I crawled out, and the moment I stood up, a loud siren rang.

Chapter 7

From the window, I saw many of the bedroom lights in the West and North Wing were rapidly being switched on, one by one. Camilla and Rosa got up, trembling a bit, looking slightly scared.

Rosa looked at me. 'Kendra, *please* tell me you know how to properly teleport to a distance.'

'I don't,' I replied, feeling more frightened as the wailing of the siren grew louder. I went towards the window and saw pixies crowding onto the field between the hostels and teleporting away.

Camilla muttered something under her breath and then said, 'Never mind, we'll lend you the strength.'

We ran out to the hallway, where girls were rushing for the stairs. Miss Everly and Madam Felicity kept telling them to not panic but teleport as fast as they could. They blocked the elevators and told everyone to use the stairs.

In the melee, I heard two girls talking - or rather, shouting.

'What's happening?' the first one frantically asked.

The second one grunted in frustration. 'Anna, for once in your life, just *think*. A 5 point something magnitude earthquake happened and we're near the *sea*. *What* do you think is going to happen next?'

The tsunami warning nearly deafened everyone and we needed to shout to hear each other.

'We need to get down to the open air at once,' Rosa yelled. 'From there we need to get to a safe house which is far away from here.'

'Why don't we just teleport from here to the safehouse?' I shouted trying to keep up with them in the ocean of girls running here and there.

'Because we will be teleporting really far away from here, so we need to get to an open space,' was the reply.

We reached the field. It was packed with pixies teleporting away, one by one with incredible speed. It no longer smelt of spring but the scent of thunderstorms was growing and I didn't like it one bit. By now a loud roaring noise like a jet plane was ringing in the air. That meant the tsunami was close.

The teachers were trying to get everyone to stay calm and teleport as fast as possible. I saw Josh in the crowd. He tried to get to us, but a master told him to leave at that instant.

The field emptied with great speed. When the last of the students teleported away, it was only us, Master Hemmingworth and Miss Julina, the teacher who taught what humans would call Science.

'What are you waiting for?' She screeched. 'Go! Now!'

Rosa and Camilla each grabbed one of my hands and closed their eyes in concentration. Then their hands started glowing like it always did when teleporting to lend strength to someone else. My body felt weightless like it always did. The two teachers, satisfied that we would reach there in time, disappeared in a flash. I closed my eyes to reduce the dizziness, which I was expecting. I felt nothing. I opened my eyes and let out a strangled gasp.

I was still standing all alone in the great field, not a single soul nearby.

Judging by the sound, I guessed the water was really close. I looked at Aternalis' building. And that was when the stuff of my nightmares happened.

I saw a raging wall of water crashing over my school, destroying it to its foundation. The water wall seemed the height of two apartment buildings and drowned anything, including trees, in its way.

I wanted to gaze at it some more, but my legs were obviously smarter than me, because they made me run in the opposite direction.

I knew that running wouldn't do any good, because the crashing waves were rapidly gaining on me.

But I had to try. I didn't see any higher ground to get to but I kept running. I swerved through trees and deserted houses, looking desperately for buildings high enough to protect me. There was nothing.

My legs were getting tired but I didn't dare stop.

'*Not now,*' I told myself. '*Keep going.*'

I made the mistake of looking behind me. The tsunami was dangerously close. If I waited for even one second I would be dead.

So, of course, I got so scared my legs gave out. I fell to my knees as the tsunami swallowed me alive.

I held my breath and tried to dodge all the rubble coming my way. I covered my head, so that it wouldn't be struck by any debris, but at the same time, I was desperate to hold on to something.

I was carried along with the turbulence of the water. I figured that survival at this point would be pure luck. I felt objects hitting and colliding with me from all directions, making me want to yell in pain, but I held my breath the best I could.

I tried to swim up to the surface because I couldn't hold my breath for very long.

I was practically drained when I got to the surface. I clung on to a huge piece of debris and began to cough uncontrollably. I think some water went in through my nose.

So this was a tsunami.

"A series of waves which can also be caused by an earthquake or a volcanic eruption."

Okay, so . . . wait. A *series* of waves. Uh oh.

Right on cue, another wave crashed over me, pulling me underwater. My head might as well have hit a concrete pavement from a great height. I felt dizzy and started to sink. I let go of my breath.

I wasn't sure if what happened next was real or my imagination, but just then I saw someone swimming towards me, their hand taking my wrist and pulling me up.

I figured it was some life-and-death hallucination and I closed my eyes, giving in to unconsciousness.

Chapter 8

I opened my eyes and tried to sit up, but my body refused to cooperate. I think I was in a cavern, judging from the high ceiling and the musty smell of a closed off space. I assumed there might be a tiny stream nearby, because I heard the sound of water from somewhere. There were muffled voices nearby, which sounded painfully familiar.

'She's been out for some time now. Should I be worried?'

'You can't expect someone who was struck by a tsunami to heal overnight, Rayson. You gotta give it some time.'

Rayson! That was Camilla's last name! The first voice who spoke was definitely her.

The second one was also familiar, but it couldn't be Josh. For one, he would never call his cousin by her last name. He usually called her Cam.

Before I could contemplate further, I felt drowsy all over again and closed my eyes.

When I came to, I could sit up. Before I could take in my surroundings, I was smothered by a hug.

'Oh my God, you're alive!' Camilla mumbled, hugging me and then slapping my back. 'This is the happiest day of my life.'

She stepped back, revealing that Josh was with her too, smiling in relief.

'Oh . . . you guys died too?' I said dumbly. 'I'm sorry. But I thought you made it to the safehouse.' Then I looked around.

The cavern was huge. Far away, I could see the entrance. I saw a rock pool from which a tiny waterfall was pouring water into a slightly bigger pool. My afterlife was beautiful.

'We're not dead, Kendra, and neither are you,' Josh said, smiling.

'I'm . . . not?'

'Nope. Ivan saved you.'

It took me a solid five seconds to realize what he just said.

'Wait,' I said. '*Ivan* saved me? I thought he hated me.'

Camilla shrugged. 'We didn't see that coming either. But it's true.'

'How did he even save me?' I asked. 'The waters were too rough for him to navigate.'

'Remember when I said that Ivan can control seas, oceans and any water body?' Camilla said, 'Well, the tsunami didn't harm him at all. He just sent all the debris away from him with a jet of water. He said that when he tried to teleport, he didn't get to the safehouse. He was stuck there just as the tsunami was coming, same as you.'

I shuddered. I would never act the same around beaches now.

'I didn't see him,' I said.

'That's because he was probably somewhere out of your sight,' Josh said. 'Anyway, he said when he was swept up with it, he tried to control it, but it was too strong for him. Then he saw you and he saved you. He got up to the roof of a building as the water passed by it and from there, he tried to teleport you and him both to the safehouse, but instead he got teleported to this cavern, like us.'

My head felt slightly dizzy from all that information but I managed to say, 'You never made it to the safehouse?'

They shook their heads. Just then, I heard footsteps. I turned around to see Ivan coming towards us. He looked at me blankly.

'You're awake,' he said. 'What a surprise. I'm glad you survived.'

He sounded neither surprised nor glad.

I cleared my throat. 'Um . . . thanks for saving me.'

That seemed pretty inadequate for what he had done but he just shrugged it off and sat down.

All of us were quiet for some time, until Josh broke the silence, 'Okay so we've got to go back to Zantoris now. I guess after Kendra regains her strength, we teleport back?'

'Why would we go back so fast?' I asked. 'Shouldn't we wait for all the water to go back into the sea?'

'Yeah . . . see, about that. . .' Josh said, looking like he was wondering where to start.

'You were in a coma for a month,' Ivan said, flatly.

'*What?!*' I yelled, but then instantly regretted it because I went into a coughing fit.

'You. Were. In. A. Coma. For. A. Month,' Ivan said slowly, enunciating each word, as if he were talking to a three-year-old.

'See, we had to make sure you were completely alright before teleporting back to Zantoris,' Camilla said, ignoring Ivan. 'We normally would've teleported back with you, but we assumed that your condition might be a bit fragile. Teleporting when your health is not good could be a bad idea. It already worsened your condition when Ivan teleported here with you. And you kinda passed out for longer than we estimated.'

'And trust me this has been the longest month of my life,' Ivan muttered.

'You were no picnic to live with either, so why don't we call it even, and you can do us all a favor and shut up,' Camilla snapped.

Judging by the way they scowled at each other, I guessed that I missed an epic fight between these two.

Ivan laughed sourly, and looked like he was going to retaliate.

Josh muttered something under his breath which sounded

suspiciously like, 'Here we go again.'

'*Anyway*,' he continued in a louder-than-necessary voice. 'Kendra, you better eat something.'

He handed me a pack of chips. I took it and stared at it.

'Where did you find food from?' I asked.

'My emergency pack,' Josh replied. 'I took it before I teleported. It had rations to last a long time but most of it got spoiled. Chips and peanut butter cups are all we have left now.'

I hungrily gobbled the chips in a most undignified manner, but I didn't care as much as I normally did.

As everyone ate dinner—which was really just more chips—I asked them, 'If I was in a coma for a month, how did I survive? I mean, usually coma patients get food through a feeding tube, so that they don't starve or dehydrate.'

Camilla pulled something out of her pocket. It looked like some sort of a sponge the size of a granola bar.

'We call this Medeema,' she explained. 'If something happens to someone, because of which they do not get enough nutrients or can't eat well, like if you're unconscious, you can simply place this on their forehead and they will not only give them their essential nutrients but it will also increase their chance of coming out of the coma alive.'

'Okay, but I've also heard that in a coma, the patient can hear everything going on outside. I couldn't hear anything.'

'You're a pixie, Kendra,' Ivan said. 'Forget everything you think you know about yourself.'

I slowly started regaining my strength over the next few hours. And I also realized that if this had happened on earth, we would be declared missing for a month then.

I voiced these thoughts to the others, and Josh shifted uncomfortably. 'There is a fifty per cent chance we're on Earth.

Whatever distance we've gone, it looks a lot like Zantoris, but we haven't met any people, so we don't know.'

My mouth hung open. 'Why didn't you go any further? You know, get some information.'

'There seems to be no one here every time we go out,' Josh replied.

I buried my face in my hands. 'Josh. Don't you remember? On the beach near our house, there is a restricted area. What if we're in there? That would explain why you couldn't find any people.'

Josh bit his lip. 'I . . . forgot.'

'Well, no wonder,' Camilla sighed. 'We spend most of our time in Zantoris, so we forgot the way things work around here.' She stood up. 'I'm going for a walk.'

'I'll come with you,' I said, standing up.

It was dark. From the distance, I heard waves lapping onto the shore and I could see hazy shadows of bats flying above us. I severely hoped that this beach was the one in Zantoris, not the one half an hour away from home.

Not a soul was around, and everything was quiet. We were walking for a long time before we reached a barricade, and we jumped over.

'Let's see if we can find any shops,' Camilla suggested in a low voice.

We walked along the dark shore, a lighthouse sending out a beam of light in a circular motion.

I noticed something and pointed. 'There.'

We jogged over and saw a souvenir gift shop. The minute we walked in, a dreadful feeling settled in my heart. Most of me already knew the worrying truth.

A young woman in a leather jacket sat behind the counter. She was scrolling through her phone, and didn't realize we were there until I cleared my throat.

She looked up, slightly surprised to find two girls out at that time. 'May I help you?, she asked.'

I considered a clever way to find our location without her thinking we were crazy.

'Where are we?' Camilla sure didn't beat around the bush.

'Palm Beach,' the woman replied after a moment's pause. The way she looked at us closely made me feel a bit uneasy.

Camilla looked at me knowingly and I came to two conclusions, good news and bad news each.

Good news: we were half an hour away from our homes.

Bad news: we were missing for a month.

'Are your names Kendra and Camilla, by any chance?' she asked, looking at us suspiciously.

I'm pretty sure my tense posture gave everything away, but Camilla didn't drop her gaze and asked just as suspiciously, 'Why do you want to know?'

The woman reached into a drawer and pulled out two fliers and put them on the table.

I read the first one, eyes widening at once.

MISSING!

Name: Camilla Rayson
Age: 12 years
Height: 5' 3" inch
Description: Brown hair, gray eyes, blue jeans, red shirt, white sneakers
Last seen: Aheart Private School

IF FOUND, PLEASE CONTACT THE NEAREST POLICE STATION IMMEDIATELY

A picture of Camilla was attached to that. Next to that, there were similar posters, featuring Josh and me.

We were missing for over a month. I looked at the last line. Then I realized something.

The woman at the counter was tapping something on her phone and suddenly put it to her ear.

Camilla and I agreed on one idea simultaneously, almost as if we were connected telepathically.

We ran.

Hearing the woman say "hello" into the phone was faint by the time we were twelve feet away from the store. She was staring after us as she frantically said incoherent ramblings into the phone.

When we reached there, we told the boys everything. Ivan listened wide-eyed, while Josh frowned, and looked down at his hands.

I sat down and took a shaky breath. 'We should go back tomorrow, at seven o'clock.'

'I'll teleport back around then,' Ivan murmured.

We ate our last dinner of peanut butter cups and water and went to sleep in silence.

Chapter 9

I had never felt so nervous and jittery in my life. Sure, I wanted to meet my family again and I still do. But one cannot just disappear for over a month and casually walk into their house again.

We teleported and reached Camilla and Josh's house first because it was the closest. Their families had been living together for a while, since Camilla's house burned down because of a fire.

We walked up the drive, and the brownstone townhouse stood quiet. Camilla rang the doorbell, and banged on the door thrice when no answer came.

I looked around. Their car was gone.

'Maybe they've gone out,' I said.

'All of them?,' Josh said, before realizing something. 'Oh God, today's Mikey's birthday.'

Mikey was Josh's stepbrother. We decided to go to my house, which would have been another thirty-minute walk, if the police hadn't forced us inside their car and driven us to the station.

The sound of the wailing sirens reached our ears, and two cops, a man and a woman, in blue uniform emerged. They addressed me first.

'You need to come with us,' the woman said, her tone telling me it would not be wise to argue.

'You too,' the other one gestured to Josh and Camilla to get in the car. We obeyed reluctantly.

Not even a minute had passed, until Camilla decided to ask, 'Where are you taking us?'

'The station,' was the curt reply.

'Um . . . why?' Camilla prompted.

The man looked at us through the rear view mirror. 'There are some questions you need to answer.'

We cast concerned glances at each other. We couldn't tell them about Zantoris. But I wasn't crazy about lying either.

The station was only a short distance away. When we pulled over, I recognized my brothers' and Josh's parents' car in the parking lot.

I got nervous butterflies in my stomach as another car pulled over and my parents got out.

They were hysterical. They hugged me and kissed me, making me a little teary-eyed myself.

'I'm sorry,' I mumbled into my mom's shoulder as she hugged me.

She pulled back and smiled, wiping a stray tear off her cheek. 'Why are you sorry?'

I shrugged as my dad pulled us both in a group hug.

Camilla and Josh had already gone inside the station, and the lady cop led us to where they were.

I felt slightly overwhelmed at the number of people there were.

Camilla's parents and her younger siblings, Agnes and Chris, looked elated, and Josh's dad and stepmom Liza, stood at each side of Josh protectively, as if daring anyone to come take him away again. Josh's stepsister, Jennie looked amazed, as if something interesting finally happened in her life, while five-year-old Mikey just jumped around excitedly, wearing a party hat. This was probably the best birthday gift he had gotten so far.

I looked for Cole and David, and I found them in the back filling out some forms.

David was ecstatic beyond words, while Cole had a casual grin, as if welcoming me back from summer camp.

'Now,' a police officer said, 'I would like to question these children, if you don't mind.'

We were herded into a room, and made to sit on the chairs opposite the one behind the desk.

The officer sat down and began, 'Now, I want you to answer my questions honestly. What happened?'

'Can you elaborate the question?' Josh asked, probably trying to stall as much as possible.

The officer frowned, wondering what more elaboration we needed than those two words. 'Why did you go missing? Were you kidnapped, or did you run away?'

'Kidnapped,' I replied, receiving strange looks from my friends. But that was technically true. Camilla and Josh took me away against my will, so that's kidnapping.

The officer nodded. 'Can you please describe your kidnappers for me?'

'I can't,' I answered. 'They'll kill me if I do.'

True again.

The officer frowned. 'Where were you taken?'

'I can't tell you anything,' I told him. 'It's not going to be a pretty scene if I tell you anything.'

He tried extracting information from Camilla and Josh but they just mumbled, 'What Kendra said,' in response to everything.

Eventually he let us go, but had a *long* chat with each of our parents. My phone thankfully got reception. (I had taken it with me before evacuating the East Wing. Somehow it survived with me.)

I played a video game while my brothers watched and gave me tips to move onto next levels.

Suddenly, the room went dark. I resisted the urge to yell, '*This* cannot *be happening right now.*'

I jumped to my feet at once. I couldn't see anything. Something covered all the windows in the waiting room, so that no light came in.

'What's going on?' Josh said.

Just then a candle flickered in all four corners of the room. Through the light I saw that no one was moving. It was like they were frozen in time. Everyone except me, Josh, Camilla and . . .

'*Cole?!?*' I exclaimed. 'Wait . . . you're not frozen.'

'Bravo Sherlock,' he replied dryly.

All the candles went out, leaving us in absolute darkness once again. A light shone in the middle of the room, like a spotlight.

In that, stood a ghastly woman.

She was skinny and pale. A tattered and old white dress hung off of her shoulders. Her nails were long and white. Her eyes were puffy and bloodshot, like she'd been crying. Her stringy black hair was an absolute mess. The grief and heartbreak her eyes held was terrifying. She clutched her heart as if it pained her.

'Everyone, cover your ears!' Cole shouted. I obliged a bit too late. The woman started weeping. She fell to her knees and wailed in agony. It was heartbreaking to listen to, but it was also very loud.

I clasped my hands over my ears. Even then I couldn't tune out the screams of the lady.

When she stopped, I was pretty sure my ears had been scarred for life. A buzzing noise was stuck in my head. I looked up again, and I saw that the screaming lady was replaced by a man frowning down on me.

He was wearing a black robe-like thing, along with a purple velvet cape. The irises of his eyes were pure yellow and his hair looked as if it were styled with great attention to detail. In his hand, he held a black staff, topped with a silver skull resting on what looked like a black flower.

'*I can't believe it,*' he said, in Zanarian. His face looked beyond furious, as if planning revenge in his brain. '*She has returned? This has to be a joke.*'

He raised his staff over my head, but before he could strike me or whatever he was planning to do, he disappeared.

The lights were back on and sunlight came in from the windows again. Cole, Camilla and Josh looked at me with shock and horror, while the others seemed more confused.

'What happened?' David asked. 'Why are you all standing?'

'Nothing,' all of us mumbled and sat down. But I caught the horrified look everyone was giving me.

Later, to celebrate our return, we went to a restaurant for lunch.

When I came out of the bathroom, I heard someone say, 'Pssst.' I looked around. I saw Cole standing behind a tall potted plant and I tilted my head in confusion. He beckoned me over.

'Why didn't you tell anyone you've been hearing explosions and feeling earthquakes?' he asked with his arms crossed.

'I *had*,' I told him. 'Don't you remember, once at breakfast I told Dad and you about that earthquake? And you said that there was no earthquake?'

'I thought you just moved your bed or something,' Cole said. 'I didn't know you felt them repeatedly. Never mind, I need to talk to you about something else. I hope you have a plan on what to do after that banshee.'

'A banshee?' I said. 'Is that the screaming lady?'

He nodded. 'In Irish legend, a banshee's wailing warns of death in houses. But the type of banshee *we* saw also gives a curse through her howling to someone who hears it loud and clear.'

I frowned. 'Wait, how do you *know* all this? Are you a pixie too?'

He shook his head. 'No, but you are one, right?'

My mouth fell open. 'You're not a pixie? What are you then?'

'A human.'

'What –'

'Hey, what are you doing here?'

We turned around to see David.

'Everyone's getting ready to leave,' he said. 'Now come on, before they think you've disappeared again.'

As we left, I was a bit quiet. Mom got a bit worried that I wasn't feeling well, but I assured her that I'm fine.

When we got home, I said goodbye to Camilla and Josh, who promised to visit the next day. I wondered whether Ivan had teleported back to Zantoris

I went to bed, and had my parents checking on me at least five times. They only went to sleep when they were assured that I had fallen into a deep sleep, probably when I started drooling. (I do that sometimes when I'm really tired)

I overslept a little. It was nine a.m. I didn't get out of bed, but my eyes were wide open and I stared at the ceiling for at least forty-five minutes for no particular reason. It felt like I was a normal girl waking up to a typical Saturday, and it felt like *heaven*.

My room was not much to look at. It was pretty neat, which was unusual because I normally looked like I preferred living in the midst of a garbage dump. The sun was shining brightly through the windows, making it impossible for me to go back to sleep. There was always a faint scent of lemon in my room, mainly because I read that lemon repels spiders. (Don't judge me, all Astors have a fear of spiders)

I eventually got out of bed and went down for breakfast.

'Morning, honey,' my mom chirped. 'Sleep okay?'

I nodded and sat at the table, where I started munching on my cereal.

'Since when did we get Lucky Charms?' I asked.

'Well, I figured since you liked this so much, I bought it for you to eat *just this once.*' Mom was a little uptight when it comes to having a "nutritious breakfast", and apparently, marshmallows don't count as healthy.

David cleared his throat and looked at Mom pointedly.

'Oh, and your brothers both got good grades in their exams, so this is their treat,' she said.

'Part of it,' Cole said, grinning. 'We get to go to Miami with our friends.'

Woah, their grades really must have been something. Dad didn't even trust Cole with the thermostat.

After some time, David and I were watching a movie on Netflix in my room. It was a So-Bad-That-It's-Funny movie and David's sarcastic commentary left me in stitches. I almost forgot the past few months. I didn't even *feel* like anything out of the ordinary.

All that came crashing down when the doorbell rang. Neither of us made any move to go see who it was.

I heard some voices, and a minute later, Cole was in my room saying, 'Hey, Josh and Camilla are here, along with Isaac.'

I stared at him. 'Who?'

'Isaac,' he repeated.

'Oh, you mean Ivan?' I realized.

'Whatever,' he replied, walking out.

I raced downstairs and saw all three of them sitting on the couch, looking confused.

They greeted me and by "they" I mean Josh and Camilla. Ivan didn't so much as glance.

I sat down. 'So, what happened? Weren't you going to teleport back?' I made the last remark looking at Ivan.

'That's the problem,' Josh replied. 'He can't teleport to Zantoris.'

Chapter 10

I raised my eyebrows. 'What do you mean?' 'I can't leave Earth,' Ivan said, looking pretty calm for a guy who just found out he can't return home. 'As much as I tried, I couldn't go back. It's like I'm cursed to never leave this place.'

'Are you serious?' I exclaimed. 'Does that mean that *we* couldn't do it either?'

'If I couldn't do it, what makes you think you would be able to?' he snapped.

'No, Kendra,' Camilla said. 'We tried and we couldn't reach Zantoris either. We've just ended up back here.'

We all sat there in silence for some time.

'Guys,' Josh finally spoke. '*Something's* definitely happening. First the tsunami, then the banshee and the dude in the cape, and now this.'

'So, what are we going to do?' I sighed.

Ivan shrugged. 'I'm going to find a way home. What else?'

'Alone?'

'Um . . . yeah?'

'You do know you could get killed if you do this alone,' Josh said.

'Who will get killed?' Liza said, suddenly entering the room. I assumed she came with Josh and Camilla to keep an eye on them.

'No one,' I said, quickly. 'We're just . . . reenacting a scene from a movie.' I saw Josh facepalm from the corner of my eye.

Her look told us loud and clear that she didn't believe me. She put down the plate of cookies on the table and went back into the kitchen to chat with my mom, but after sometime, they shifted nearer to us, looking worried.

'Maybe we should go outside to the garden,' I suggested.

No one answered, but everyone got up and headed to the backyard, grabbing cookies along the way.

We sat down on the neatly mowed lawn. A white cat crept up behind Ivan. I smiled.

'Come here, Cottonball,' I called.

The cat hesitantly came my way and purred on my lap.

Josh smiled and reached out to stroke her head and Cottonball miraculously didn't scratch his eyes out. Ivan stared at the cat. 'Is it yours?'

'S*he*, not *it*,' I corrected. 'And to answer your question, yes, she's my friend. I've had her since she was a kitten.'

Cottonball apparently got bored with me, because she suddenly leaped on Ivan. She sprawled on his lap, looking up at him with curiosity. Then she gazed around at us.

'Meow?' she asked.

'Maybe later,' Camilla replied. 'Anyway, as Josh was saying, Ivan, is that you can't go alone.'

Ivan scoffed. 'Why do you care?'

She rolled her eyes. 'Because I don't have an interest in seeing anyone die, no matter how much of a jerk he is. It's also one of the laws that if a group is together outside Zantoris, it's each pixie's responsibility to look after the others' wellbeing. I doubt you even *know* the way back. Besides, your parents are probably here on Earth looking for you. What are we supposed to tell them when they find that you have gone on a crazy mission?'

He groaned. 'So, you're basically saying that I should stay put in case my parents are looking for me, even though they're probably not?'

I tried to be optimistic. 'Well, you don't *know* they're not looking for you.'

He shook his head. 'Members of the Zantorian Senate are forbidden from coming to the Land of Humans for safety purposes.'

I frowned. 'Safety from what?'

'People like you.'

'Oh . . . okay,' I said, not really knowing how to respond to that.

'Anyway,' Josh said, 'We never got to talk about what happened at the station.'

Camilla looked at me. 'Kendra, you know what a banshee is?'

I nodded. 'Yeah, I know. So, I assume I'm cursed now.'

'Please don't take this lightly, Kendra,' she pleaded. 'Many things have happened to the people who hear her wailing. They've gone absolutely insane! They become wanderers, who go place to place, mourning and spreading misery until it becomes too much for them and they reduce to a banshee themselves.'

'Oh,' I said.

'But it's okay,' Josh said quickly. 'There is a way to reverse it.'

'There is?' I said, excitedly.

'There is?' Camilla repeated, confused.

Josh blinked repeatedly, as if he had just been slapped. He frowned and massaged his head with one finger, like he was getting a headache. 'Never mind.'

Just then, Cottonball meowed with joy, as she pounced on a bowl of milk my mom was carrying. Mom smiled at us, put down the milk, and went away.

'Anyway, what were we talking about in the first place?' Ivan asked, probably petulant that the subject wasn't about his issue anymore.

'We'll get you back home,' Josh promised.

'But how?' Camilla groaned.

Well, that was just the question of the century, wasn't it?

Remind them of their Physiography class, a tiny voice said inside my head.

'What about your Physiography class?' I blurted.

Camilla frowned. 'What about it?'

'I don't know,' I murmured. 'Something in that might give us a lead, or something? What even *is* Physiography?'

Josh absent-mindedly stroked Cottonball. 'It's where we learn about Zantoris. Not like History. It's more about its geography, landmarks, things like that.'

"How is that supposed to be helpful?" I asked my inner voice which had suggested this in the first place.

When I say that I didn't expect it to answer back, I really didn't.

It's not my fault they can't remember what they need to.

"Who are you?" I asked.

Your inner voice, dummy. The "inner voice" said, probably rolling its eyes.

"Inner voice? You've got to be kidding me," I thought. "I think I've officially lost my mind."

You haven't. Inner voice is one way to put it. The actual concept is more complex, but the bottom line is that I will be with you whether you like it or not. Oh, and your friends have been calling you for the last two minutes.

Sure enough, they were.

'Kendra?' Camilla called, sounding slightly frustrated. 'Earth to Kendra!'

'Yeah?' I replied, slightly shaking my head. 'Sorry, I zoned out for a minute there. What were you saying?'

'Your mom's calling us,' Camilla said. 'It's time for lunch.'

'Already?' I got up groggily.

It was really hot by now. Cottonball basked in the sun and Josh was slumped against a tree trunk, looking half-asleep. Where I lived, the sun had that type of effect on people.

While I had my lunch, I kept up a conversation with my inner voice.

"Maybe I should give you a name," I thought. "I don't like calling you "it". Do you have a name?"

Nope.

"Okay, how about Deirdre?"

Sorry, I have trouble pronouncing that name.

"Matt?"

No.

"Lizzie?"

Nah.

"What about . . . Riley?"

There was a pause.

I like that name. From now on, my name will be Riley, my inner voice decided.

I felt a bit relaxed after that, for some reason.

The atmosphere at the lunch table was much more vibrant than that of the garden. Mom and Liza chatted like old friends, Josh hungrily wolfed down his pasta, Camilla and I annoyed Cole by singing "99 Bottles of Beer" at the top of our voices, while Ivan stared at us like we were little green men from Mars, not touching his food.

After lunch, all of us except Ivan sprawled on the couch, thoroughly exhausted and full. Cole got a call, so he headed out to take it. That pretty much left us four to discuss again on what we have to do.

Tell Josh and Camilla to try and remember something from their Physiography class, Riley urged.

"What should I tell them?" I asked her. "They'll probably think I'm crazy."

Come on, trust me, she said. *I promise, there is something in there which will help you.*

I sighed. Here goes nothing . . .

'Guys,' I started, 'Can you *try* to remember something from your Physiography class? Something, anything that can help with this.'

'What do you want us to remember?' Camilla asked, looking genuinely confused. 'I really don't get what you're talking about.'

'Unless,' Josh said, looking like he was trying to remember something. If he had a beard, he would probably be stroking it.

'To get there, we're going to have to cross all the barriers . . .,' he muttered.

'What?' I said.

Josh looked at me, 'We haven't told you everything about Zantoris.'

'No, really?' I said, sarcastically.

'Zantoris is actually heavily protected,' he went on. 'It's bordered by five barriers which ensure its security. To get into Zantoris, people have to first go through all the barriers. Each one poses a trial of some sort, like the traps someone might put to keep a thief away from their house, only that the ones which we have to face are more dangerous. These barriers collectively form our Borders.'

All of us were silent. Then Camilla quickly composed herself and said, 'Okay, then. Looks like we're going to the Borders to get into Zantoris.'

I frowned. 'I have one question. No, two, actually.'

'Go ahead.'

'How do we get to the Borders? And assuming we *do* find a way, how are we going to convince everyone to let us go? They might not be so crazy about letting us go anywhere alone after we disappeared for over a month. And told them that we have a death threat.'

'Ugh,' Josh groaned, as he flung his legs over the arm of the couch, pressing his forehead. 'Why is it that every time a problem is solved, a new one comes up?'

Everyone fell silent again, scouring their brains for a solution.

Suddenly, I had an idea.

'Guys,' I said. 'I think we have a solution.'

Chapter 11

'Okay, let me get this straight,' Ivan said. 'Your brother is not a Terran, nor a pixie, but a *human* who knows about our existence?'

'Yes,' I mumbled, getting a little sick of answering that question over and over again.

'How is that even possible?' he shrieked, genuinely terrified. 'No, this has to be a mistake. Humans *cannot* know we exist. The last time that happened –'

'Kendra, *please* tell me Cole hasn't said anything to anyone,' Josh pleaded, sounding pretty scared.

I shrugged. 'I don't know. We're going to have to ask him.'

When I told everyone that Cole knew about everything, they had a fit of terror, calmed down and then panicked again. I was the only one who wasn't all that affected, but the way they worried, fidgeted and looked outside the window got me caught up in the mood.

Now, I was scared too, even though I didn't really have any idea what to be afraid of.

All of us made our way to Cole's room. He was on his laptop with headphones plugged in. We stood there awkwardly for a few minutes. I cleared my throat and he ignored me. He only paid attention when I knocked over several things from his desk.

He glared at me. 'What did you do that for? Pick it up. Now.'

I was about to say no, but then he gave me that look that advised me to suck it up and just do what I was told.

'What do you want?' Cole sighed.

'We kinda need your help,' Camilla said.

'What kind of help?' he said.

We told him everything. In the end, he got up and said, 'So, you want me to take a bunch of twelve-year-olds with me to my friends' trip so that one could find a way to get back to their magical fantasyland and the other could find a way to reverse something which is basically irreversible, without any adult tagging along.'

'The curse *can* be removed,' Josh insisted. 'It's just that, it will take time and we have got to face a few obstacles.'

'How much time will that take, exactly?' Cole inquired.

Josh shrugged. 'That would be a maximum of one or two months.'

'But don't worry,' replied Camilla hastily, when Cole raised his eyebrows. 'The Borders are outside of Earth, so the same rules of time apply there.'

Cole looked at us for five whole minutes before letting out a long sigh, 'Fine. But I'm *only* doing this for Kendra. There are also going to be some ground rules. Expect them in writing by this evening.'

Ivan got up and said. 'I need to ask you a question.'

'Shoot,' my brother replied, turning his attention back to the laptop.

'You're clearly not a pixie,' he stated, in a dangerous tone. 'How do you know about us?'

'Why should I tell you?' Cole demanded, looking slightly annoyed at being interrogated by someone who is four years younger than him.

'Because humans aren't supposed to know that we exist,' Josh said, sounding sick of saying it again and again.

'Well, I didn't want to know this myself, so I guess we're both disappointed,' he replied, shortly.

'At least tell us that you haven't told anyone what you know,' Camilla begged.

Cole thought for a while. 'My friend Sean knows. But I didn't tell him. He was there with me when I found out.'

Apparently that was it. All of us got up and left the room. I led everyone to my room which once again looked as if a tornado swept through it.

I flopped onto my bed, while Josh and Camilla sat on the floor. Ivan settled on a chair, looking around distastefully.

'Well,' I started. 'I guess we should ask our parents if we can go with Cole and his friends.'

'Yeah,' Josh agreed.

Just then Liza came in and said that they've got to head back home. Josh and Camilla said goodbye and Ivan went back to his campout.

Just then a familiar buzzing noise came in my head.

"Hey Riley," I greeted, "where have you been?"

Sorry, I dozed off after lunch. What did I miss?

"We're going to find a way to get Ivan home, and also reverse the curse I got from the banshee. We will be going with Cole on his Miami trip, so that we can slip away to the Zantorian Borders without any adults looking out for us."

Ooh, sounds exciting. But what makes you think your mom will let you go with your brothers? She's not going to let you go, especially after you told the officer that your kidnappers are out to get you.

"Well, I'll say that this could be a sort of a bonding trip?"

But she will have questions as to why Josh, Camilla and Ivan need to bond with Cole and David. Besides, she'll probably have this idea of a bonding trip in her mind for who knows how long, and she'll probably make you three go on a trip of your own.

'Ugh,' I groaned out loud. 'When did my life get so complicated? I was going on the right track before. Where did I go wrong?'

Probably when you forgot that you had a choice to return to Earth instead of staying on in Zantoris, Riley offered.

'Not helping,' I muttered.

I took a deep breath, grabbed my phone and hit play on the music. Finally my nerves seemed to calm down.

I was in my room for a long time until I was called down for dinner. I didn't ask permission for the trip, because I still had to think of a reasonable excuse to go, but when I went to my room, I found a piece of paper with the "ground rules" Cole was talking about.

The rules included not speaking unless spoken to—basically all the rules you need to make yourself invisible. I was fine with that.

I quickly emailed the rules to Josh and Camilla, and decided that I would show this to Ivan when he would (probably) come the next day.

I started thinking about ways to get my parents to let me go. Pretty soon I had a list which went something like this:
1. There's a Beyonce concert.
2. A science project required me to observe the ecosystem at the coast.
3. My favorite author will be visiting the beach.
4. I wanted to visit a friend.

And more like this.

I thought the first two were the best ones, which was sad. But the third sounded stalker-ish and my parents would want to meet this "friend" they've never heard me talk about. The others were so ridiculous, it's embarrassing to even think about them.

I went to Cole to hear *his* thoughts. I saw that David was in his room scrolling through his phone.

They both looked up when I entered.

'Cole, can I talk to you?' I asked.

He came outside.

I handed him the list and said, 'Which of these will make the most sense to Mom and Dad to let me and the others come with you guys?'

Cole ran his blue eyes across the paper. '*None* of these make any sense.'

He kinda has a point there, Kendra, Riley piped up. *Like, seriously, why would your parents let you go because you had a science project when you missed school for more than a month?*

'Ok, fine, I know these ideas are pretty stupid,' I admitted. 'Do *you* have anything?'

He thought for a moment. 'This trip is a reward to me and David for passing our midterms. You never gave yours, so maybe you can ask mom and dad if you could take that test in school with permission from the principal. And if you pass with good marks, mom and dad will *surely* give you a reward of some sort. *Then* you could say that you want to go on this trip with your friends.'

I frowned. 'But we need to get Ivan back to Zantoris as soon as possible. He's probably been declared dead by now. Studying the entire course, getting permission for a retest, all of it is going to take up time. Besides, who knows what my curse will do until then.'

'You guys really have no choice,' Cole said. 'Unless you want to tell Mom and Dad the truth.'

'No way,' I refused at once. 'Camilla, Josh and Ivan already were panicked when I told them that you knew. It's one of the most ancient laws to prevent the news of our existence reaching human ears. I have a feeling something *really* terrible will happen and the reason there is no havoc right now is because you're technically still a teenager. Adults may be less open-minded about things like this.'

Cole shrugged. 'In that case you're going to have to take all your exams and so will Camilla and Josh.'

I groaned and went to my room. I got ready for bed and didn't realize how sleepy I was until my head hit the pillow.

In the morning, over breakfast, I cleared my throat and all the attention promptly came to me. Cole discreetly gave me an encouraging nod.

'Mom, Dad,' I started, with a somewhat shaky voice. 'You know how I missed all my mid-term exams?'

They slowly nodded.

'Well, I was wondering if I could take them now with the permission of the principal,' I finished.

They looked surprised but also slightly pleased.

'Sweetheart, it's great that you want to take the exams,' Dad said. 'Actually, Principal Jameson called last night and said that you will have to take your exams if you want to graduate to the eighth grade. Now this is completely optional and you don't need to feel pressured –'

'I'll take it' I decided, firmly. I could only imagine their shock. As far as they remembered, I was the one who complained more during exams than actually studied. This was new territory.

David was looking at me with a suspicious expression, and Cole followed suit, probably to avoid suspicion himself.

After a while, Camilla and Josh came over, along with Ivan, whose campout is close to their house. I told them the plan. Josh and Camilla groaned.

'We ask you to do one simple thing of finding a way to get into the trip, and you land us with exams?' Camilla exclaimed. Ivan snorted, apparently enjoying this plan.

'Do you have a better idea?' I snapped.

They shook their heads.

'I thought as much,' I muttered, before turning to Ivan. 'All of this will take up a lot of time, and will delay us returning to Zantoris. Are you okay with that?'

That was a silly question to ask. *Of course,* it's not okay. Ivan put down his guard for a second, looking crushed and desperate. Then he became aware that his emotions betrayed him, and quickly put on his usual aloof expression and shrugged.

I went to my desk and grabbed a textbook from there.

'Guess I should start studying,' I murmured.

Josh and Camilla sighed and grabbed a book from my desk. I was going through Arithmetic I, when I noticed Ivan sitting awkwardly.

'You could pick a book too,' I said, waving my hand towards my bookshelf.

He got up and chose a novel. Pretty soon, my room turned into a reading club.

For lunch, Josh and Camilla went home and Ivan left with them. Over at the table, Mom said, 'Great news, honey! Principal Jameson says that you can definitely take the exam. Since it was the flu season, many students had fallen sick and are now asking for a retest. Their parents are, anyway. They will be getting one after two weeks. So, he says that three more can be arranged.'

'Three more?' I said.

'Well, Josh and Camilla didn't take the exams either, and Principal Jameson had just gotten calls from their parents about this.'

I nodded and closed my eyes. This was going to be a *long* week.

Chapter 12

The next week was a busy one for me and my friends. We kept studying and revising material every chance we got. After school, instead of relaxing in front of the TV, we trooped off to the local branch library and studied. Torture, yes, but also necessary.

When we returned to school, all eyes were on us. We were known as the 'Kids-Who-Went-Missing'. Thankfully, the teachers were lenient with us and gave us extra coaching to help us catch up.

Ivan was becoming nicer to us. He didn't refer to us as Terrans for two days. He asked us questions from our notes as revision, and if we got one answer wrong, he made us write the question and its answer fifteen times. Brutal—and a waste of paper—but effective.

As the day of my exam drew close, I got increasingly nervous. I absolutely *had* to pass this with good grades, or we would *never* get back to Zantoris. Josh seemed more relaxed and confident, while Camilla betrayed no emotion. Ivan didn't show it, but I could tell he was freaking out. Before we left for school, he came to see me after visiting Camilla and Josh. I thought he was going to give a pep talk or something, but he just said an awkward, 'Good luck,' and left.

Half an hour before the regular classes were over, I had to go to an exam hall along with the rest of the kids who had to retake their midterms.

We had to take two exams in one day, Math and Science. I found it slightly difficult, but I circled what I thought was the answer and moved on. Before I knew it, it was time to hand in the papers. We were allowed an hour's break and then were given the Science paper.

Science was simpler. I finished ahead of time, and gave it a once over. I peeked over at the others who mostly seemed to be doing fine, except Josh, who looked like he was ready to tear the paper in half. I couldn't blame him. The seventeenth question *was* kinda tricky.

After it was over, we headed home, almost in time for dinner. But, my family waited for me. Well, my parents did, anyway. Cole and David had already eaten and were lying on the couch, looking half-dead.

'So,' my mom began, 'How was it?'

I took my time in chewing and swallowing, then I said, 'The Science one was pretty easy compared to the Math one.'

'Well, I'm sure you'll do well,' Mom assured. 'You and your friends have been working really hard for this.'

Next up was History.

I don't know if I had ever mentioned that History wasn't my strong suit. To make matters worse, the school decided to give us the exact same questions which I *always* faltered in. Ivan could make me write the answer fifty times, and I still wouldn't get it.

I decided to calm down, and first complete the questions I did know. I did those as quickly as I could, and was left with twenty minutes. I thought hard, but couldn't come up with enough to get me full marks in that question. Then I had an idea.

"Riley, I need your help."

What?

"I don't know the answer to this, this, this, and that question. Oh, and also the last two ones."

What do you want me to do?

"Do you remember the answer?"

I do.

"Great, tell me what they are."

No.

"Why not?" I groaned inwardly.

Because that would be cheating, Riley declared.

I huffed. "Can you at least give me a clue?"

No.

I clenched my fists. "If I fail, that's on you."

Good to know.

I quickly filled out the last question as the teacher came to my desk to take the paper. I sank into my chair and sighed with both relief and tension.

I looked over at my friends. Josh grinned and Camilla did likewise, which told me they did well in their test. Or at least, they *thought* they did.

Fifteen minutes later, it was time for English. It was pretty simple. I had always been good at English; it's just how I speak.

I felt a bit lightheaded after that. I had Spanish, and after that, all exams would be over.

I was not the best in Spanish, but Camilla, who was fluent in it, agreed to help us out.

After school, I went over to Camilla and Josh's house, because Cole and David had a party over at mine.

The house was again bursting with life and music. There was an arm-wrestling match between Agnes and Chris, with Mikey cheering them like mad, and Jennie yelling at them to be quiet and let her read.

Josh, Camilla and I relaxed for a while before playing Monopoly. Ivan, who was there too, refused to play until he saw what the game was about. That is quite possibly the smartest move he ever took.

Eventually, he decided to join us. Needless to say, Riley was a huge help throughout the game

'Maybe we should stop,' said a very grumpy Camilla as she sold her last property.

'Nope,' I smirked.

We went on. The fights increased, we went bankrupt and Ivan was using us as rolling ATM machines, because somehow, *everyone* landed on his property. I think next time we need to make someone else the treasurer.

As I walked back home, I thought that maybe we got this after all. We just have to pass my Spanish test, convince my parents to let me go, get into the Borders, get Ivan back home and find a way to reverse my curse.

It's as simple as that.

When I got back later that night, I found that the house was neat and tidy. I was pretty surprised. I was kind of expecting a mess. But then, if Mom and Dad were back home, they probably would've chased everyone out and hustled my brothers to clean up themselves.

I quickly wolfed down my dinner and went to bed. I tossed and turned for half an hour, until I fell asleep.

The next day, I revised my Spanish thoroughly and Camilla helped Josh and me. Ivan, who naturally knew nothing about the language, claimed to come only because he wanted to read the next book of the series he had started off of my shelf.

The exam was incredibly easy. I felt relieved.

I skipped home, happily. I knew this feeling would vanish on result day, but I tried to enjoy it while it lasted.

The world always seemed to get better and more vibrant whenever exams were over. The slightly warm weather which I once thought as annoying and distracting, now felt welcoming and gentle against my skin.

'I'M HOME!' I yelled happily as I walked through the front door.

'Hey,' Dad greeted. 'How was it?'

'Great,' I replied. Then I headed to the kitchen and drank three glasses of water consecutively. My throat was parched and I hadn't drunk any water for the past two-and-a-half hours.

Mom came back from shopping and, on my begging, agreed to make my favorite dinner.

'So,' Mom began, 'When are the results expected?'

I shrugged. 'Probably next week?'

For the next few days, me, Josh and Camilla were relaxing like there was no tomorrow. Ivan kept coming over from time to time to return a book or start a new one.

The days passed by quickly, and before I knew it, I found myself sitting at my desk with the school website open, tapping and fidgeting nervously.

The results were due at six thirty, and I was reloading the page every two seconds at six twenty-eight.

Suddenly, a link - "Exam Results" - popped up.

I could feel my heartbeat increase tenfold. I stared at the link for two minutes like a doofus, and suddenly remembered I'm supposed to click it. I slowly dragged my cursor and watched silently as the page began reloading and redirecting me to a form which asked me to fill in my full name and class.

The clicket-clackity sound of the keys was all that was heard in my room as I filled in all the information and pressed enter. A list of links appeared for me for each subject.

I decided to start with the ones I thought I did a bit lousily at. First up was Math.

93.

At least it wasn't as bad as I feared. Next, I checked out Social Studies.

84.

I sighed. I *knew* I'd mess up those History questions. I then moved over to Science.

95.

Yay. Feeling slightly more confident, I went to English.

97.

Awesome. Now that just left Spanish. This determined the future. I *need* to get high marks in this because I know that your overall percentage has an annoying habit of going up by two per cent if you get good marks, and then sinking like the Titanic when you get low marks.

After two deep breaths, I opened the link and my eyes quickly started searching for the result.

99.5.

I quickly did calculations. I wasn't sure if it was correct or not, but I got 93.7%. I did the calculations again and this time got 98.75%.

Puzzled and pretty sure I had gotten something wrong, I did it again and got 85%.

Do you even know how to do this? Riley commented, probably shaking her imaginary head in despair.

"No," I admitted.

Well, the important thing is you got passable marks Riley said, cheerfully. *And really good ones too!*

I grinned. This was certainly a huge leap from the past years.

I took a print out and skipped happily to the living room where everyone except Dad and David were.

'MOM!!' I shrieked.

She looked up in surprise as I shoved the paper under her nose.

She read it and, with Cole looking over her shoulder with a cocked eyebrow, looked at me beaming.

'Well done, sweetie! Oh, I'm so proud of you!' she exclaimed.

'Are you sure you didn't cheat or something?' Cole said.

'Cole!' Mom looked at him with stern eyes.

'Good job,' he sighed.

Dad, too, was really happy with my results. I raced over to Josh and Camilla's house, calling Ivan to tell him that the results were out.

When I reached, I saw that they hadn't yet seen their grades.

'Stupid Wi-Fi isn't working,' Josh grumbled. 'We have to call someone. What about you?'

I excitedly thrust my print out in his hands, and Camilla and Ivan peeked over his shoulder.

'Oh. My. Goodness,' Josh said, enunciating each word. 'You got a 93.7!'

I knew the first one was correct.

'Is that a good thing?' Ivan asked.

I vigorously nodded my head.

Ivan smiled a real, genuine smile for the first time since I met him. His usual dull, green eyes lit up to a brighter shade and his whole face radiated hope and excitement.

'KIDS, THE Wi-Fi IS FIXED!' Mr. Hannigan's voice came from downstairs.

There was a scramble for the laptop and Josh reached it first. He quickly opened the website, typed in his information with lightning speed and went straight to the overall report.

I looked at it and smiled.

'89.5, not bad,' I said.

'But I could've done better,' he replied mournfully.

'Come on, we went missing for more than a month,' I reminded him. 'We've been out of practice.'

'Easy for *you* to say; you got above 90!'

'Anyway, let me see mine,' Camilla interrupted, pushing Josh off the chair. She, like her cousin, went to the overall report. She grinned.

'80,' she announced happily.

'See, she got lesser marks yet she's happier than you,' I said to Josh.

At this he cracked a smile and said, 'Well, to her, anything above zero is good, but okay.'

Josh got his parents upstairs, and they saw the grades. They were happy and invited Ivan and me to stay for dinner.

Ivan reluctantly accepted but I didn't because I told my mom I'd be back for dinner. I hung out there for some time and then skipped joyously back home. (I was so happy, I forgot how to walk so I guessed I'd be skipping around for some time)

I did most of the talking at dinner. My parents listened patiently while my brothers had more of a 'When-Is-She-Gonna-Shut-Up' look.

'So,' Mom said when she got a chance to speak, 'Your dad and I were thinking about what to give you as a treat.'

I straightened a bit. 'I'm listening.'

'Well,' she continued, 'We remembered how much you wanted to go to Miami with your friends, and since your brothers were already going, we decided that you can go with them.'

I grinned. 'How did you know that?'

Dad shrugged. 'I overheard you talking to your friends about how much you need to go there two days ago.'

I froze. 'How much did you listen?'

'Don't worry, not much. Just that one thing.'

I heaved a sigh of relief before realizing that we did it. We're going.

I squealed like a six-year-old girl who got presented with a unicorn, nearly knocking my parents off of their seats while hugging them.

Cole and David started protesting, but I quickly said, 'Don't worry, I won't do anything. You won't even know we're there.'

'Who's we?' David asked, narrowing his eyes.

I hesitated. 'I was wondering if I could bring three of my friends along. Is that okay?'

'Of course, it is,' Dad replied.

I went to bed feeling ecstatic. Now all we need to do is go on this trip and hope our teleportation takes us to these . . . Borders. Cole and the others were also attending a concert so they booked a few hotel rooms. I guessed Mom and Dad expected me to be with them at all times. Letting me out of their sights was already a very big step for them.

In the morning, when I woke up, I found that Josh and Camilla and Ivan were already there.

We all sat at the table while I ate my breakfast.

I told them everything and their faces lit up after each word. When I told them about the concert, Josh's face contorted in concentration.

'So we need to book tickets and hotel rooms?' he asked.

'No, not really,' I said. 'I mean, we can *pretend* to pay, and forge tickets if possible.'

'But if we come back, we're still going to the concert and the hotel,' he countered.

I tried to ignore the "if". 'Didn't think of that.'

'Anyway, never mind that now,' Ivan said. 'What are the admission fees for this place?'

I put my plate in the sink and raced up to get my laptop. I

opened it and typed "cost of tickets to Miami Beach Pop Festival".

Camilla leaned in. 'It's a music festival?'

'Yes,' I replied.

'But I thought your brothers didn't like this type of music.'

'They don't,' I agreed. 'They're only doing this for some of their friends.'

Ivan poked his nose in my laptop from the other side. 'It's in Miami? How will we get there?'

'We'll take a train, I think.'

Ivan whistled. 'A bunch of sixteen-year-olds alone? Your parents sure give you a lot of freedom. And trust.'

'I think someone's mom is chaperoning us,' I said, sighing.

'But isn't the point of this trip avoiding adults?' Josh butted in, concerned.

I threw up my palms. 'I don't know, we'll find a way.'

'Do you think we should ask Cole to help us with this?' Josh said. 'He's already going next weekend, so he might be able to help us look in the right website and all.'

'You seriously think he will help?' I asked.

'Maybe I should ask,' Ivan suggested. 'I'm a guest so it might be hard for him to say no.'

'It's worth a shot,' Camilla said.

I beckoned Ivan with my head to go upstairs and find him.

After a few minutes, he came down with Cole. I don't know what he did, maybe he asked nicely or threatened to drown him with his hydrokinesis.

My brother pulled up a chair. 'What do you need help with?'

I pushed the laptop towards him. 'What website did you and David use to book your tickets?'

Cole scrolled down a bit and clicked on a link. I peeked in to see what he was doing.

'Cost for one person is 325 dollars for a three-day pass,' I read out, doing some quick calculations on a paper side-by-side. 'So for four people, it would cost one thousand three hundred.'

'We don't *have* that much,' Camilla said, as if that weren't obvious.

'Mom and Dad already paid for Kendra,' Cole piped up.

'We still need money,' Camilla reminded.

We were all quiet for some time, before Josh spoke up: 'Do we even *have* to go? I mean, we'll say that we're going but we never enter the park, and just leave.'

'Do we *have* to go to Miami to get to the Borders?' I wondered. 'I mean we could just go to the garage and teleport from there. If we're gone for two minutes, no one will notice anything.'

'No, Kendra,' Ivan said, 'See, if we're on Earth then we need to get to a place which closely resembles our destination. I don't know what the Borders look like, but this beach looks like the one we have in Zantoris. Just like when you were in your school, the field resembled the one in Aternalis.'

'O . . .kay,' I said, trying to take it all in. 'So ditching this trip is out of question.'

'We still don't have enough money,' Josh complained.

'How much *do* you have?' Cole asked.

'My current allowance right now is fifty, I think,' I recalled.

Josh and Camilla told us their allowance and some quick calculations showed we were exactly hundred dollars away.

'Great,' Josh slumped back on his chair. 'Where are we going to get it from?'

Cole suddenly got up and started walking away. We stared after him, not really sure what to make of that. He came back holding an envelope. My brain didn't know what was happening, but Riley, who was obviously smarter than me, gasped.

Cole thrust the envelope in my hands, saying, 'Here, keep it.'

I opened it to see a hundred dollars lying there.

I looked at him, a huge smile tugging at my lips. 'Really?'

Cole shrugged.

'Thank you *so, so* much!'

I tried to hug him, but he put his hand on my forehead, slightly pushing me away, saying, 'You touch me, and I'm taking it back.'

'But really, Cole, thanks a lot,' Camilla said, grinning.

He shrugged. 'David did something too, you know. We each gave fifty.'

I made a mental note to give David a thank you Post-It along with a bag of chips.

Ivan frowned. 'How do you all have so much money? Do you work?'

'It's pocket money saved over the years,' I replied. 'Why? Is it not a thing in Zantoris?'

He shook his head. 'And why should it? It doesn't make sense to have any money other than what you've earned.'

'Huh,' I said, frowning. Considering how Ivan's parents were richer than mine, Camilla and Josh's combined, I was a little confused as to how he never had any money to spend for himself.

'Now, as for how to get there,' Josh said.

'Oh yeah, you probably don't know,' Cole suddenly said, 'Mom made me and David take you guys with us on the train journey. And don't worry about that, your parents have paid. You'll get your tickets this evening.'

I heaved a sigh of relief. 'Okay, so I guess everything is settled now? No more plans to make?'

'Nope,' Josh replied, looking as if the whole world's weight had been lifted off of his shoulder. 'All we need to do now is start packing.'

Saying that, everyone went from sitting in perfect, tense posture to slumping back into the chair in the most undignified manner.

One phase of the plan was complete. Now we needed to teleport to the first Borders, survive all the challenges and . . . wait.

'Guys,' I began, 'if the Borders are technically a part of Zantoris, and we can't enter Zantoris, then how do we know that we will be able to access the Borders?'

'We don't,' Josh said comfortably, as if that were no big deal. 'We've just got to try and if we don't succeed, then . . . oh well, we tried.'

Everyone seemed disturbingly calm with that idea. We all sat in silence until Camilla lightly slapped the table and said, 'Well okay, everything's done now, but when do we leave?'

'This weekend, early morning, so be up by 5 a.m.,' David said suddenly entering the room. We watched as he journeyed to the fridge, scanned for snacks, visibly got disappointed when he found nothing and waddled back to his room.

Unfortunately it was Sunday, so to us, the weekend took its sweet time in coming. Josh and Camilla got permission for the trip but it took a *lot* of convincing. After they did, my mom gave my brothers a long lecture on how they need to look out for us and that we should be within their line of vision at all times.

I was relieved. I was afraid that Camilla and Josh wouldn't be allowed to go, but then if they weren't, it would make sense. They disappeared for a month, so letting them go on a trip is a miracle.

We got our tickets on Wednesday.

My curse didn't show itself in any way, making me think that the banshee must have been a dud. We had almost forgotten about Bob. (We had gotten a bit bored of calling the guy in the robes that, so we named him Bob). Everyone had now made peace with the fact that Cole and his friend, Sean knew about pixies. We made them promise not to tell anyone. Not that anyone would believe them, but still.

Ivan was now neutral with all of us. He didn't mock or insult us. His face refused to show any emotion. Though out of all of us, he got along best with Josh. I'd take it as a win, because as long as we're getting along and not fighting, everything should be easy.

I started packing on Friday. I packed a huge suitcase with clothes. That would be the one I will be leaving behind.

I then took a backpack which I *would* be taking with me, and packed a first aid kit (I had no idea how to do first aid, but hoped the others could help me), canned rations, a toothbrush and toothpaste, some breath mints, a towel, my phone and its charger, a pair of earphones, and five pairs of clothes for every season (I didn't know whether seasons in the Borders are the same as Earth). The end result was an overstuffed, bulging, odd-looking backpack.

As I lay in bed, I thought over everything that had happened over the week. Everything was going smoothly. A bit too smoothly.

Seems pretty suspicious, doesn't it? Riley said.

"Mm-hmm," I mumbled. "I have a feeling something is going to go wrong."

Riley was a bit silent after that.

"Riley?" I called, "Hey, you there?"

Y-yeah, I'm here, she said quickly. She said nothing other than that.

And after that, the whole night passed in silence.

Chapter 13

'WAKE UP! YOU'RE LATE!' David barked as he pulled the blankets off me, leaving me to wake up with a leap and start shivering.

'What do you mean I'm late?' I mumbled sleepily as I rubbed the gunk out of my eyes.

'You were supposed to be up at five,' Cole said, as he threw a pillow at me to keep me from falling asleep. 'Didn't you set your alarm clock? It's ten minutes to six.'

The moment I heard that, I probably set the record for the fastest person on Earth. I showered within two minutes and patted myself on the back for packing everything beforehand. I grabbed my backpack and suitcase and hugged my sleepy parents tightly as if that was the last time I was going to see them—because that might possibly be true.

'Take care, sweetie,' Dad said, kissing my head.

I wasn't able to make any reply to that.

After all the goodbyes, I climbed onto the back seat. We drove to Josh and Camilla's house to pick them up. Josh's bright and fresh-looking face was at odds with the dull bluish-gray color of the early morning sky, while Camilla's matched it perfectly.

'Just go a bit down the street, and you'll find Ivan's campout,' Josh instructed.

We drove down the street and saw Ivan waiting with a backpack.

We scooched over for him and he found some room in the tiny space.

'Where did you get that backpack from?' I asked.

He shrugged. 'Don't worry, I left something for that kid to make up for the loss. And he still has his stuff, I just needed the bag.'

'You stole it?!?' David raised his eyebrows, turning around in his seat to look at Ivan.

'Yes.'

Well. At least he was honest.

We made it all the way to the train station, where we met Cole and David's buddies.

'There you are,' Sean said. 'What took you so long?'

'*Somebody* forgot to set the alarm clock the night before,' David replied.

There were ten of us in all, including my brothers' friends Sean, Brad, Jada and Carlos. Jada's mother was chaperoning us. She was discreet, yet she managed to give us the feeling that we were being watched.

Sean kept a respectful distance from my friends and me probably because he knew that we were pixies and Sean felt intimidated. Brad just nodded to us and didn't say anything else to us for the rest of the trip. Carlos was a bit more easygoing. I had known him for a while, so he kept popping his head in our carriage asking if we wanted anything from the train stewardess. Jada ignored us like we weren't there, and the only contact she made with us was when she told Josh that his bag would fall on his head if he didn't push it further away in the luggage rack.

Camilla, Josh, Ivan and I had a passenger car of our own. A friendly stewardess kept coming along every five minutes asking if we wanted any peanuts. I was feeling very irritable, though. Maybe it was the lack of sleep.

Riley hadn't said much last night, but the way she spoke two or three words had me convinced she knew something about this whole trip but refused to tell me.

"Why won't you tell me?" I demanded. "It could save a lot of trouble, you know."

Because I can't, she replied, firmly. *Don't ask me why, I just can't. It's one of the rules. Besides, even though I can't tell you, I **will** help you, I promise.*

I let the matter drop. Now, I looked over to my friends and wondered if I should even trust Riley at all. I hadn't known her for that long, yet I was willing to put the lives of my friends, whom I have known longer, in her hands.

Camilla sat at the window seat, her brown hair fluttering about her face from the breeze which came in through the open window. The sun had risen high by now, and the light made her gray eyes turn pale blue.

Josh twiddled his thumbs to keep himself occupied and occasionally took a swig from the juice box he got from the stewardess. Both cousins looked a bit identical, with the same marble gray eyes, and dark brown hair. I remember being fascinated by their eyes when I first met them. I had read somewhere that gray eyes mean they are connected to supernatural beings. I had dismissed it as a silly superstition, but now, after everything that had happened, I was careful not to think of anything as silly and fake.

Ivan leaned his head back against the wall with his eyes closed. Now that he didn't have his judging look, I realized how much he looked like his mother, Cordelia. His emerald eyes definitely belonged to his father, sure, but the way he kept his hair parted from the side, and the sophisticated shape and structure of his face and nose reminded me of Cordelia.

Suddenly, without any warning, my vision went black. The

most disturbing part? At this point, I wasn't even surprised anymore.

When I could see again, I saw that I had floated out of my body - literally.

I could see myself looking straight ahead with unblinking eyes, and the others didn't look my way, so they didn't notice anything. I glanced at my hands and yelped. It was like I was a ghost or spirit. Every time I moved, it evaporated in a small cloud of mist and became solid after a few seconds.

Suddenly, Ghost Me was shot out of the train and zoomed across the place. Everything was zooming by faster than a cheetah and was too much of a blur to me to see which way I was going. When my vision steadied, I found myself standing in the middle of a throne room.

Chapter 14

Whenever someone said throne room, I always envisioned a humongous room with big golden thrones, everything brightly lit with chandeliers, a well-carpeted floor and the regal and kind face of a king or queen at the throne.

I never pictured a huge Goth cathedral-like chamber, dimly lit with torches and walls dripping with what suspiciously looked like blood. Through the high dome glass ceiling, I saw that the sky was dim gray. The room had a musty smell, like it had been locked for centuries. I was standing behind one of the pillars which stood in two rows, leading to the far end of the room, where two big chairs were placed. The room was freezing. The chairs were obsidian black and the cushions that lined them were blood red. And sitting on them was our very own Bob and a woman who was probably his wife.

I could tell because they were wearing identical rings, with an onyx stone on which was carved a clover. From my time in Zantoris, I learned that a clover signifies marriage.

My mouth went dry once I saw Bob. My legs decided that it was the perfect moment to get stuck to the floor, when my sworn desire was to run away from this creepy place. Fortunately, I was invisible to them. At least, that's what I hoped.

Bob looked the same from what I last saw of him. Same perfectly styled hair, same intimidating yellow eyes and same dissatisfied expression.

'*We must stop them,*' he said in Zanarian, creasing his eyebrows. '*But how?*'

'Azmaveth, my dear, is it really necessary to do all this?' the woman enquired. She was sitting on her throne with incredible poise, wearing a long black dress. Her blonde hair was piled on top of her head and her eyes were pitch black. I didn't know what to make of the fact that in her hand she held the same orb-like thing I had found with Cole and Sean when I bumped into them on the day I got sucked into all this drama. On the other hand she held a dagger which was black as darkness, and the grip was encrusted with rubies which seemed to blaze brightly, like fire.

As for Bob/Azmaveth, he turned to his wife in surprise. *'Now, now, whatever do you mean, Mallory?'*

The woman hesitated. *'They might be no trouble to us at all. Maybe we're just jumping to conclusions. After all, all they want to do is find a way back home. Although, the girl with the banshee's curse is going to have to go to another path.'*

Azmaveth rolled his eyes. *'This is why I'm the patron of my people, not you.'*

'But –'

'I hope you remember what happened to the last person who tried to oppose me,' Azmaveth threatened, a dangerous glint in his yellow eyes.

Mallory's lips tightened. *'Alright then, let's go through with your plan.'*

Apparently, that was it. I zoomed out of the place and my ghost was put back in my body with such force that my head slumped back and hit the wall. Hard.

Josh and Camilla caught the movement and Ivan woke up with a jerk at the loud knock.

'Kendra?' Josh said, frowning. 'You okay?'

'Huh?' I mumbled, only half-listening and rubbing the back of my head. 'Oh, I'm okay. Just . . . owww.'

Ivan stared at me. 'Did you have a vision?'

'That's what it was?' I said. 'What's a vision?'

'What did you see?' Camilla asked, ignoring my question.

I described everything. By the end of my story, everyone had gone white.

'What's a vision?' I repeated my question in what would barely be considered a whisper.

'It's . . . well, some might call it a guidance,' Ivan replied. 'They happen when someone is starting a new phase in their life. They show stuff which will be relevant to your situation. But . . .' Ivan hesitated and looked me in the eye. 'It's weird that we're having them at this age, because it's more common in young adults who are starting their careers or something of the like. The vision you saw? I had the same one last night.'

'I had that one a few days ago,' Josh said.

'I saw this on the day our exams started,' Camilla said.

I frowned, trying to keep my worry in check. 'What did we just get ourselves into?'

No one had any answer to that so I tried a different statement. 'Why are we keeping secrets from each other?'

'What do you mean?'

'These visions and dreams are related to all this,' I said. 'And some might help us too. So we can't keep these visions a secret.'

'That makes sense,' Camilla agreed.

'Okay, from now on, we won't keep any secrets which might help us,' Ivan agreed. 'But now, one thing's clear: This guy—Azmaveth—has a hand in all of this. And I have a feeling that he's not on our side, so we need to steer clear of him.'

'He wants to stop us from going to the Borders,' Camilla recalled. 'And his wife, Mallory, said that the one with the banshee's curse was going to have to go on another path.'

All eyes turned on me.

'We'll look into that later,' I decided. 'Maybe we should forget about Azmaveth. We'll be careful, yes, but it could also be that this guy tries to stop *everyone* who enters the Border.'

I looked outside the window. The rest of the five hours was spent either sleeping or staring out of the window, contemplating life.

I think there was one point where everyone, including me, fell asleep. No one stole anything from us, which was a relief, but then we didn't really have anything at hand which was *worth* stealing.

We only reached our destination at night. Josh was shaking me awake.

'We've reached,' he mumbled, sleepily.

We grabbed our bags from the rack and got out of the train. The railway station was deserted. No one was there except the station master. The sky was pitch black and the lamplight gave the whole place an eerie touch.

We waited for my brothers and their friends to exit the train. It took a while since their passenger car was a bit far away from ours, so Ivan and Camilla leaned on the headlamps back-to-back, and started to doze off.

Cole, David and their friends certainly looked tired and bleary-eyed, but definitely in a better condition than any of us. They picked up our bags for us, and managed to stuff everything in the taxi.

Needless to say, all of us barely got any space to sit and were squashed like tomatoes. The road was a bit rocky, and our heads kept banging each other every time there was a speed break. On the bright side, it *did* keep us from falling asleep.

At the hotel, each of us had to share a room with someone. My roomie was Camilla and Josh and Ivan shared a room.

I threw myself on my bed and was just starting to drowse off, when Camilla decided to think.

'I've been thinking . . .' she started.

'What?' I mumbled, lifting my head.

'Isn't this a bit too easy? Why would our families even *think* of letting us go after we disappeared? Especially after you said we had a death threat.'

I sighed and sat up. 'You're saying someone else is having a hand in all this?'

Camilla shrugged. 'Seeing as we already have Azmaveth as a rival, that's a possibility.'

'You know what, let's not overthink,' I said. 'If we do, we'll get even more scared.'

'Oh, I'm not scared,' Camilla told me, slipping under the sheets. 'Just thinking.'

Breakfast the next day felt more like a funeral. At least to me. Cole, David and their friends seemed happy and content, completely oblivious to what we were about to do.

The plan was simple. Get to the beach and teleport.

All we could do was hope that everyone would be distracted by something when we reached the place.

After breakfast, I went back up to the room and quickly took a shower. I pulled on a pair of jeans and a sleeveless yellow shirt and kept a slim black jacket at hand, since I didn't know the weather conditions. I tied my hair in its usual messy ponytail.

Jada's mom got us a minibus in no time. She struck up a friendly conversation with me and my friends who were huddled at the back. As for the rest, they acted more like kids than sixteen-year-olds. They stuffed their faces with snacks, sang karaoke at the top of their voices and would've stuck their head out of the window into the moving traffic for some "aesthetic" pictures for their

Instagram stories and hit their head by a truck if Jada's mom hadn't stopped them.

Then we stopped for some time at a café. My brothers and their friends went off on their own, leaving the rest of us behind, but every now and then, David and Cole occasionally glanced at us to see if we're okay.

My friends and I chose a table which was a little away from them, but within each other's sight. We couldn't eat much, and I kept thinking about how much I would have loved hanging out in this place with Josh and Camilla if the reason wasn't because we have to go on an impossible mission with some creepy weirdo of a pixie watching our every move.

I got a bit bored, so I took out my phone and started surfing the web.

Ivan poked his nose into the screen. 'What's this?'

'This is a phone,' I explained. 'It's a device in which –'

'I know this is a phone,' he interrupted. 'I meant "what's this" as in "what are you doing".'

'Well, I realized that ever since I discovered this whole pixie thing, I never really searched "pixies" on Wikipedia,' I replied.

Camilla looked up from her pizza. 'Kendra, I've told you, don't believe everything the world says about pixies.'

'Then I'll go over the facts and you tell me what's true and what's not,' I suggested. 'Number one: Pixies are famous for stealing children and frightening maidens and leading travelers astray.'

'Wrong,' everyone said in unison.

I moved on to the next fact. 'Pixies aren't supposed to lie.'

'That's not written here,' Ivan said, still peeking into my phone.

I shoved his face away with two fingers and said, 'I heard this in Aternalis school. I just needed an elaboration on this rule.'

Camilla looked amused. 'You could've just asked? Never mind. So yeah, pixies aren't supposed to lie, especially to an Elder.'

'Who's an Elder?' I asked.

'Pixies usually live up to a thousand years,' she explained. 'After that, they die. But there *are* several cases in which pixies live beyond a thousand years. They are called Elders. They have to be treated with utmost respect above all else.'

I nodded. After some time, we were on the move again. As we piled on to the bus, my stomach started churning. When we reached the beach, that would be it. On the drive there, I leaned against the window and looked outside, when, without warning, a familiar voice said, '*Morning, Kendra.*'

"Riley, where have you *been*?" I demanded. "You've missed out on so much."

Sorry, I was sleeping.

"Wow, you sleep a lot."

I like to sleep, is that such a crime?

"Fine, fine."

*Although, I did catch that view from five minutes ago. This place is **gorgeous** isn't it?*

"Yep. It's times like this when the occasion *has* to be a death warrant."

It reminds me so much of Zantoris . . .

"Wait, you've been to Zantoris? I thought you were just an inner voice."

Inner voices can travel anywhere they want, but in spirit.

Neither of that made any sense to me, but I decided to let it go. I chatted more with Riley in my head.

The bus screeched to a halt and all of us piled out. My friends and I were the last ones to leave, mostly because we were glued to our seats in terror.

David and the others went off, while Cole stayed back, trying to persuade us to come out.

'Come on, you guys,' he said. 'You got this, alright? I know this is what many people say and the results *always* vary, but I know you can do this. You've gone through incredible lengths to get here, with all the retaking exams and giving up allowance and all. I'm not going to let you just *sit* there and let all that effort go to waste. Even though I don't know you all that well, I *can* tell that you're strong, okay? You survived a freaking tsunami, for Pete's sake!'

Ivan frowned. 'How do you know that?'

'Kendra told me. See the point is that you better get out *right now*, because I'm not accepting that me and my brother gave money to strangers, only for them to wuss out at the last minute. Also, I don't have another pep talk planned.'

So, slightly more confident from Cole's "pep talk", we stepped out of the bus. I could only imagine how weird all that was for the bus driver, who stared at us with a look that said *what on Earth was all that about?*

Naturally, we took baby steps, literally, procrastinating as much as possible.

The pearly white sand got into my shoes the second I started walking on it. I grunted and dusted my shoes. The waves lapped onto the shore with a gentle *whoosh*, and I saw some five-year-old boys and Carlos screaming and running away from the waves. The sun beat down at full capacity, making the water look tempting.

'So this is it, huh?' Cole gently put a hand on my shoulder. 'Take care, all of you. Good luck.'

I gave him a hug, and mumbled thanks for all the help he gave, and Cole shook hands with the rest.

Ivan looked at me. 'You still don't know how to teleport?'

I shook my head. All of us held hands. My head was hit by that familiar feeling of dizziness. Cole watched silently as we all started to glow brightly. My heartbeat thundered as I closed my eyes to cope with the vertigo. A bright light enveloped all four of us as we entered the Borders.

Chapter 15

I wasn't sure if everyone felt that way, or if it was just me, but I was pretty disappointed when I opened my eyes. I was expecting something more dramatic than a conference room.

'Is . . . is this it?' Camilla wondered, perplexed.

'I've got no clue,' I said.

'Josh, what's going on?' Ivan asked.

Josh frowned. 'Why are you asking me?'

'You're the nerd who knows everything about Zantoris.'

'I don't get why you're asking me,' Josh protested. 'Just because I'm academically smart doesn't mean I know everything. I've never been to the Borders before, so I had no idea it would look like a conference room.'

I looked around. The room looked decent. A semi-circular glass table surrounded us. The walls were divided in columns and each of them were painted white and sandy brown. A potted plant stood in the corner and there were several lights around the room, but only the one in the middle was switched on, giving it the aura of an interrogation room. There were no windows, and the only escape from this place seemed to be the door at the far end.

I stared at it thoughtfully, before it opened.

A woman with dark curls and an orange evening dress stepped inside. She glanced at us, as if four kids standing in the middle of a conference room were perfectly fine.

She had a clipboard in her hand, and grabbed a pen from a pen stand on the table.

'Your names, please?' she asked as she uncapped the pen.

We all stared at her like doofuses. She looked at us and cleared her throat.

'I *said*, your names please? You do want to enter Zantoris or Devuniake, right?'

'Zantoris, yes,' Josh replied, nodding.

'For that, the king and queen of both sides need to know who it is,' she went on. 'I don't know if your intentions are good or not, and I don't *want* to know, but at least give me your names.'

Ivan went first. 'Ivan Calder.'

The lady nodded, and looked at Camilla. 'And you?'

'Camilla Rayson.'

'Right,' the woman jotted it down, and then looked at me, expectantly.

'Kendra Astor.'

The pen stopped inches from the paper when I said my name. The woman looked up at me. 'Kendra Astor, is it?'

I shifted my feet nervously. 'Yes.'

She jotted it down without another word

'Joshua Hannigan,' Josh said, when it was his turn.

The lady nodded. 'Right, stay here and I'll get back to you.'

She was gone for a long time. All of us sat on the chairs or lay down on the table. It was awkward for a long time, so I decided to break the silence.

'What did that lady mean by the king and queen of both sides?' I asked.

'The king and queen of *both* Zantoris and Devuniake,' Josh said. 'But, it's pointless for the king of Devuniake to know, he never lets anyone enter his kingdom anyway.'

'Who's the king of Devuniake?'

Josh frowned. 'His name is Ciar. He used to be a Zantorian, before he took over half of Zantoris and named it as his own.'

'What's the deal with him?' I asked, getting interested. Something about the name "Ciar" rang a bell in my mind, but I couldn't figure out from where or why.

Josh shrugged. 'Nobody knows what he even looks like. No one comes out of Devuniake, and anyone who goes in never comes back alive. But there are rumors that Ciar was secretly in love with Ardella, and defeated Zantoris in a fit, when Ardella married Alazar.'

I heard a loud snort from somewhere. It didn't seem to come from anywhere.

Just then the woman in the orange dress came back, and this time, she had in her hand a green locket filled with some sort of liquid.

All of us got up and hefted our backpacks. The woman went straight to a basin, which I didn't notice before, and smashed the locket against it. A faint sizzling sound was heard. She muttered something under her breath for a few minutes, and suddenly a portal with a green aura opened beside the basin.

She faced us, her eyes solemn and her expression looked like she's attending a funeral. She disappeared with a flick of her hand, leaving us with a debate of who will go first into the green portal.

'Perhaps we should go in alphabetical order,' I suggested. All heads turned to Camilla.

'I hate you guys,' she murmured.

She took a few steps towards it, poked her toe inside the portal and withdrew almost immediately. Then she took a few seconds of gathering courage, long enough for me to say my ABC's to find out who goes next. Then, apparently deciding to get over with it quickly, Camilla jumped into it without warning.

Ivan was the same, only a bit more hesitant. His arm went inside the portal, and slowly but surely, so did the rest of his body.

Josh went next. He casually walked through it as if he was just entering his house. Sometimes the guy's calmness in doing things amazes me.

Finally, it was my turn. Riley tried to encourage me.

Come on Kendra, you can do this! Just jump in and get over with it, or take it slow and steady, completely your choice.

But what amazed me at that moment was the amount of uncertainty I was hiding inside me. As I stood at the portal, all my doubts rose to the surface.

What if this fails?

What if something goes wrong?

What if we never get Ivan back home and my curse never gets lifted?

What if Azmaveth plans on doing something really bad and destructive?

What if this is a trap and we never-?

I shook off the what ifs, which had no business being in my brain in the first place. My instincts took over completely, as I threw myself into the portal.

Chapter 16

So, going through a portal is *not* fun. It feels like you have jet lag, only ten times worse.

First, all the energy from your body gets drained, and you feel like sleeping but the second you close your eyes, the whistling wind forces them open. You can't even *see* anything. It's like you have closed your eyes, and the fact that you can't see where you're going gets you paranoid. You're flying through the Dark-Tunnel-with-No-End at more than a hundred and fifty miles per hour.

At one point you either feel like crying, or feel dizzy, or have an excessive desire to throw up, or all of the above at the same time.

Suddenly, green lights danced before my eyes.

That means we're close, Riley explained calmly.

Just when I was considering giving in to unconsciousness, I suddenly found myself sitting on top of a huge rock.

Cold wind whipped against my bare arms from all directions. I shivered and wore my jacket, wrapping it firmly around me. Stormy gray clouds hung above me, and rumbling thunder startled me every now and then.

The rock I was on was one of many standing in unorganized rows. A huge lake stood before me, and judging by its raging torrent, it was going to destroy anything which came in it.

'Kendra!' Camilla called, leaving me startled. I almost slipped off the rock, but she was at my side at once and steadied me.

'Are we in the Borders now?' I asked, keeping my eyes on the horizon.

'Yes. Now I'm assuming to keep going, we need to cross this.'

One question hung in the air, too obvious for anyone to voice it out loud: How were we going to do that?

Walk around the shore, Riley instructed. *You'll find something that can help you.*

'We need to walk around and see if we can find anything,' I said.

We carefully trod over the rocks, and there had to be someone around me after the first three times I slipped. After a few minutes of walking and aching feet, we were ready to give up. Camilla exhaled heavily through her nose, as if trying to keep cool. She looked around and saw something in the distance. 'There.'

She darted off in the direction and we tried to keep up. But when we reached the spot, I wanted to cry with frustration.

Camilla raised her eyebrows, clearly unimpressed. 'There's no way *that* is going to help us survive.' She pointed to the shabby, poor-conditioned boat. It had enough space for all of us, but I had a feeling that it would disintegrate if a baby sneezed on it.

'We have no choice,' Ivan said. 'So, who here knows how to maneuver a boat?'

No answer.

'Nobody?' Ivan huffed. 'Fine, all of you just do what I say, got it?'

I didn't entirely understand what Ivan was telling us to do, but clearly he knew what he was doing, so I trusted him. He told us to do some things like putting up the sails and all. And finally, it was ready.

Together we managed to carry it on the water. A current started tugging it, before we could even fully board. Fortunately, Josh and I quickly got in before we could get left behind.

I wasn't much help at all. Ivan yelled orders to Camilla and Josh to help but didn't say anything to me. I guess one look at my terrified face assured them that I was in no condition to do anything.

The huge waves reminded me of the time I was trying to escape the tsunami and barely survived. I clung to the sides of the boat and tried to push down the horrific memory. I glanced over at Ivan several times. He had also been stuck in that disaster, but now, no wave or current seemed to faze him.

He, Josh, and Camilla were trying their hardest to keep the already-weak boat intact, with all the currents and rocks we kept crashing into. I felt embarrassed and ashamed that I couldn't do anything, but really, it was all I could do to keep myself from fainting from the familiar visions of the tsunami which kept flashing in my brain.

Suddenly, a wave crashed into the boat breaking it into two and pulling Camilla under.

'Camilla!' I screamed, somehow finding my voice.

Until that moment, I had never seen Ivan's water powers up close. He thrust his hand towards the water, and two seconds later, a sea-green jet of water contrasting with the lake's murky waters placed a coughing Camilla on the other half of the boat, which was miraculously still afloat.

Although, that went to waste because, two seconds after she stopped coughing, she went under again, and this time, so did the rest of us.

I couldn't see anything at all, and the flashbacks became more vivid. I frantically tried to swim up to the surface, using every little bit of energy I had.

I gasped and coughed uncontrollably when I reappeared on the surface, desperately searching for Camilla, Josh, or Ivan. It was raining heavily now, and the thunder and lightning didn't reassure me at all.

I tried calling out for them, but my voice failed me.

Suddenly, one of them appeared next to me, gasping and flailing. I tried to swim over to them, but the currents kept pushing me away.

Suddenly, I was pulled underwater without warning. And I mean, *literally* pulled.

It felt as if five pairs of strong hands grabbed my ankles and were trying to drown me. Since I was caught by surprise, I didn't have time to hold my breath, so I took in a lot of water through my mouth and nose.

I freaked out and broke out to the surface before I went too deep. I breathed heavily and hoped for the millionth time that my friends were okay. Well, as okay as you can be in this hellhole.

I heard some of them shouting and flailing when they managed to break to the surface, and that's all I needed to know they were still alive.

I was pulled down again, but this time, I managed to hold my breath in time.

Underwater, I looked around desperately for my friends. I heaved a sigh of relief inwardly when I saw the silhouette of three figures beside me, struggling.

I froze when I saw what was at their feet. Two wispy hands were grabbing hold of their ankles and pulled them deeper every time they tried to swim up.

I looked down at *my* feet and nearly shrieked. For the same ones were at mine too. I didn't know whose hands they were, but the only thing my mind told me to do was keep swimming.

But for some reason, Riley was telling me the opposite. She kept telling me to stop trying to swim up, but I was too busy trying to swim up to heed her.

It was exhausting. There were several times where we almost

made it, but then the hands pulled us down into the deep parts again.

Camilla was the one who did it better than the rest of us. She was the only one who even managed to break out to the surface, much less stay there for fifteen seconds. That was when I realized how strong she was.

I could tell that Ivan was trying to control the water but even he could not do anything about it.

Kendra, stop struggling!

This command was so firm that my hands and legs went limp. I looked around wildly and found nothing. When I looked again, I saw something silver shimmering in the distance. Then it struck me.

These hands weren't making things hard for us. They were actually trying to *help* us. When we tried to swim upwards, they pulled us down, hoping that we would find that we were going the wrong way.

Many people have this misconception, Riley explained. *That's why this is tough for them, and they eventually die. They jump to conclusions.*

"How do I tell the others?" I asked.

Leave that to me.

With that, the familiar buzzing noise I get in my head whenever Riley talked to me, disappeared. The silence felt weird.

The tugging feeling at my ankles was gone. I watched as my friends stopped struggling, and looks of confusion appeared on their faces.

I didn't know what Riley did, but their sights got fixated on the same thing I had seen. The buzzing noise in my head returned.

They got the message. Now keep swimming there and don't stop until you see a symbol.

"What symbol?" I asked, as I started swimming towards that silver shimmery thing. This time, nothing stopped me.

You'll know.

We realized that thing was far away and kept swimming for a really long time. The waters were still and calm now. Ivan was the one in the lead. He seemed relaxed and at home underwater.

He occasionally put up a show for us by making some moving figures of beautiful sea creatures, using bubbles. He swam effortlessly for a long time. He didn't even seem tired.

The rest of us at the back were exhausted. My arms and legs ached. Sometimes I felt like giving up and sinking. The only reason I persisted was because Riley kept yelling in my head to keep moving if I dared to pause for a minute.

Camilla was probably the most tired, but she absolutely refused to stop at all.

Josh didn't hesitate to stop. Several times it seemed like he had decided to sink and die by not working his arms and legs, but five seconds after, he came back to his senses, and frantically swam again.

Once, Josh nearly sunk so low, it caught Ivan's attention. He acted quickly, sending turbulence to lift him and send him towards our destination at top speed.

He looked back at us and that was the moment he realized all of us were tired. He did the same thing to us, and once we reached he was already there.

I had some questions, like, how did he get here so fast? And how long was he planning to make us limp with all the swimming before he pulled out this technique?

But we were more worried about how a necklace with the initial "G" hanging from it, sitting on the seafloor was going to help us get to the second challenge.

"Riley?" I called. "Any thoughts?"

I got nothing, Riley admitted.

What complicated matters even further was the fact that we couldn't talk to each other.

Josh picked it up and suddenly dropped it at once. He nursed his fingers against the palm of his other hand.

I, like an idiot, decided to pick it up and check what was wrong with it. I hadn't even fully enclosed my fingers round the chain and I withdrew.

The whole thing was searingly hot.

Suddenly, I noticed that Josh's hand was fading to dust. We watched in horror as his whole body began turning to dust. Soon, the same started happening to *my* hand. I inwardly shrieked.

"Riley, what's happening?" I asked.

I think this is leading you further, she said, but the doubt in her voice wasn't helping.

I felt queasy and the sight of Camilla and Ivan reaching for the necklace was the last thing I saw before I blacked out.

Chapter 17

I was the first one to revive. I opened my eyes with a groan, still nauseous but a bit better than what I had felt before.

Sitting up slowly, I took in my surroundings. I was sitting in a dingy alley. All my friends were lying next to me, unconscious. I figured they would wake up soon.

My gaze drifted to something on Camilla's right cheek. Dark bluish-black goo was dripping off. I stared at it for two minutes before something Camilla had told me came back to me in a flash.

'Pixies' blood is dark blue, not red.'

I widened my eyes. Where did that come from? I also noticed that Ivan's sleeve was torn and an ugly gash was on his arm.

"What on Earth *happened* to them while me and Josh were away?" I thought as I dug through my backpack for the first-aid kit. Miraculously, my backpack, which I thought was lost for good, had been transported to me, and so had everyone else's.

Josh woke up and I heaved a sigh of relief.

'Josh! Oh, thank goodness. Can you help me?'

'With what?' he asked, sounding tired. It was soon replaced with concern when he saw the injuries.

'Oh my...how did this happen?' he exclaimed, as he gently placed one hand on his cousin's cheek and carefully scrutinized Ivan's arm.

'I don't know, but do you know about first aid?' I asked, as I opened the kit.

Josh nodded.

'Good. I don't. Tell me, what do I do?'

Camilla's cut was bleeding, but it was easier to stop compared to Ivan's. Josh bought a bottle of water from a shop nearby and cleaned the wound. I grabbed a pair of tweezers to remove gravel from the cut.

Ivan was the problem. The gash would just not stop bleeding. I tried to put pressure on it using a wet compression, but it did nothing.

(Ok, so honest confession. It was also a bit fascinating to watch because it was the first time I had seen pixie blood. It was a smooth dark liquid. Just like Camilla's. But the fact that so much of it was coming out of Ivan's wound was slowly freaking me out.)

'This much bleeding is not natural,' Josh frowned. 'We are usually supposed to call a doctor if something like this happens, but –'

'There's no doctor available now,' I finished.

After some time, it reduced a little. Josh put a bandage around Ivan's arm, and then told me to put some ice around Camilla's cut to prevent swelling.

My hands were soaked in Ivan's blood (gross), so I took the ice between tweezers.

The moment the ice touched her skin, Camilla's eyes flew open. She yelled, and sat upright, her face streaming with sweat.

'Woah, there, easy,' I said as I placed my hand on her shoulder.

'Lie down,' Josh instructed. 'You still have tiny bruises and cuts which have to be treated.'

Camilla slowly lay down and started breathing heavily and rapidly. After Josh put on the band-aids for the tiny cuts, and I finished applying ice, Josh helped her to sit up.

'Now,' I started, 'what happened?'

'Huh?' she mumbled, looking up.

'What happened?' Josh repeated. 'Why do you and Ivan look like you've been mauled by an animal even though there are supposed to be none in this place?'

'I don't remember,' Camilla said.

'You don't *remember*?'

'No,' she replied.

I frowned. How was forgetting something which attacked you five minutes ago possible? If I were Camilla, I would have nightmares for at least a year.

A few minutes after all of Ivan's injuries were treated, he came to. He looked pale and in shock but recovered quickly. Even he claimed that he remembered nothing.

'How is that possible?' Josh exclaimed. 'Unless someone or something is working against us.'

Camilla gave a subtle eye roll. 'Hadn't we established that a long time ago?'

Ivan was up on his feet after a while, and we were on the move again. When we got out of the alley, we realized that this place was quite possibly the saddest one we had ever been to.

Almost everyone was wearing black or gray. And if not either, then brown. The weather was the same by the lake; gloomy gray clouds, chilly wind whipping back and forth and the feeling of dread so thick, one could cut it with a butter knife.

I wrapped my black jacket firmly around me, partly because my bright yellow top looked awkward among people who seemed to be ready for a funeral.

'Do we need to change into other things so we blend in?' I whispered.

'We'll be fine, I think,' Josh whispered back.

And so we kept going, hoping to be discreet. We had strange looks come our way. Clearly, onlookers were horrified. But we looked straight ahead and marched off to -

'Wait,' Ivan stopped. 'Where are we going?'

Camilla shrugged. 'Nowhere. Just looking for anything that might help us.'

No sooner had she said that, trouble arose.

It all started with a blood-curdling scream coming from a nearby house.

On instinct, all of us ran inside to see what happened, along with a couple of neighbors. The sight I saw inside left me dumbfounded.

The whole house was scanned, to see where it came from. One of the neighbors called everyone to the bathroom, saying it was from there. My friends and I were at the back of the tiny crowd in the bathroom.

I got on my tip-toes.

For in the bathtub, lay the dead body of a child who looked no older than we were. His eyes were glassy, and navy blood, which sprouted from his stomach, stained his gray shirt and black trousers. A woman, probably his mother, sat next to him, holding his hand and weeping.

My hand flew to my mouth in shock. Next to me, I heard Josh mutter, 'Oh my God,' while the others were too stunned to say anything.

The Infirmary was called, while a pixie comforted the grieving mother. Suddenly, someone exclaimed and pointed to the wall.

Now that was something we had *definitely* not seen before. The symbol looked painfully familiar.

It was a pristine skull resting atop a black flower. People started talking about it, when someone beside me gave a strangled gasp. Only later, I had thanked my lucky stars that it had been Camilla, otherwise I would have been in huge trouble.

I turned my head sharply, only to see *all* my friends staring at my forehead, a look of horror on their faces.

I frowned and mouthed 'What?'

Camilla fished a tiny mirror from her bag, and I froze when I saw what was on my face.

For the *exact* same symbol was on the left side of my forehead. It looked like a tattoo applied permanently.

I looked at my friends and we now knew one thing: We needed to get out of there *right away*, or else people would see that and assume that I had done it.

We discreetly managed to exit the house. I swept my hair over my forehead, which made me look weird. Quickly, we ducked into an alley.

'Guys, I promise that I didn't do *anything*,' I started. 'I don't know what –'

'Don't worry,' Josh interrupted. 'We believe you.'

I blinked. 'You do?'

Ivan nodded. 'You were with us the entire time. When could you have *possibly* done it?'

I sighed in relief. 'Thank you *so* much. But, what do you think is happening? The same symbol was on the wall. Why did it come to my head?'

'Oh,' Camilla said, in a low voice. '*Oh.*'

All of us turned to her. 'What?'

She took a deep breath. 'Okay, Kendra, don't freak, but . . .'

She hesitated.

'But what?' I prompted.

'I think it's your curse.'

Chapter 18

All the blood rushed to my feet. Ivan looked at me, concerned, while Josh tried to calm everyone down.

'H-hold on, we don't know for sure that it is the curse,' he said.

'Yeah,' Camilla said, looking regretful that she ever said that. 'I could be wrong.'

Kendra, Riley said in a low voice. *It **is** your curse.*

"How do you know that?"

What other explanation do you have for that?

"Maybe, this is, um, something Azmaveth is doing to us. One of us gets framed for crimes which happen."

Or, your curse's first mutation is starting to show, and you need to make it out of here without letting the townspeople execute you.

"Execute?! Wait, Riley, how on Earth do you *know* all this?"

*Ken, inside voices don't only have the knowledge **you** have. There are times when they can help you through a situation. And when I say that it's your curse, it **is** your curse.*

There was no difference between my heart and a drum at that moment. I drew a shaky breath.

It was no use getting scared like this. I knew this was bound to happen sooner or later.

'It's my curse,' I announced, with so much confidence, it surprised me.

Camilla looked devastated. 'Kendra, I said that I *think*. There's a good chance that I could be wrong.'

'No,' I replied, firmly. 'My instinct tells me that it is.'

'Well, this sure was a surprise,' Ivan said quietly. Then he shook his head. 'Don't worry, just cover that thing with your hair and we should be good to go.'

'That would be no use,' I responded. 'Look.'

I covered the symbol with my hair, but a cold wind kept blowing it back.

Josh ran his hand through his hair. 'What do we do then?'

Before any of us could answer, everything combusted in a shade of bright red.

It happened so fast and without warning, it took some time for me to realize what exactly happened. Strangely, the explosion didn't hurt or burn me in any way, but the force *did* throw me away from my friends. I landed on my right arm, a sickening crunch sounding in my ears.

I got up and tried to move the arm I landed on. I yelled a few questionable choice of words as a shrieking pain stabbed my shoulder. My face beaded with sweat as I tried to call out, but no sound came out.

The air was unbearably hot, and the smell of smoke filled my nose. There were tiny fires all round the alley. If you could call the place an alley.

The walls were knocked down and smoking, and pixies from all corners of the street were staring, aghast. That was when I realized that my hair was brushed back, and the symbol was there, as large as life.

Suddenly, I was surrounded by yellow smoke.

"Riley, what's *happening*?" I asked desperately.

I don't know. Someone must have noticed that symbol and planted a bomb while you weren't looking. What's happening now, I have no clue.

I felt someone take my arm, (my good arm, thank goodness) and hiss, 'Come with me. Now!'

I looked up and shrieked. 'HELP SOMEBODY! HE'S KIDNAPPING ME!'

In my defense, to my twelve-year-old mind, that was the only reasonable excuse why a grown man was trying to take me away.

I couldn't see his face because it was covered by a faded black mask, and his hood was up.

'Shut up!' he hissed. 'I'm not kidnapping you! I'm trying to help!'

'I don't believe you!' I yelled. 'SOMEBODY-'

'I have your friends.'

That made me go silent. The smoke was slowly dying down around us and I saw hazy figures of pixies.

'Are they fine?' I asked.

'Sort of,' he muttered. 'But you and I won't be if you don't come with me.'

Having no desire not to be fine, I did as he said. I know I shouldn't follow strangers, but he knew where my friends were. It might've been a trick, but I deemed it too risky *not* to see for myself. Besides, I wasn't above throwing some punches and kicks if he tried any funny business.

He led me to an abandoned crumbling building. I didn't know what to pay attention to, the pain of my broken arm, or my nerves which decided to make a list in my brain of the million things which could go wrong.

'Are you *sure* they're in there?' I asked, as I chewed my lip nervously.

'Yes,' he relied, before frowning. 'Your friends are the brunette, the blond and the guy who got a lot of burns, right?'

'*What?*' I squeaked. 'Who got burnt?'

'The boy with the long-ish curls,' he said, pulling me to the entrance. 'Although, the girl is no better off either, and neither is the other guy. What's confusing me is as to how *you* survived.'

He added the last remark while glaring at me suspiciously. The truth was, I was freaking out completely. Not that I *wanted* to get hurt, just the fact that I didn't was odd.

I stepped into the building through a revolving door, trying to ignore the random creaks and squeaks I kept hearing. It looked like the lobby of a hotel, except everything was old, abandoned, and dusty. My vision tunneled to my friends in the corner and at that moment nothing mattered more than the fact that they were alive and okay.

I jogged closer and saw that they were *clearly* not okay. Camilla's cut on the check was oozing blood again along with new injuries. Ivan looked fine, except his face was red from the explosion, and dirt and grime covered his arms. And Josh . . . oh no.

His face had cuts and bruises and there was burnt tissue at the tip of his mouth. The worst part was that everyone was covered in dust.

I looked at the man. 'Why haven't you cleaned their wounds yet? It could get infected!' Saying that, I dug through the first aid from my backpack, which again, had not been harmed.

Meanwhile, the man cocked an eyebrow. 'Strange way to say, "thank you for saving me from the wrath of the townspeople", but you're welcome.'

I sighed and looked at him. 'Look, thank you for saving me from the wrath of the townspeople. I really appreciate it. But can you *please* help me one more time and treat their injuries?'

'Fine,' he huffed. 'But don't worry about that boy.' He pointed to Josh. 'I already put cold water on his burns.'

We spent the next few minutes treating their injuries, though it was mostly him who was doing it. I forgot that my arm was still broken—a fact that I was reminded of the hard way.

He made me sit in the corner and drink an elixir which could apparently mend broken bones in an hour.

After he was done he washed his hands in an old sink in the corner, and announced that everyone was going to be unconscious for some time, but they were going to be alright. I was still worried but nodded and said nothing as I sipped the elixir, which tasted as delicious as rotting frog skins and mushrooms. I had no idea how this man knew so much about what happened to them without any official medical help, but he seemed to know what he was doing.

He removed his mask to reveal his face and put down his hood so I could see his mane of messy silver-dyed hair. I estimated him to be between twenty and twenty-five. He was paler than the moon, and his dark eyes were constantly flitting about as if expecting an attack.

He sat at the other end of the room, and we said nothing for a while. I finished my elixir and noticed that my pain had subsided. It only hurt if I moved.

'You have strange eyes.'

I looked startled. 'Excuse me?'

'You have strange eyes,' He repeated. 'I've never seen a pixie with eyes of different colors.'

'Oh,' I said, 'Okay, fair enough. You know, there could've been a polite way to say that. I mean, you can't just tell people that their eyes are weird.'

'Sorry.' He didn't sound very sorry.

'Why did you save us?' I asked him.

'You'd rather I let you die?'

'You know what I mean.'

He dropped his eyes. 'I was in your position once.'

I raised my brows slightly. 'You were?'

He nodded. 'I was a mere traveler like you. A bearer of a banshee's curse.'

I hitched my breath. Should I tell him I had a curse too?

Probably not, Riley said. *You just met him.*

There was no need though, because he added, 'And I know you have the same one.'

Questions flooded my brain, but I decided to go one at a time. 'How did you get the curse?'

He winced as if it were not a pleasant memory. 'Long story. I, uh, well . . . the banshee was disguised as someone I knew, and I automatically went towards her. As soon as I got near, she started wailing, and I didn't have time to cover my ears. Then, another man came to me and teleported me to these Borders and told me to keep going till I reach a palace.'

I nodded my head. 'Has your curse acted up yet?'

'Yes,' he said, as he lifted his sleeve to reveal the sign of the skull resting on a black flower. 'I think this came to frame me, so that the townspeople thought that I was responsible for all the accidents which happened.'

'How did the bomb explode?' I asked.

'That was planted by some pixie who already saw your symbol, there is always one,' he replied.

'How is it that you haven't been reduced to a banshee?' I asked.

He shrugged. 'I don't have a clue. The moment I decided that I would stay here and not advance further, it just *stopped*. I don't know what happened, but I'm not really complaining either.'

I furrowed my eyebrows. 'Why didn't you want to go further?'

'All the townspeople had my face and name memorized,' he explained. 'Going out now would be suicide. And even if I *do* get out, I avoid crowded places and wear a face mask.'

'Does that mean my friends and I are safe?' I asked, hopefully.

'I mean, if they think that you are the mastermind behind these events, they wouldn't think it's me, right?'

'Oh, no, not at all,' he replied. 'See, all of these pixies are very gullible. As long as they have someone to blame, they're set.'

'Really?'

'Uh-huh. They're easily influenced to change their mind when they see something which goes against their previous beliefs. So, when they see you with the symbol, they are going to forget about me and target *you*. Everyone is that way, except the Prince of Zantoris. He was sent here by his parents to maintain order.'

'Oh . . .,' I muttered. Then I thought of something. 'Wait a minute, if they forget about you and focus on me, then you can definitely continue your mission without attracting any attention.'

He shook his head. 'I can't. I actually took a sacred oath to never advance further.'

I frowned. 'Why would you do that?'

'Why not?' he replied. 'I'm safe here. My curse doesn't mutate further.'

'Don't you have a family or a home to get back to?' I blurted, without thinking.

'My family abandoned me, I was homeless on the streets of Earth and still am, but in a different place,' he scowled. 'But thanks a ton for reminding me of all that. Any more questions?'

His eyes sent a silent message: *Stop getting personal.*

I thought for a couple of seconds whether my next question was personal. 'What's your name?'

He tilted his head, as if I were the biggest question in the world. 'I'm Griffin. What about you?'

'Kendra,' I replied. My eyes fell on something around his neck.

A silver chain. With the initial "G" hanging from it.

Before I could give it any further thought, I felt someone stirring.

Chapter 19

'Camilla!' I exclaimed, as I rushed over and suffocated her with a hug. She hugged me back before muttering, 'Can't - breathe.'

'Oh, sorry,' I pulled back.

Camilla put her hand to her head as if it hurt. 'What happened?'

'Someone saw Kendra's sign on her arm and planted a bomb when you weren't looking,' Griffin said, as he came over.

That's when she noticed the burn on her hand and slowly looked at all her burns and bandages.

Her eyes drifted to the boys and widened them when she saw Josh's state.

'Oh my –' she covered her mouth with one hand. 'Josh . . . is he –?'

'Dead? No,' Griffin said. 'Is he going to be out for a while? Yes. So is this guy.'

Camilla suddenly put her hand on her stomach and moaned, 'I think I'm gonna be sick.'

Griffin, quick as lightning, helped her up and led her out through the revolving doors. From there, I could hear her throwing up and belching, while Griffin stood to one side, looking polite, but queasy.

'You done?' he asked in a low voice. She must have nodded because he called out to me, 'Kendra? There are two bottles of water in the corner. You see them?'

'Yeah,' I yelled back.

'Bring one of 'em to me,' he said.

I got up and passed a bottle to him, trying to ignore the throbbing in my arm. I handed him the bottle and listened as he instructed Camilla to drink some water. After she came inside, she looked fine but a little embarrassed. She sat down beside Josh and rested her head against the wall. 'So, uh . . .'

'Griffin,' I whispered.

'Griffin,' she said. 'Thanks for dragging us away from that explosion there.'

He simply shrugged.

'How long are the boys gonna be out for?' she asked.

Griffin looked thoughtful. 'A few days, maybe?'

I sighed. I was willing to sacrifice any amount of time if it meant that they were going to be fine. Griffin plucked a strand of hair from each of their heads to make Medeema, that thing pixies use to make sure unconscious patients remain hydrated and well-fed.

'After they wake up, they should rest for some time,' Griffin instructed as he put the granola-bar thing on their foreheads. The one on Josh's head started giving off a silver aura, while Ivan's was more of a greenish-blue color, like the ocean. (According to Camilla, the one which I had glowed red.)

'The bomb was a really small one,' Griffin continued. 'The effects weren't as bad as to expect death, but they are going to be slightly weak for some time and so are you Camilla. Kendra, how's your arm?'

I moved it. It didn't hurt a bit. I rotated it and tried swinging it back and forth. It felt as good as new.

I grinned. 'All good.'

He looked surprised. 'I wasn't expecting it to happen so quickly. Guess you're a fast healer.'

'How is it that you didn't get hurt in any way?' Camilla wondered. 'Aside from your arm, of course, but it wasn't directly caused by the explosion, was it?'

'No,' I replied. 'When it threw me back, I landed on my own arm, so it was me. And, really, I don't know how it didn't do anything to me.'

'Guess these Borders are making you invincible, huh?' she teased.

Deep down I knew that the answer was yes. I normally take a long time to recover from *anything*. But ever since I came here, I've been the one in the group to be completely fine. I noticed that when all of us became conscious in the alley after escaping from the river, I was the only one not feeling weak, while the others were walking tiredly and sluggishly.

'And how is it that our bags are not getting harmed in any way?' she asked, as she drew hers close and pulled out her phone.

'I don't know,' Griffin replied, as he sat down at the other end of the room, far away from either of us.

Camilla frowned. 'Ugh, there's no reception here either.'

Griffin simply shrugged and went outside, saying he's going to get dinner.

'You have money?' I said.

He looked at me. 'Who says I'm buying?'

'You're stealing?' I exclaimed.

'What? No!' he replied. 'There's a 24-hour diner nearby, which gives free food to homeless people.'

'What if they ask you to remove your mask?'

'They won't,' he said, confidently, as he headed out.

Once his footsteps faded, I scrambled for my backpack and got out a notebook and a pen.

'What are you doing?' Camilla asked, looking amused.

I held up the notebook. 'In this, I have written all the questions I had ever since I came to Zantoris, which I never got the answer to, and to which you will give an explanation right *now*.'

Chapter 20

Camilla laughed. 'Guess I'm not going anywhere until you have answers, huh?'

'You are *so* smart,' I replied as I flipped through the pages. 'Alright, number 1: Why was Ardella looking at me weird when I met her?'

'What do you mean?' Camilla chuckled.

'Oh, come on, you saw it too.'

'I'm not sure of the *exact* reason,' she replied, hesitantly.

I snorted. 'No wonder pixies are forbidden to lie. You are terrible at it.'

'That's all I'm going to say about this,' Camilla stated.

'Fine,' I grumbled. 'Number 2: Where have you and Josh been sneaking off to, at Aternalis?'

Camilla's smile faded slightly. 'I guess we can't hold it off for much longer.'

I waited.

'Remember when Josh went off to talk to Atticus and Cordelia when we were at their house?'

I nodded.

'Well,' she continued. 'He told them about the color of your blood, and how you heard loud noises before we realized you were a pixie. We thought they would know what was the case, because they are descendants of the very first pixie families ever in creation. Therefore, the Calder clan knows a lot about pixies and the unique and rare things which have happened. But when they said that they got nothing, they decided that going to Alazar and Ardella would be best. In case you're wondering, Alazar is our king and Ardella's husband.'

'All this time you have been going to secret conferences about me to the *king and queen?*'

'Yes,' she replied, avoiding my eyes. 'They had a hard time figuring out what the matter was, but they did find one major discovery.'

'And that is . . .?' I prompted.

She pressed her lips together. 'I've already said enough. I wasn't supposed to tell you *anything* to begin with.'

'Oh, come on!' I protested.

But she remained adamant. I huffed, and scribbled down the question in my notebook in my rough handwriting: What was the major discovery about me that Camilla thinks too worrying to share with me?

'Get some sleep,' she told me. 'Griffin probably won't be back until long.'

I did as she said, but looking back, I really shouldn't have closed my eyes. Because that was when the nightmares started.

I found myself standing in my old room in the Infirmary. The place looked the same since I left it; huge chandelier, heavy curtains, walls painted brown.

Over by the cabinet, stood none other than the same person I saw on my first day. I had dismissed it as a strange dream, but that was to reassure myself. Outside the window, the same lightning I saw on my first day flashed three times.

The scene changed to the very place I wanted to avoid with a burning passion.

Azmaveth's room.

The chamber sent feelings of beetles crawling up my arm.

I saw Azmaveth sitting on his chair, but Mallory wasn't there next to him. Instead, standing before him was a girl who looked to be about twenty. She wore a long black dress, with a silver belt fastened at her waist.

I couldn't make out anything about her except that her long black hair fell loose below her shoulders and her skin was paler than snow.

But when she lifted her face, I saw her yellow iris eyes narrowed with anger. She looked so similar to Azmaveth I guessed that she was his sister. Or daughter, as she looked too young to be his sister.

'Thana, I assume you know why you're here,' Azmaveth said, in Zanarian.

'Yes Father,' she replied through gritted teeth. *'I'm here because you are an arrogant and pompous imbecile who cannot bear to be wrong about anything.'*

Azmaveth exhaled sharply. *'You are here because you disobeyed my wishes. Thana –'*

'You mean your orders to torture innocent people,' Thana interrupted, crossing her arms.

'You should be ashamed of yourself,' he hissed. *'You bear the name of such an honorable ancestor and you disgrace it with your foolish ideas that I am apparently "out of control with insanity".'*

'You are,' Thana said in a low voice. She looked her father in the eye and suddenly, her tone softened. *'Don't listen to him. Please. His words are of no worth.'*

Azmaveth pinched the bridge of his nose. *'You know why we are doing this. I raised you better than this.'*

'You raised me to be just like you!' she fumed. *'And for that, I have paid the price! I - '*

'That's enough!' Azmaveth thundered.

Thana screamed in rage and stomped off. After that, everything went black and I got a weird feeling as if I was gradually sinking in deep waters, until my eyes flew open.

'Kendra?' Camilla frowned. 'What's the matter?'

I took a few moments to catch my breath, all the words I heard were swimming around in my head. The gist of what I saw was Azmaveth getting into a fight with his daughter but it seemed to be much more than that.

Just then Griffin came back and yelled, 'Dinner!'

We both scrambled to our feet and surrounded the boxes like hungry puppies.

He gave us medium-sized boxes and a spoon.

Inside the box were tiny silver balls, very similar to the ones used on cakes. They are actually very crunchy and once you bite into it, the taste of spinach dipped in white sauce fills your mouth. Not really the taste I would prefer but I choked down that disgusting thing.

'This is Amartok,' Griffin explained. 'It's a very healthy and nutritious meal of Zantoris. Very useful when a pixie is sick.'

'I would say that this is delicious, but pixies are not supposed to lie,' Camilla said, as she put the empty box away.

Our next course was served in disposable cups. It was a soup-like thing. It was so hot it burnt my lips, and even after an hour of blowing into it and applying ice on my upper lip, it was still piping hot. It was very spicy too. My spice tolerance was hanging by a thread when I drained the cup. Camilla, on the other hand, gulped an entire bottle of water, making Griffin mad that she didn't leave any.

After that Griffin went for an after-dinner stroll leaving me to tell Camilla about my nightmare.

Some time later, Griffin returned and all of us went to sleep. I drowsed off after a few minutes of chatting with Riley and comparing my life before versus after pixies for the millionth time. The boys remained unconscious. Sleep overtook me the minute I closed my eyes.

Chapter 21

I was in for a surprise in the morning. 'Josh?' I mumbled.

'Morning,' he greeted me. He looked as good as new, as if nothing ever happened to him. Ivan, who was sitting up beside him, looked the opposite. He looked pretty miserable and, for some reason, ignored me completely for the rest of the day.

According to Griffin, Josh woke up first at 3 a.m., and accidently knocked Ivan's head. This resulted in two puzzled boys wondering where the heck they were.

Our breakfast was the remains of yesterday's dinner. The mood was pretty upbeat and even Griffin chimed in the conversation every once in a while.

The only person who didn't say a word was Ivan. Like I said, he ignored me completely and even when he *did* look at me, his eyes held. . . fear.

When I tried to talk to him privately, he just pushed me aside and went about his business.

To be honest, I felt kinda hurt that he was behaving this way, but I soon noticed that it just wasn't me. He kept his distance from Josh and Camilla, too, though neither of them noticed.

I shrugged it off, thinking he'll be fine.

'So, when are you all leaving?' Griffin asked.

'Ask them,' Camilla jerked her head towards Josh and Ivan. 'I'm ready to leave anytime they regain their strength.'

'I feel okay,' Josh said. 'This evening might work out for us. What do you say, Ivan?'

'Works fine,' he replied quietly.

'It's settled then!' Griffin exclaimed, apparently glad to have us out of his house.

He packed us a bag with extra food. He gave me a brown hoodie and a mask, just in case. Camilla brushed her hair and tied it into a rope braid, while telling Josh and Ivan of my nightmare about Azmaveth and Thana.

'Why would he be torturing innocent people?' I asked, sitting in a cross-legged position. 'Thana told Azmaveth that he didn't have to listen to *him*. Who's "him"?'

'Don't know,' Josh said. 'We still have to be careful. We've managed to avoid him so far, but –'

'What do you mean?' Griffin interrupted. 'You haven't avoided him at all.'

'What do *you* mean?' I said, frowning.

'That mark,' he gestured to my forehead. 'That is Azmaveth's most famous symbol.'

'*What?*' my friends exclaimed in unison. I was too stunned to say anything.

My mind flashed back to the time Azmaveth appeared after the banshee gave the curse. The staff he was holding had the same symbol. A skull perched atop a black flower.

Griffin nodded. 'Azmaveth has the ability to control anybody's curse. He normally doesn't, but he helps a lot with the first mutation. All the crimes? He's the one who is actually responsible.'

Camilla muttered some "*sophisticated*" words about Azmaveth and interesting places where she would like to kick him. Josh buried his face in his hands and Ivan simply scowled at me, as if it were somehow *my* fault.

I frowned. What is the *matter* with this guy today?

I wouldn't worry about it. Riley said. *The only thing I can say here is . . . just go easy on him. His childhood hasn't exactly been the best, you know.*

"How do you know?"

There have always been rumors around him. Why he hates Terrans specifically.

"Is it something personal?"

Well, yes.

"Then stop!" I said, before she could say anything more. "It's not right that I know it without his knowledge."

Suit yourself.

Lunch was kind of subdued. That evening, we would step out again, facing a lot of angry townspeople. Word must have spread a fair bit by now, about how a child was murdered and that a young girl was responsible for it.

'How is it that when you went out, no one noticed the symbol?' I asked Griffin, as I gave him the plastic plate at the sink to wash and reuse.

He didn't look at me as he spoke. 'I already told you, I took a sacred oath to stay here and never advance further. So, as I took that oath, the curse stopped completely. The symbol was still there, but I could easily cover it.'

I nodded and returned to my spot, lost in deep thought until Riley spoke.

Really?

"Really, what?"

You seriously don't notice anything suspicious?

"About . . . ?"

About him. Griffin.

"What's so suspicious about him?" I was confused. I'd say that Griffin was actually pretty considerate rescuing all of us.

*Don't you see how he's clearly **lying** about everything?*

"Riley, I think you're mistaken. I'm pretty sure he is who he says he is."

I wasn't sure where the defensiveness was coming up from but I decided that it is what it is.

Riley seemed to sigh. *I guess this group has got to have a clueless one. Thank goodness the others aren't as oblivious.*

I really had no idea what she was *on* about, but after she said it, I noticed that Camilla avoided him whenever possible. Josh seemed unsettled by the guy, while Ivan stole suspicious glances at him. But somehow, I couldn't bring myself to believe that Griffin possibly meant any harm for us.

The evening came quickly. It was not long before all of us were shouldering our backpacks and hesitating to go outside.

Okay, I did most of the hesitating.

'C'mon Kendra, if anything happens to you, we'll protect you,' Camilla said.

'I don't *want* anyone protecting me,' I mumbled.

'Well, then come *on*,' Ivan said, impatiently. 'You're wasting everyone's time with this drama.'

Camilla scowled at him. 'Would it kill you to be gentler? How would you feel, stepping out of some place, knowing that everyone out there is waiting to kill you?'

'I would stop being a coward and making such a fuss,' he snapped back.

Before a fight could break out, I hastily said, 'You know what, you're right, I should just go.'

And with one smooth step, I went out through the revolving door. Riley clapped inside my head and cheered exaggeratedly. I kept my hair over the sign, but something kept blowing it back. All three of them surrounded me like some sort of barrier and I could feel myself getting anxious every time someone looked my way. I kept my hand firmly on the symbol to cover it, but something was going on there, as well.

For every second I covered it, it grew searingly hot, like an iron which had just been submerged in fire. I stubbornly kept my hand over it, but it was too much for me. My eyes welled up.

Suddenly, I heard tires rattling, like that of a train and people screaming. I knew that I had to look back, or get out of the way, but I kept walking with my eyes staring straight ahead.

Josh chewed his lips nervously. 'Guys, should we -?'

'LOOK OUT!' someone screamed.

I was pulled out of its way by a passerby while my friends hopped to the other side of the road. In front of me, I could see a carriage-like thing driving itself at full speed.

'How is it driving itself?' I wondered aloud.

But one look at everyone's shocked faces (and I mean *everyone*) I realized that I had bigger problems. The pixie who had pulled me aside had disappeared, so had the car and my forehead was visible to everyone clear as day.

I gulped. Azmaveth must have created more ruckus while we were away, because all pixies were glaring at me with fury and hatred and fear.

A pixie with a buzz cut was the first one to recover.

'What are you waiting for?' he snarled. 'Seize her!'

Two people dived in. I ducked and wildly looked for places to run. I couldn't since I was now cornered by pixies from all directions. Someone grabbed me, but Camilla appeared out of nowhere and kicked him in the shin, while I punched him right across the face. I doubt it hurt him much, but it was enough to surprise him.

We ran as fast as we could, dodging the confused townspeople who were slowly taking in what the chasing pixies were yelling. We reached a bridge which was crossing a wide stream. We almost made it before a lady grabbed my wrist.

Unfortunately, she was really strong. I struggled a lot and stomped on her foot as a last resort. She yelped but didn't let go of me.

I saw Josh, Camilla and Ivan cornered. My gaze suddenly fell on the gushing waters in the stream and I had an idea, but Ivan was way ahead of me.

He thrust his hand towards the water and a huge wave rose to the height of a tree. It crashed over the townspeople, drenching us as well, but that was the least of our worry. It startled them for a moment, and the lady let go of me. Since we saw it coming, we took off as fast as our legs could take us.

We left the bridge and I struck up a conversation with the rest.

'Which way do we go?' I yelled as I ran.

'How are *we* supposed to know?' Josh shrieked.

'What's the plan then?' Camilla shouted.

'Can we first keep ourselves alive right *now?*' Ivan screamed as something whizzed past his ears.

I widened my eyes. Now they were throwing rocks at us, and some of them were really big.

We kept running as more stones collided with us. It was a miracle as to how we were still alive.

But that doesn't mean none of us were harmed. Josh got an exceptionally sharp stone strike at the back of his head. He yelled and dropped to the ground and muttered something under his breath. All of us turned around and rushed to him at once. Needless to say, the townspeople caught up.

'Get up!' the buzz cut man snarled as he tugged at Josh's arm.

'Careful!' Camilla warned, still supporting her cousin.

'You keep quiet!' snapped a figure in green robes. He wore a silver circlet on his head which passed his forehead and had a regal posture.

'You have no right to speak, especially after all the crimes your friend has committed,' he continued, waving his hands dramatically as he spoke. 'You will be answering to the Prince himself. In the meantime, I charge you with imprisonment. All of you!'

'Wait, you can't do that!' Camilla blurted, before turning to us. 'Can he?'

'How *dare* you question the authority of the most prime officer of the Senate?' he roared. 'I demand an execution!'

'NO!' Ivan yelled, the authority and power in his voice silencing everyone at once.

The officer's eyes seethed with anger. 'What do you mean no?'

'I mean, *no*,' he replied, not dropping his gaze from the officer's. 'I happen to know that you are not the only member of the Senate. My father, Atticus Calder, has a more prestigious title. He is the senior-most officer.'

The name and the title had the crowd shifting their gaze. I guessed that I had underestimated the popularity and power of Atticus.

'My Lord, Serban,' someone whispered to the officer. 'If the boy's parents are truly what he says they are, then maybe we should avoid execution unless we are given that as an order from Prince Trevino.'

Serban stared at us with utter contempt for a few seconds, before clapping his hands and yelling, 'Guards!'

From nowhere a carriage appeared. Four massive cages with spikes facing inwards were being towed along. Guards clad in steel armor and holding javelins clasped chains around our hands and shoved us inside the cages.

The spikes were extremely sharp, and unfortunately for me, my shoulders were slightly broad. One of them poked into my arm, allowing a single drop of crimson blood to trickle down. I didn't get to know until I felt something on my arm. Once we stood in the tiny space, we couldn't move or do *anything.*

I looked at Josh. His face was pale and my only fear was that he'd lose consciousness and get stabbed by the spikes.

But thankfully, he was able to put up till we reached our destination.

I closed my eyes. This was it. This was rock bottom. Our situation cannot get any worse than this.

Now it's all going to get better from here . . . right?

Chapter 22

Wrong. I was totally wrong. I knew that once I saw a massive gray building with six towers looming in front of us. The creeper growing against the wall was so tall that it reached the window which was two feet away from the main balcony. We drove around it until we reached a sloped path, which led to a massive iron gate.

We entered it and with a crash, a gate sealed the entrance.

Torches lit up the dark path as we passed it. It was like an underground tunnel. We walked until we reached another gate. One guard got down and knocked seven times, tapping his foot lightly along with each knock. I guessed that that was their secret knock.

The whole place groaned as the gate rumbled open and a gust of cold wind blew into our faces.

The chariot advanced further and with each step, I was convinced that my heart's only ambition was to beat its way out of my chest.

We entered a massive cavern, very similar to the one we had stayed in after the tsunami. There were chambers and dungeons as far as the eye can see. Some cages were even hanging from the ceiling. A metallic smell was in the air and the sound of agonized grunts and groans of the prisoners filled the whole cavern.

All the prisoners in the cells stared at us as we went by, and the way they held their weapons didn't scream friendly.

Suddenly, we stopped. Our cages were opened one by one and we were shoved in.

'Your trial will be tomorrow morning,' one of the guards said as he banged the door shut.

We didn't care - for that moment. The minute Josh got down, he collapsed and hit his head against the wall. He fainted halfway through the treatment, and we gently put him on the hollow space carved from the rock. We placed our jackets below him so that it would be more comfy than rough.

I sat down and considered sleeping. All that running and standing still made my back ache. I was exhausted.

'Why is your blood red?' Ivan suddenly demanded in a dangerous tone.

I looked up and remembered my shoulder got a tiny cut from the spikes. The blood had stained the sleeve of my white shirt.

'O-oh,' I stuttered, desperately trying to think up a story. 'Well, I . . . um, it's, uh . . . –'

'It's none of your business,' Camilla finished for me, handing me a band-aid.

'I was talking to her,' Ivan snapped.

'Nevertheless, you have your answer,' Camilla replied calmly. 'It's none of your business.'

He rolled his eyes and muttered something under his breath. I didn't catch what he said, but Camilla did, and whatever it was, it made her marble gray eyes snap to a color of storm clouds.

'I heard that,' she said.

Ivan looked at her. 'And I should care because . . .?'

Now, I always knew how to predict a fight. What I *didn't* know was how to stop it.

Camilla's shoulders tensed, like it always did when someone had signed a death warrant.

'Shut up,' her voice had a dangerous undertone. *If you know what's good for you.*

'Oh, I know,' his voice was drenched in fake sympathy. 'The truth hurts.'

Normally, Josh is the peacemaker of fights, but since he wasn't available at the moment, I was left wracking my brain, thinking, *what would Josh do? What would Josh do?*

I know I should probably stop saying that, and ask what Kendra would do, but all Kendra would do is watch in horror as she thinks about what Josh would do.

Camilla narrowed her eyes. 'I'm not going to waste my time arguing with you. Last time I did that, I went short of fifty brain cells.'

Ivan's nostrils flared, but he said nothing.

I sighed through my nose. At least *that* was settled. I wondered what he had said to make Camilla so furious and hurt. There was a *reason* he was being so hostile. The dream he probably saw had much more to it than I thought. I rubbed my head, feeling the beginnings of a migraine.

Camilla caught the movement. 'You have a headache?'

'Yeah,' I replied. 'A little.'

She dug through her backpack and got out aspirin.

She tried to give it to me, but I refused.

'It's okay, it doesn't hurt that much. But thanks.'

She nodded and put it back into her bag. 'Do you want to cover the mark? Now that we're caught, maybe it won't expose itself.'

'How?' I asked. 'It's not like I can get fringes right now.'

Camilla smiled a little, and rummaged through her bag. She took a scissor out of the first aid kit. I was a little skeptical, but then decided that life was more valuable than style.

Pretty soon, I had bangs almost covering my eyebrows. I looked in the mirror and it was actually not that bad for someone with no experience.

'Thank you,' I smiled.

'That is a stupid haircut,' Ivan snorted.

Suddenly, a knife flew in through the gap of the bars. It nearly stabbed Ivan through the cheek, but he jerked his face away, and we heard the knife stab the wall at the far end.

'Great!' He growled under his breath as he scrambled back. 'Backs against the wall, you two! Don't move!'

We did as he said, but the space was narrow. Another one flew in, and I saw that the prisoners in the opposite cell were having a wonderful time messing with us.

'How long are they gonna keep doing that?' Camilla asked nobody in particular.

'Probably till morning,' Ivan replied before scowling at me. 'Thanks a lot, Kendra! If it weren't for your stupid curse we would never be stuck here. It's because of you we're doing this in the first place. I should have just let you drown in Zantoris.'

His words stung. A lot. A lump formed in my throat as I mumbled, 'Sorry.' But Camilla had other ideas.

'Hang on,' she frowned. 'How is this *her* fault?'

'How is this *not* her fault?' Ivan said. 'Be ignorant all you want, Camilla. You know deep down that if it weren't for this *wretch* - '

'The only wretch here is you!' Camilla shouted, clenching her fists as though holding back from punching him. 'Just get over yourself, okay? You're not the only one with problems.' She took a shaky breath and looked at him with red eyes, though she wasn't crying. 'I don't even know what to expect from you. You're the same arrogant low-life you were three years ago.'

Something happened three years ago, I realized. Ivan's face became impossible to read and I realized something else. *He regrets it.*

I looked around. It had been strangely quiet this whole time and I understood why. All the prisoners were watching and listening silently (almost like a moment of high suspense in a drama movie). Although, the way Camilla yelled *was* pretty dramatic. Either way, Ivan and Camilla didn't seem to notice at all.

'Ivan,' I said in a much softer tone of voice than Camilla's. 'All we're saying is that you'll have to put up with whatever problem you have with us till we get you home. After that, we can ignore each other as much as you want.'

'Oh, *please*,' he scoffed, his emerald eyes looking at me with such pure hatred, I might as well have murdered his entire family. 'This has *nothing* to do with getting me home. All you have in mind is to remove your curse, and you, –' looking at Camilla – 'to retrieve the ring.'

Okay, now I'm starting to get worried about this guy.

'Wha - . . . I –' Cam stammered in surprise before exclaiming. '*What ring?*'

'And yet, you are shamelessly breaking the tradition of honesty,' Ivan sneered. 'Isn't it bad enough that the ring you look for is used by the one who has the blood guilt of millions?'

Correction: Now I'm *officially* worried about the guy.

An audible *shink* from knives was heard from the opposite cell.

A woman with wrinkled skin and an eyepatch scowled at us with lazy disgust. 'As much as I would *love* to see this fight continue, most of us have tribunals tomorrow which are likely to end in execution. I am sure that *I* don't want to spend the last night of my life hearing this pitiful party squabbling, so *zip it.*'

One of her minions threw another dagger at us to emphasize the point. This one nearly pierced my nose, but I saw that coming because I shrunk back to the wall at once.

After that, all the lights went off. The fire from the torch subsided to give off a dimmer glow. I guessed that that was their bedtime signal.

One by one, we dozed off to sleep but before I did, I tried to figure out how on earth we were to survive if our team would get torn apart like this.

"Riley?"

Yeah?

"What would you wish you had done differently in your life if you knew you were going to die tomorrow?"

There was silence for a bit. I felt my eyes well up. I was so scared at that point that I didn't even care that someone might see me crying.

*Oh, Kendra. You are **not** going to die tomorrow. I promise.*

I closed my eyes. "You don't know that. Now, answer my question."

Another moment of silence before she spoke.

*Well . . . there **are** things I have regretted. Many. But, if I had to choose to reverse one thing, it's not standing up for myself.*

"Aren't you an inner voice? What do you need to stand up against?"

Riley let loose a nervous laugh. *Oh, you'd be surprised. The point is, I learned the importance of not just sitting back and letting people take advantage of you a little too late. What about you?*

I thought for a while. "Well, being more confident has always been on my bucket list."

Really?

"Yep."

Well, you can still complete that because you're not going to die tomorrow.

"Really?"

Of course! Any fool could see that.

I snort-laughed through my nose. "Thanks, Riley."
Welcome. Now, can we sleep? I'm tired.
"Night, Rile."
Good night.

||||

Josh woke up in the middle of the night. Or that was what he claimed. He told us that he didn't want to wake us up.

We ate a subdued breakfast. The only thing that was said was a comment on my new haircut by Josh. None of us felt like dessert, and that was a shame. If I were to die, I would definitely want that mango sorbet to be the last thing I eat. We occasionally had to toss some food to the other hungry prisoners to keep them from killing us with their daggers.

Oddly, Griffin had packed us more than enough, as if he saw all this coming. We sat in silence, either brooding about our hearing with the prince, remembering the good old days when life was yet to start for us or just reading a book.

Josh quickly seemed to detect that there was something going on between Cam and Ivan. He didn't look surprised, but had more of a *oh boy, here we go again* look.

As the eye-patch woman had said, many of the prisoners *did* have tribunals. And the fact that the sight of guards dragging them off to court was the last I saw of them wasn't assuring.

After several hours of waiting agitatedly, finally, it was our turn.

Chapter 23

The guard's keys jangled as he fit one into the keyhole. We sat frozen in our spot as he grunted when he realized he was using the wrong key. He found the right one and swung open the door with a flourish.

As he entered, he announced in a deep, baritone voice, 'Prince Trevino will see you now.'

I just had time to think 'What kind of a name is Trevino?' before four other guards appeared from behind him, and clasped chains around our wrists. I stared down at it. It was very similar to the one I had seen on Thana's hands in my dream.

'Get up!' one guard growled as he held my shoulders and tried to pull me up.

I did as he said. We walked through the cavern. Almost all the cages were empty. I gulped.

'Dude,' I heard Josh whisper to Ivan. 'Aren't your parents going to be there?'

'No,' Ivan whispered back. 'Senior officers are only supposed to attend hearings in the court of Alazar and Ardella. That comment I made yesterday was simply stalling.'

'What if someone recognizes you or any of us?'

'They won't. This is the court of the Borders. They barely have contact with Zantoris, so to them we're just criminals thanks to *somebody*.'

Ivan scowled at me.

I wondered why the Prince of Zantoris was in the Borders, but before I could ask Riley about it, we reached the great iron gates, where yesterday's chariot was waiting. We were shoved in the same cages we were in yesterday.

The doors opened with a wave of cold wind washing over us. The chariot advanced and the gates closed with a bang. That was when I realized I had left my black jacket back in the cell.

I shivered in the cold and tried to keep myself from falling over.

Again, torches lit the passageway when we passed them. The main door opened as the chariot went up the sloped path. I squinted when the sun reached directly in my eyes. We drove round to the front of the palace. The copper doors opened automatically for us.

A wide path was bordered by well-trimmed hedges and beautiful gardens. We reached the flight of stairs where the chariot stopped with a jolt. One of the spikes poked the same place I was stabbed yesterday and the patch of red on my sleeve got bigger. I hoped that no one would notice it.

It hurt like nobody's business, but I managed to keep myself from screaming in agony.

My friends, Ivan and I were dragged out of our cages. I glanced at Josh to see how he was getting on. He was limping a lot but looked fine, otherwise.

Serban was waiting for us.

He smirked as if he looked forward to beheading each of us.

'Prince Trevino is waiting,' he stated.

We trudged up the stairs and by the time we were at the top, we were thoroughly worn out. Serban and the guards had teleported upstairs but forbade us to do the same. Probably their own way of punishing prisoners.

We reached *another* door. Serban knocked on it seven times, but didn't tap his foot, like they needed to in the prison.

It was opened by nobody in particular. We turned through

countless great halls, which were made with every precious metal imaginable. Intricate statues and portraits of all the past kings and queens hung on the walls, forever unsmiling in oils.

We stood before a high gate with huge handles. Finally, trumpets blared from all four corners.

Serban went off somewhere leaving us with our guards. We waited for a few minutes when the doors slid open, making a sound similar to that of a prison bar opening.

And we entered the throne room, the very place which decided whether we lived or died.

It was huge. Four chandeliers brightly lit all the corners. The floors were thickly carpeted, and a maroon carpet led from the entrance to the throne, which was resting on the raised platform at the end of the room. The room was chilly, as if the aircon had been blasting for hours, and the air smelled of death. Actually, it smelled of green apple scented candles, but the way Serban and the other officers who were in attendance looked at us, we knew that an execution was due, no questions asked.

The officers' chairs were made of mahogany, lined with green cushions. They were laid in two rows, facing each other along the edges of the carpet.

On the golden throne at the end of the room, sat a man who looked well into his thirties. His brown hair was left in a kind of a Kurt Cobain-meets-Harry Styles hairdo, and his brown eyes scrutinized us as we advanced further and knelt after we reached a certain distance away from him. He seemed to favor his beard because he scratched on it repeatedly throughout the hearing.

'State your names,' he commanded.

'Joshua Hannigan,' Josh stated.

'Ivan Calder,' Ivan announced.

'Camilla Rayson,' Camilla said.

'Kendra Astor,' I squeaked. My voice was a pitiful mess compared to my friends' confident voices.

Prince Trevino stood up, his cape swishing behind him as he came forward and looked down at us, who were still kneeling and apparently were supposed to kneel the whole time.

'Before we get started,' he motioned to Ivan to stand up, ignoring the rest of us, 'Do you know why you are here today?'

'Yes, Your Lordship,' Ivan said, with his head bowed.

'Do you know the severity of the crimes your companion has committed?' Trevino said, sternly.

'With all due respect, Sire, in no way is she my friend,' Ivan retorted. 'And, yes, I am aware. She murdered a child, and, uh . . .'

'Don't bother,' the prince turned around to go back to his throne. 'Countess Arabeth will read out all the charges.'

A tall, stern looking woman with a pair of glasses perched on her nose stepped forward. She held a scroll in her hand, and like the rest of the officers, wore an iron circlet round her forehead.

'Kendra Astor,' she began, her loud and clear voice ringing through the silent room. 'Guilty of committing twenty murders in less than forty-eight hours, for robbing five banks, leaving thousands of people homeless. Guilty of planting explosives on more than thirty schools and public gatherings, for stealing from fifty houses and shops respectively, for the assassination of two officers and for ransacking the room of the Prince himself.'

She gave me a subtle contemptuous look, before returning to her seat.

As for me, every shred of hope that I could survive vanquished at once. All those actions deserved execution without a doubt.

But it was *Azmaveth* who deserved that, not me. I took a deep breath. This was my fate. I had accepted that. Now, the only thing on my mind was what would happen to my friends and Ivan. They certainly didn't deserve death.

Prince Trevino spread his hands, again referring to only Ivan. 'Well? Tell me, what should I do with the likes of you?'

'I will leave the judgment to you,' Ivan said, submissively.

'Sire, if I may,' Serban spoke, standing up.

Trevino motioned him to speak and if it was possible for my heart to sink further, it did.

'As all of you are clearly aware,' Serban began, 'there are not enough words to describe how vile and corrupt this girl's actions are. She has disrupted the peace of our town, and replaced our comfort with misery. Although, I *will* attempt to bring to your consideration that all this seems quite suspicious. Why would a criminal put on *her* symbol at every disaster site and then one day walk out of her home, fully knowing that she will be recognized? Wouldn't that be the behavior of someone who *wants* to get caught?'

Everyone started murmuring amongst themselves while Trevino motioned me to stand up. 'Explain yourself.'

I stood up, my knees shaking so badly, I almost fell down to the ground. 'Well, Your Majesty, um . . . I –'

'And don't even *think* of lying,' the prince warned. 'If something besides the truth escapes your tongue, that will only seal your fate.'

My knees stopped shaking, and a sudden wave of confidence washed over me. He wants the truth? Fine. I'm hitting him with the truth.

'I am not responsible for these crimes,' the steadiness of my voice surprised me. 'I am a bearer of a banshee's curse, and the first mutation is that I would be framed for disasters which neither me, nor my friends, nor Ivan is guilty of. This symbol doesn't belong to me. It formed the moment it appeared on the site of the murdered child. I hope you will believe me.'

Everyone shifted nervously. I said, 'I rest my case.'

Countess Arabeth studied me closely. 'Your Lordship, she is telling the truth.'

Prince Trevino looked too stunned to say anything. Then he regained his composure.

'I believe you. You are not lying. But . . . *someone* has to pay for all the crimes.'

'Does it *have* to be us?' I asked, softly.

The prince stood up, looking genuinely disheartened. 'Forgive me. I know it isn't fair, but the people want justice. They think it is you, and if we reveal that it wasn't, it will cause more confusion than there is already.'

'Wait,' my eyes widened slowly as I realized. 'Oh my . . . this is actually *happening*? Are we –?'

Everyone stood up, and Prince Trevino unsheathed his sword. 'By the laws of the Zantorian Senate, and the power passed down by our ancestors, I hereby sentence you, Kendra Astor, and your compatriots to execution.'

Chapter 24

All of us scrambled to our feet, as Prince Trevino menacingly advanced forward, his sword point glistening dangerously.

We started to back up, our eyes fixed on the prince. I tried to think of a plan to stall our death, but at the moment, my brain felt like the knife to my soup: absolutely useless.

Everything seemed to happen so fast. Prince Trevino quickening his pace, us almost reaching the end of the great room, and the brilliant blackout which saved our lives.

The chandeliers snapped off the ceiling, and the flames of the fires were snuffed out of the torches. This was our cue to run.

It took all our might to open the gate, and needless to say, everyone noticed.

The two guards outside the door locked their javelins to prevent us from escaping but we ducked underneath.

As we ran for our lives, we could hear the sound of guards from all corners picking up the chase.

'Over here,' Josh suddenly motioned us to follow him through the door.

Even today, I'm not quite sure what that room was for. It was a musty, old room, with everything caked in dust. A huge picture lay in the corner, covered with a white tarp. I felt strangely *drawn* toward it even though I had no idea what it was, but I managed to stand my ground.

We waited with baited breath as the guards shouted and yelled, zooming past, convinced they were still chasing us.

We dared not breathe. At the count of fifteen seconds,

Camilla's gaze fell on an old key on the floor. She grabbed it and fit it in the keyhole, and the door locked with a click. She tucked it away safely in her jeans pocket.

Ivan sank to the floor, his back leaning against the wall. 'Wow, just . . . wow.'

'Hey, he told me to tell the truth,' I protested. 'If I didn't . . . well, the outcome wouldn't be any different, but still.'

We waited in silence, wondering what to do next. I looked at the covered picture again. My fingers *itched* to remove the tarp.

'I wonder what that is,' I muttered, but somehow, the others heard it.

'Probably some old portrait of someone?' Josh guessed.

I walked over to it and touched the cover with two fingers. It felt silky, but also cold. I withdrew my hand and saw that dust covered it as well. I wiped it off my fingers with my thumb.

Others had soon caught on to what I was planning to do, and they looked curious about it as well. Only Ivan looked bored. He really did not seem to care less.

With one smooth move, I pulled down the tarp, only for my freaking headache to come back. The same one I got on the day I discovered pixies.

I couldn't get a good look at the portrait, as my vision got blurry and I fell a few steps back.

'Kendra!' Josh and Camilla were at my side at once. Ivan looked at the portrait, frowning.

'Who's Aithne Einar?' he wondered.

My headache worsened. 'Stop . . . please.'

Josh quickly got up and covered the portrait with the tarp again, and the pain subsided.

I took five deep breaths and closed my eyes. Josh gave me water but I couldn't have any.

'Ivan, what was the name you said?' I asked.

'Aithne Einar,' he pronounced it like A-thh-naa *AY*-naar. 'Why?'

'That name is really familiar,' I mumbled. I got up and went straight to the portrait.

Josh knew instantly what I was going to do. 'Kendra, no. Wait- NO!'

It was too late. I pulled down the white sheet so I could get a closer look. My head started throbbing, but it was not as bad as before.

The picture gave me a strong sense of déjà vu. And I guess that would make sense, since the person in the portrait was the same person who was in my Infirmary room on my first day.

The overall impression this fierce-looking woman gave was that she wanted to crawl out of the painting and kill everybody.

Her intense brown eyes stared straight ahead, and her mane of flaming red hair spilled freely across her shoulders. A gold chain hung on her neck and from that, a ring. The ring was studded with a ruby, the same color of Aithne's hair. Her right hand was on her throat, near the necklace in some sort of a style, as if she were posing for the front page of a fashion magazine. Her nose was slightly wrinkled and her lips curled up, showing no doubt that she was angry.

Below the copper frame, were the words in Zanarian Script:
AITHNE EINAR
?-1939

I noticed two obvious things: Aithne was dead, and that no one knew her date of birth.

If that was the case, then no one could know how old she was when she died. But by the looks of her, I *could* tell that she was a full-fledged grown up. Also, for some reason, I found it disturbing that she died during World War II.

'What are you *doing*?'

Knowing that that voice belonged to neither Josh, nor Camilla, nor Ivan, I turned round sharply.

Standing before us was the very person who had tried to kill us, five minutes ago.

The prince didn't attempt to do that now. He simply covered the picture and sighed, looking at us. 'You shouldn't have done that.'

I shrugged. 'Sorry, I just wanted to see what was in there.'

Prince Trevino shook his head. 'Well, Aithne is not much worth seeing.'

'Who *is* she?' Camilla asked, looking slightly disturbed by gazing at Aithne.

'A former comrade,' Trevino said, a bit too quickly. 'But nothing you should bother yourself with. Now what is your plan?'

Josh hesitated. 'Plan?'

'To escape,' the prince prompted.

I frowned. 'Aren't you going to kill us?'

'That is not what *I* want, that is what the *people* want,' he explained.

'But aren't you the prince?' I said. 'You can do whatever you want.'

Trevino sighed. 'If only it were that easy. The last time I passed a judgment which went against the citizens' wishes, it almost triggered a mutiny. Since then, I have been forced to execute every criminal regardless of whether they are guilty or innocent.'

We were silent at that, not knowing what to say.

Ivan broke the silence. 'We don't have a plan as of *yet*, and we were told we couldn't take the help of anyone-'

At this I felt guilty, since I had asked Riley to help out so many times.

'-but I'm sure we can bend that rule a little,' Ivan continued. 'Sire, can you please announce that we have been killed, but we were actually drowned in the river because we left you no choice, and that was why you couldn't show them the bodies?'

Prince Trevino frowned. 'But pixies are not supposed to lie.'

'Well, can't you twist the words around a little bit, to make it technically sound like a truth, but people interpret it in their own way?' Ivan said, impatiently. 'Pixies are good at that.'

The prince looked thoughtful. 'Yes, I suppose I could do that. But how will you sneak off?'

Suddenly I remembered something Griffin told me. These townspeople's minds were like robots, they were quick to believe in anything which opposed their previous beliefs.

'We can manage that,' I assured him.

The prince nodded and teleported away with a flash and without a word. Everyone looked at me with raised eyebrows.

'How can we manage that?' Ivan asked.

'Like this,' I took the key from Camilla, unlocked the door and walked out, cool as a cucumber. But before I could go beyond even half a foot, Ivan pulled me back in.

'Are you out of your mind?' he hissed. 'Do you *want* to get us killed?'

I rubbed my head. 'I think I know what I'm doing. Now, *be quiet* and follow me.'

'Wha-?'

But I didn't hear the rest of what he was going to say, because I was out of the room, with Josh and Camilla following me obediently like little ducklings. The grumpy duckling stayed adamantly in the room for five whole minutes, but then realized he can't be separated from us and rushed to keep up.

'We will die. We will die. We will die,' Ivan muttered as we walked through the suspiciously empty hallway. 'We're gonna die. We're gonna die.'

'I don't know about "we", but *you* definitely will if you don't shut up,' Camilla snapped.

We continued to walk silently (and aimlessly it felt), because none of us had any idea where the entrance was. We were clueless about where we were heading, until we reached the balcony where Trevino was giving a speech.

Camilla and I immediately ducked behind a curtain while Josh and Ivan hid behind another curtain.

'My good people!' Prince Trevino yelled. 'I bring tidings of joy! It is my immense pleasure to announce that the rogues who disrupted our peace have got what they deserved!'

A massive cheer erupted. I figured what the prince said was technically true. We got what we deserved, and that was not death.

'This is a new start for us!' Prince Trevino boomed. 'The reign of fear and terror is over! The worry about who the criminal is going to target next has come to an end! So in honor of that, we will celebrate!'

A bigger cheer went up even before he finished his speech. I wondered how we were going to escape.

I poked my head out of the curtain and saw Ivan peeking out too, looking impatient and annoyed. He gave me a stink eye and popped his head back in the curtain. I did the same, and looked outside the window. We were several floors above and an army of pixies stood before the balcony from where Trevino was still hyping them up by giving details about the celebration.

My eyes suddenly caught something. The tower on which the huge creeper was growing against was the tower we were in. And the top of it was just beside our window.

'Camilla,' I whispered, not tearing my eyes off the plant.

'What?' she whispered back.

I discreetly pointed to the creeper, and she quickly caught up on what I was planning to do.

'Alright, let's tell the boys,' she told me in a low voice.

She peeked out of the curtain and whistled a familiar tune. Sure enough, Josh poked his head out and Camilla beckoned him over. Josh said something to Ivan and both of them darted over to join us behind the curtain. By now, it was like a tiny crowd and I had no doubt that, from outside, we were making it way too obvious.

'What happened?' Josh whispered. 'Have you got a plan?'

'Yeah,' I replied. 'Well, sort of. Do you see that creeper? I'm thinking that if we can tie it to the operating arm of the window, we can climb down to the garden and find our way from there.'

Josh frowned. 'But how do we know that this thing supports our weight? And what if someone sees us?'

'I don't think anyone will see us, but I'm with Josh on the weight thing,' Ivan said.

'We don't know if this is strong enough,' Camilla admitted. 'But we have to try.'

She opened the flap as quietly as possible, pulled down the tip of the plant and tied it to the operating arm of the window. She knotted it five times.

'So, who's gonna go first?' she asked.

'I'll go,' Ivan announced. He carefully climbed onto the ledge and placed his foot on something I couldn't see from where I was standing. And then he slipped.

Chapter 25

I let out a strangled gasp while Josh leaned over the window sill, frantically looking for Ivan.

After a few seconds, a faint shout said, 'It's okay! Just slide down that thing, it's as sturdy as a pole!'

I chewed my lip nervously. 'Who's going next?'

'You,' Camilla promptly replied. 'We can't risk any of the heavier ones, because then it could tear off. Josh and I can come down last, and if this thing breaks off, then at least all of us are safely down.'

'But Ivan just went down, and he's the tallest out of all of us,' I complained. 'I'm pretty sure you guys will be fine.'

'Yes, and so will you,' Cam replied, pushing me to the window sill. 'Now go!'

I flung my legs over the sill and wrapped them around the stalk. I grabbed hold of it with my hand and suddenly, an invisible force (probably Camilla) pushed me off the ledge.

I slid down that thing, breathless and hands burning from the friction between my palms and the creeper. I closed my eyes and suddenly found myself at the bottom. Putting one foot gingerly on the ground, I felt my way around with the other foot.

It was unfortunate that I didn't take my hands off it in time, because barreling down the creeper was Josh. He landed right on top of me.

'Get off me,' I muttered, as I pushed him over to the side. I got up and brushed off the dirt from my clothes, only for Camilla to fall on me.

'Ugh, get off!' I groaned. I threw her over to the side and got up.

'Sorry,' she murmured. 'Where's Ivan?'

'I'm here,' he said.

We looked around. Now all we had to do was find the main gate and sneak off.

Suddenly, a voice from behind us said, 'Who are *you*?'

We turned round sharply and froze in our spots.

It was Countess Arabeth, the woman who had read out my charges, standing with one hand on her hip and a cocked eyebrow. Since she asked us who we are, I assumed that she was convinced that we were dead.

'W-well,' I began. 'We, uh, we were just trying to find our way home, and since we're new around here, we got lost. Can you help us find our way out of here?'

All that was technically true, but the meaning she assumed was different.

The countess sighed and looked at us through her thick-rimmed glasses. 'Trespassing into palace grounds should usually result in imprisonment, but since you are just children and you seem to be telling the truth, I will give you another chance.'

It took me all my willpower not to roll on the floor and laugh. This was the same woman who was in favor of chopping my head off just twenty minutes ago.

The others didn't seem too sure what to make of that but we obediently followed her as she led us out. She reached the gates, before which a bewilderingly vast mob of people were listening intently to Prince Trevino.

I looked up to the balcony and he caught my eye. I mouthed "thank you" to him, to which he nodded.

Countess Arabeth said something to the guard in Zanarian

and, after glancing at us briefly, he opened the gates a fraction and we walked out.

And finally, we were free.

Countess Arabeth bade us goodbye, and we returned it. We dodged the people who stood around until we reached the end of the crowd.

Suddenly, everyone roared in a cheer and confetti started to pour from the skies as cheerful trumpet music began to play. Prince Trevino gave a stylish wave to the crowd as his cape swished when he turned to go back.

'Let's get out of here,' Josh said in a low voice.

Our grim faces were at odds with the jovial atmosphere. We passed a fountain, around which people were dancing, shops were buzzing and there was a general air of celebration.

Suddenly Josh stopped dead in his tracks.

'Hey, what's wrong?' Camilla asked.

'We are *so* stupid,' he declared.

'Oh yeah?' I shifted my weight from one foot to another.

'All this time we could have used teleportation!' he exclaimed.

Ivan rolled his eyes. 'We *can't*. That's the whole reason we're making this trip in the first place.'

'No, not to Zantoris,' Josh replied. 'But to other places, like we could have bailed ourselves out of prison.'

'Huh,' I said, furrowing my eyebrows. 'You know what, you're right. We could have used it this whole time. Shall we try and see if this leads to another place?'

'Sure,' Camilla agreed. No one else seemed to have a problem with it.

'But first, can we go back to our prison cell?' I asked, hesitantly. 'I left my jacket there, and our supplies are there too.'

'Of course,' Josh replied, taking hold of my hand.

'Not,' Ivan muttered. But nevertheless, he joined the link.

I closed my eyes, as our palms grew warmer. This time, instead of dizziness, I got the feeling as if I wanted to throw up, roll on the grass and chase butterflies, all at the same time.

It felt interesting.

'Uh, Kendra?' Josh called. 'You can open your eyes now.'

I did. We were back in our cell. The opposite cages and cells were empty. Looked like everyone except us got executed.

I grabbed my jacket and tied the sleeves at my waist. Hoisting my backpack onto my shoulders, I looked at the others to see if they were ready to go.

That was when I noticed the smell.

I wrinkled my nose slightly.

'Do you guys smell it too?' I asked.

'Smell what?' Camilla said, frowning.

'You know, the burning sage,' I replied, looking around for the source. 'Where is it coming from- aha!'

I spotted a tiny aroma diffuser in the shape of an owl standing in the corner. Now that was *definitely* not there when we were here before.

'You think that's our ticket to wherever we need to go next?' Ivan inquired.

'I don't know,' Camilla bent down and touched it. 'I wonder if – oh yeah, this is definitely taking us somewhere.'

She made the last remark when her finger started fading, like mine and Josh's did when we touched the gold chain.

Soon, nothing was left but dust.

We glanced at each other, and passed around the diffuser, bracing ourselves for the unknown outcomes.

Chapter 26

The unknown outcome was a gorgeous five-star hotel. Not that I was complaining, of course.

Once again, it was left to me to be the first person to gain consciousness. People who were going in and out wore bizarre expressions, seeing four passed out kids in front of the main entrance.

I yawned and took in the whole building. It was a tall building with roughly thirty floors. There were huge windows and the walls were pure white. At the top floor in huge letters were the words NIVARA HOTEL.

I grabbed a catalog from the nearest magazine stand. It went something like: *Pamper yourself with everything YOU deserve, and Nivara is just the place to help you take the first step!*

A couple of sentences down told me that there is a personalized attendant for every room. Or suite, I should say.

The picture of their cheapest room looked like it was made for the President. The picture of the swimming pool was stunning and also featured a hobby room, where one could do a million things at once.

There had to be a catch somewhere. Life would never give us such a luxurious place to stay at without a price.

'Hey.'

I nearly dropped the catalog, only to find out that it was just Josh.

'Oh it's you,' I sighed. 'Are we all gonna wake up in the same order? Like Camilla will wake up next and Ivan will be last?'

'Don't know,' he said as he scooched over beside me. 'So Nivara Hotel, huh? Cool.'

'You've heard of this place?' I asked, as I turned the page over.

'Of course,' he replied, plucking the sheet out of my hands. 'This was where Isla Andilet's sister was murdered.'

'I know that story,' I recalled. 'Priska died during the riots which sparked after Isla decided to become the queen without marrying. At first I thought it was something related to gender discrimination, but it was actually because nobody believed in a ruler who had no one by their side.'

'And this is not the only sacrifice Isla had to make,' Josh went on. 'Her best friend gave up his life so that she could fulfill her ambitions. Her parents' lives were threatened by the riots which started in front of their palace, but the King and Queen refused to "get their daughter in line", as they put it. They were forced into exile and Isla was imprisoned and tortured for five years.'

'Woah,' I whispered, wide-eyed.

'On the bright side, Isla emerged victorious in the end and you know what? She is still alive today.'

'She is?'

'Oh yeah,' he replied. 'She is one of those rare pixies who have managed to live beyond a thousand years. And, boy, she is *old*.'

'How old is she?' I asked.

Josh creased his brows. 'I'm throwing a wild guess here, but probably over five or six million.'

I widened my eyes. I was going to say something but then changed the question for no reason. 'When are the others waking up?'

'Well, Cam woke up after you put ice, so . . .'

I caught up on what he was planning. With identical evil grins decorating our faces, we took a bottle of water and dumped it whole over Camilla, and she woke up with a leap, accidently punching Ivan's face in the process.

Ivan groaned and sat up. He scowled at us.

'Seriously, people, would it kill you to wake me up in a normal way?' he shouted.

'You know what Ivan, you're right,' Camilla said. 'Too bad you're not normal.'

He rolled his eyes. 'Shut up, you hag.'

'*What* did you call me?'

'Guys, cut it out,' Josh broke in.

'Nivara,' Camilla shuddered. 'Why is this place converted to a hotel?'

'Because, stupid,' Ivan replied. 'Zantoris always prefers to bury and forget all the dark parts of their history. That's why they do everything to make this place *not* look like a boarding school.'

Camilla looked like she was about to retort, but I coughed and said, '*Anyway*, let's go inside and see what clues we could get for this challenge.'

We picked ourselves up and shouldered our backpacks. That was when I realized how much stuff I had packed. My shoulders felt like they were on the verge of cracking.

We walked into the lobby.

For someone who was trying to hide the sad history, they sure did an excellent job.

It looked like a regular hotel lobby. Well-carpeted floors, ornate, high chandeliers, and a lady in a uniform behind a front desk. When she saw us, she smiled widely and sprinted over to us.

'Welcome, welcome!' she greeted. 'My, you look tired. Do you want a room for four? That can be arranged. You don't have money? Not a problem! I am more than happy to help out poor, homeless souls! Let me just check you in!'

Saying that she pranced away back to her table and started typing something.

'Uhhh,' I faltered. 'What just happened?'

'I have no clue,' Ivan replied, he and the others looking a little weirded out.

'Do you think this is a trap?' Josh wondered.

'Oh yeah, this is definitely a trap,' Camilla replied.

'*Yet* we are going to go ahead with this?' he said.

'Yep.'

'So we know this is a trap, *yet* we are going to do this?'

'The fact that you're this surprised is getting me a little suspicious,' I said.

We plopped down on the couches and put our bags on the ground. For no particular reason, I fished out my phone. But it was no use, so I swiped left to right on the homescreen.

Just when I looked up, I saw the receptionist coming over.

'Here is your key,' she thrust a card-like thing in Josh's hands. 'And I noticed that something happened to you two' she looked at Cam and Ivan '- so here.'

She gave Camilla a towel to wipe off the water me and Josh had dumped on her, and Ivan an ice pack, to treat the spot he got punched.

'Follow me,' the receptionist instructed.

We went with her to the elevators. She scanned some sort of a card and we went inside. Smooth jazz music erupted when we entered and all the walls of the elevator, even the door, were mirror-backed. It had its typical hotel smell which I could never identify.

Suddenly, a stinging pain went up in my chest. It was as if my heart was literally aching with every beat it took. I dismissed it as something which will come and go, but looking back, I really shouldn't have done that.

The elevator reached the tenth floor with a ding and the doors slid open.

But just when I had taken a few steps out, I stopped short.

'Kendra?' Josh turned around. 'Hey, what's the matter?'

The words couldn't come out of my mouth. Somehow, I don't know how, I knew that the very place I was standing was the same place Priska died

Chapter 27

I desperately wanted to get out of the place, but my feet were rooted to the ground.

'Miss, is everything alright?' the receptionist inquired.

I opened my mouth to say something, but shut it abruptly. I nodded, stuck my hands in my pocket and walked on.

The pain in my chest had spread to my shoulders. I suppressed a wince when the receptionist stopped before a door, on which was carved a beautiful peacock. She turned to us.

'I am *honored* that you chose Nivara Hotel to attend to your every need,' she said. 'If you want anything, feel free to call us *anytime*. Enjoy your stay!'

With that, she headed back toward the elevators. Josh scanned the card on the handle and a small light on it turned green and we went inside.

The air felt chilly, but it looked pretty impressive.

It was like a tiny apartment, complete with a kitchen, a living room, a dining table, two big bedrooms and four bathrooms.

I shook my head. I was more than convinced now that this was a trap. You just don't get things like this for free. Like I always say, some random person giving you things unless you haven't earned them at all is a good reason to be suspicious.

Suddenly, my neck started to hurt. I grunted. Having your chest, shoulders and neck pain at the same time is *not* something you want to experience. I decided to see if anyone had any painkillers.

'Does anyone have any painkillers?' I asked as I dumped my

backpack on a couch.

'I do,' Camilla replied. 'Why?'

'My shoulders and neck are hurting like mad . . . and now so is my stomach.' I clutched my sides as my abdomen started aching. My vision began to blur, and I sat down, hoping to stop the dizziness. A migraine came next. I whimpered in pain.

Cam and Josh looked at me in concern while Ivan wondered, 'Do you think this time your curse is in the form of physical pain?'

'Yeah, sounds about right,' I moaned, clutching my head and leaning on a cushion. 'I don't think painkillers will do anything if my curse has something to do with this.'

Camilla nodded and put the medicine back in her bag. Everyone sat down on one of the couches.

'So, now what?' Josh said.

'Well, first things first,' Cam began. 'I *need* to take a bath, I haven't washed up for two days and I'm feeling really *filthy* right now, and you guys should do the same.'

'Good idea,' Josh agreed. 'Who wants to go first?'

'Me,' she promptly replied. She carried her bag to the bedroom and I heard the sound of gushing water from the tap.

'Lie down for a bit,' Josh suggested.

I removed my shoes and did as he said. I closed my eyes, trying to ignore my aching torso.

Of course, that was the perfect time to have a vision.

I knew the setting was after the tsunami struck Zantoris. I didn't know how *exactly* I knew, but something told me it was. I also knew that I was in the safehouse, the place everyone teleported to in case of an emergency.

The safehouse turned out to be this massive theater-like place with steps carved from the stone and a roaring fire in the middle to keep everyone warm. It was early morning, but the mass hysteria I saw before me downplayed the beauty of the dawn.

It was an overwhelming sight. Hundreds of thousands of pixies were gathered in the humongous colosseum. Pixies rushed around, reporting missing pixies, frantically searching for friends and families in the frenzy. In the corner, I saw Rosa and Norman, having a heated conversation, with lots of head shaking and hand gestures. I went closer.

Norman's eyes looked wild and scared. 'Rosa, I'm not fooling around! Where are Camilla and Kendra?'

'How many times do I have to tell you?' Rosa shot back, her eyes red and puffy. 'I don't know! I teleported *with* them. Camilla and I lent our strength to Kendra because she couldn't teleport, and when I opened my eyes I was the only one standing here.'

Ardella and a man with red hair, probably Alazar, hopped about, handing out blankets and helping small children find their parents.

Suddenly, Favonius jogged up to them. He shook his head and said, 'I couldn't find them *anywhere*. No one has seen them and now, even Josh seems to be missing.'

As they started exclaiming and freaking out, my attention went to a girl standing at the top step, gazing at the horizon. I began to climb up the high steps. This took time since there were roughly sixty steps to get to the top. At one point, I sat down to catch my breath.

Eventually, I *did* get to the top. I could see the entire Land of Zantoris. Mostly I saw a huge canopy of trees, waterfalls and mountains. But all of it was submerged in water. Far off, I saw the sea which was responsible for the tsunami. Its waters had spread to all four corners and as far as I could see, it was only water.

To the side, I saw another stretch of mountains, in which there were the same amphitheaters holding thousands of pixies. Beside me, the girl muttered something under her breath in Zanarian. I tried to get a good look at her face, because the way she spoke and looked reminded me a lot of someone.

This was Ivan's sister.

She had the same emerald eyes, but her hair was pitch black, like her dad. She looked about twenty. Her expression was too calm and composed for someone who had just seen her home get flooded.

Suddenly, I heard footsteps behind me. Both of us turned around, only to come face to face with Atticus and Cordelia.

Their clothes looked rumpled and their eyes, exhausted.

Atticus spoke first. 'We can't find him.'

'We think that maybe he's in the other assemblies,' Cordelia said, frowning towards the other amphitheaters. 'But why would he go there? We have always told him to come to this one, so that the family could be together.'

'I know where Ivan is,' the girl said in a soft, low-pitched voice. 'Good news, I can reach him. Bad news, he's not safe. Neither are Kendra, Josh and Camilla.'

Her parents' expressions held nothing but shock. I myself was a little surprised over how she knew all this.

The girl lifted her eyes to the horizon again. 'I will have to teleport back there before it's too late. Before *they* realize I'm missing.' She gestured to Alazar and Ardella, who were still helping out.

Those were the last words I heard before everything went black. Lightning flashed thrice, seeming almost determined to blind me. My eyes opened and I sat up on the couch with a leap. By now, my entire body was screaming in pain. I squeezed my eyes shut to prevent tears from falling.

My stomach, head, neck, chest, legs you name it, *every* part of my body was in agony like there was no tomorrow.

There was no one in the room. The tap was still running in the bathroom, and a note on the table said in Josh's handwriting:

Gone for a walk. Took Ivan with me. Will be back in ten.

"Riley?"

I'm here.

That was all I needed to hear. I sighed as the throbbing worsened. The smell of burning sage filled my nose. That was when I noticed the aroma diffuser. It was the same owl-shaped thing we saw at the cell.

I stared at it for some time, wondering what my family must be doing. Since Earth, for us, became frozen in time, I guessed that Cole was still staring at the spot we last stood. David would still be doing whatever it is he was doing. Mom, being a lawyer, would likely be presenting a case in court and Dad is either in a Zoom meeting or giving Cottonball her bowl of milk.

'Any better?'

Camilla stood at the doorway of the bedroom, trying to dry her hair against a towel. She had changed into a gray hoodie and blue sweatpants.

I shook my head. My vision was blurry by now. All I could see of Camilla was an unclear silhouette with a strange palette of brown, tan, gray and blue.

'Well, there's hot water and free bath salts in the bathroom,' Cam said. 'Go freshen up. You should probably feel better.'

Needless to say, the bath didn't help at all. By the time I was dressed, the pain had increased to unbearable. I lay down on bed and groaned. I closed my eyes trying to focus on all the happy memories.

The time my cousins threw a surprise party for me on my

twelfth birthday.

The time Mom and Dad agreed that I could keep Cottonball.

The time –

'What the heck is *wrong* with you?! Why can't you just shut your mouth if you don't have anything worth saying!'

'I'll do that once you stop thinking you're so better than everyone else, you *traitor!*'

I sighed and lumbered off to the living room, where the screaming was coming from.

I expected it to be Camilla and Ivan to be at each other's throats, so I was in for a great surprise when I found that it was Josh and Camilla.

I tilted my head in confusion. What were they fighting about? Despite being hugely different from each other, they rarely ever fought.

'Guys, what's all the noise about?' I mumbled.

'Oh nothing, just that I have the misfortune to even be *related* to this scum of a traitor,' Camilla hissed.

'Oh *you're* one to talk!' Josh snapped back angrily. 'Don't think Ivan hasn't told me what you are *actually* here for. I know what you are up to. I know all about the ring and what you want to do with it.'

'What is *with* you two and this ring you talk about?' Cam shouted. 'You're just making up stories to get me into trouble!'

'Okay, guys let's not fight,' I said, as I stepped in between them. I turned to Josh. 'Look, Josh, I think you and Ivan are sort of mistaken with this whole ring thing. Why would -?'

'You're taking *her* side?!' he snarled.

'No, I'm not!' I hastily backed up. 'I'm not taking her –'

'So you're taking *his* side?!' Camilla shrieked.

'I'm not taking *anyone's* side!' I shouted, throwing my hands up in surrender. I meant for it to be loud and authoritative, but it came out more like a froggy croak of despair. Pain arched through my entire body and I fell to the couch. It was all I could do to keep myself from crying and screaming.

'Well, too bad,' Camilla said, crossing her arms. 'You have to choose.'

Both of them stared at me fiercely. I bit my lip to keep myself from wailing. The experience of having to pick between two of your friends *and* your entire freaking body throb and pain at the same time is ...less said the better.

I just didn't understand why they were behaving like this. I had never seen this side of them, and honestly, it made me feel a little frightened. The crazy light in their eyes, the hatred with which they looked at each other made me sick. They didn't even seem to *care* about what state I was in.

It's the voices.

"What voices?"

In some places of Zantoris, which have a less-than-respectable history, the evil souls which died there enter the minds of the living pixies and expose the very thing they don't like about each other. They turn up the hate-o-meter to full and wait for them to tear each other apart.

I looked at their faces again. They didn't drop their fierce gaze for a long time, and till then, Ivan came into view and leaned against the doorway of the door.

"How come this isn't affecting me?"

You stood in the same spot where Priska died. So Priska's spirit was the first to enter your mind. Her mind was a million times purer than the ones who killed her, so I think she is helping you block them.

I bowed my head a little. 'I don't want to be on *anyone's* side.'

'Just what I thought,' Josh spat. 'Who was I kidding? You are never able to make any decision on your own.'

'Excuse me?' I raised my eyebrows, as Riley murmured, *ouch*.

'You heard me,' he blustered. 'This *whole* trip you have always been looking at me or Camilla to do things. Well, I'm sorry, but those days are *over*. I'm done babying you two. It's time that you stop getting all up in our heads and just stand up for yourself.'

I was stunned. Is that what he really thought of me?

Well, it was.

I got up and slowly walked into the other bedroom, locking myself in. I face-planted myself on the bed and took ten deep breaths. Eleven.

I turned over as I heard all three of them screaming at the top of their lungs. I closed my eyes. I knew that the powers for Terrans only came when they turned eighteen, but I wished more than anything that for me, they would come right now. Preferably the power to melt into the ground and disappear.

I drifted off to sleep, welcoming the warm, fuzzy darkness with open arms. It felt like only five minutes had passed when suddenly, someone banged on the door loudly, nearly battering it down.

'Come out,' Ivan barked. 'It's time for dinner.'

'I'm not hungry,' I yelled. 'You guys go ahead without me.'

'Unless I suffer from amnesia, I hardly remember that being a question,' he snapped.

I groaned. 'I said, I'm not hungry!'

He marched away without a word and I closed my eyes again.

Chapter 28

I woke up at around ten in the morning. I had a serious case of pillow hair and a line of drool made its way across my cheek and on the pillow.

I quickly wiped it off with a napkin from the bedside table, and threw my broken hairs in the bin.

I flung my legs over the side of the bed, but when I tried to stand up, I immediately fell down.

The torture wasn't over yet. This time it was even more.

Hobbling miserably to the bathroom, I washed my face and brushed my teeth. Stepping out of the room, I only heard silence. I didn't have the heart to go down for breakfast, but I was also convinced that I would faint if I didn't have something to eat.

I rummaged through the kitchen for a pan and some flour, almond milk and sugar. I didn't find any vanilla essence, but there *was* a jar of cinnamon powder.

Despite my mom's saying that cinnamon goes great with pancakes, for some reason, I had always been averse to cinnamon. It made me feel nauseous. The aroma itself made me jittery.

I ultimately ended up having plain pancakes with Riley talking non-stop in my head to distract me from the pain.

About half an hour later, the front door was flung open, almost taken off of its hinges. Camilla stomped in, went for the room and slammed the door shut.

O . . . *kay.*

Two minutes later, in came Josh and Ivan.

'Great job, dude,' Josh grumbled. 'You broke her.'

'What gave you the impression that I care?' sad Ivan, rolling his eyes.

The bedroom door opened again, and this time, Camilla came outside with her backpack on her shoulders, and the fact that she was heading straight for the front door was not a good sign.

I got up, pushing my chair back with my calves. 'Hold on, where are you going?'

The way they jumped told me that they didn't see me when they entered the room.

'How long have you been there?' Josh asked, frowning.

'That doesn't matter,' I told him, before turning to Camilla. 'Where are you going?'

'Any place which isn't populated by *you* three, that's for certain,' she snapped.

'Come on, this is madness,' I groaned as I caught hold of Camilla's wrist to stop her from leaving. 'Why are you guys acting like this? Whatever you think about each other is not true. Well, technically it is, but it's not . . . listen, you've got to stop listening to those voices.'

They all stared at me.

'What voices?' Camilla scoffed. 'Can no one get around here without thinking of some stupid story? First the ring, and now this.'

'It's *not* a story!' I said. 'Well, mine isn't. You have to –'

'Why am I still here?' Camilla suddenly exclaimed and broke off. She ran towards the elevators, knowing fully well that I was in no condition to run.

I looked at Josh and Ivan. 'You aren't going to go after her?'

'Why?' Ivan scoffed.

'Because she can't split from us!' I yelled, exasperatedly. 'Who knows what danger she might get into. And on top of that, she will be all alone.'

'If she gets in trouble, that was her personal choice,' Ivan said at once. He went to the bedroom and slammed the door shut.

A clear sign of *"Leave me alone"*

I looked at Josh. At that point, I was ready to give up. Accept the fact that this was a failure, I will soon turn into a banshee, Ivan will never get back home, Camilla will either die or survive and Josh will probably just go back to Earth, announcing that we drowned at the beach and died.

But Riley wouldn't let me give up.

Just try, she gently coaxed.

But I no longer had the energy to. I was exhausted at this point. I sighed and sat down on the couch. 'At least tell me what you and Camilla were fighting about.'

Josh sat down opposite me.

'When Ivan and I went for a walk, he . . . uh, told me his whole story. The real reason he detests Terrans. It's not my place to tell what exactly it was, but that changed how I saw him.'

'So when I came back, I started talking to Camilla. Somehow or the other, the topic diverted to Ivan and she said something mean about him. I tried to defend him, saying that maybe we shouldn't judge him without knowing the backstory, but she got annoyed and called me a traitor. And you can guess what happened after that.'

My hand flew to my head, where the headache showed no intention of decreasing. Josh, seeing this, hesitantly gave me a half-filled glass of water from the kitchen.

After I finished it, I asked in a low voice. 'Josh . . . please bring back Camilla. She's your cousin. And you're older than her. Shouldn't you be the one to look out for her?'

Josh scowled. 'First of all, I'm only older by eleven months, and that hardly counts. Second, she *deserves* what she will get. I have always told her to think before she acts or speaks, but no. She *has* to say exactly what's on her mind, without even thinking about how it will affect people. Well, I'm sorry, but you can't always dump the responsibility on me, with the excuse that *I'm* the older one. She has been provided a perfectly functional brain, and the ability to think for herself.'

'Yeah, but everyone gets confused sometimes,' I retorted. 'Don't act like there hasn't been any situation where Cam literally broke the rules to help you. Like the time she ruined her own space project in elementary school, so that you could complete yours and get a perfect score. Or when she punched Sofia Vincent and got suspended when she found her calling you a - you get the point. And I could go on like this all day. Have you seriously forgotten all that?'

That seemed to quieten him.

Feeling a little confident, I went on, 'Please, just go and convince her to return. Being out there alone with no idea what to do is really dangerous. Trust me.'

At the count of 110 seconds, he got up and looked at me. 'I'm doing this *only* for you.'

With that he half-walked half-jogged out of the door.

I was so relieved I wanted to cry. Also because the shrieking pain in my body had doubled.

I curled up in a tiny ball on the couch, whimpering each time a migraine showed its symptoms. I was so desperate now, that I grabbed some painkillers and ate them.

Oddly, that only increased it. I squeezed my eyes shut, and opened them a few minutes later to familiar sounds of bickering.

'*You* are the one who foiled my plan! I had it completely under control!'

'And that is exactly why you're bleeding!'

That made me sit up. Camilla was bleeding? Why?

'Oh, please,' she scoffed. 'You *know* it would have worked. You just don't want to admit it.'

'No, what I *don't* want to admit is that I have such an idiotic pinhead as a cousin,' he snapped back.

I hobbled towards the door and saw the best sight I had seen all day.

Josh and Camilla were walking from the elevators, with Josh lugging along Cam's backpack. Camilla leaned on her cousin as her legs and arms were soaked in thick, dark gore, as she hurled comebacks at Josh's rantings.

Yes, that was the best sight I saw all day.

Cam didn't so much as glance at me as she entered the suite. I guessed she was still under the spell.

'What happened?' I asked.

'She fell into a ditch,' Josh explained, as he made her sit down. 'She tried scrambling out but there was some wire.'

Camilla scowled. Suddenly, the bedroom door clicked open and Ivan stepped out.

He took one look at Camilla and groaned. 'Why is she back? Honestly, if she wants to run far away from us, who are we to interfere?'

'Never thought that this day would come, but I agree with him,' Camilla muttered.

'Zip it, both of you,' Josh demanded, as he wrapped some gauze around her bleeding hand. 'Camilla is staying with us whether she likes it or not. In fact, no one is splitting from this group, until we complete what we came here for.'

Neither of them seemed particularly exhilarated about the arrangement.

'Why can't she just go and disappear once and for all?' Ivan grumbled.

I winced. This guy will regret it if he doesn't start to watch his words.

'No one asked your opinion,' Cam snapped.

'Hey, what did I say?' Josh said. 'Cut it out. If we are going to die, listening to you two fight is not the last thing I want.'

Silence hung in the air. I thought of what Riley said.

The voices expose exactly what you don't like about each other. If that was the case, then this thing with Camilla and Ivan is *not* going to float by easily.

I shook my head. Why were we still there? We need to find a way to the fourth challenge.

Go to the fireplace.

I looked up in surprise.

"Riley?"

Yeah?

"Why should I go to the fireplace?"

*I don't know. Why **should** you go to the fireplace?*

"You are the one who suggested it."

. . . No. I don't think I said anything like that.

"Then who told me to go to the fireplace?"

I don't know.

I leaned my head back and sighed. "I hate Azmaveth."

Oh yeah?

"Of course! We wouldn't be making this trip in the first place if it wasn't for his stupid banshee. If I didn't know any better, he's probably the one who sent the tsunami. Honestly, what is his deal with us?"

I don't know.

"Sometimes I wish that all this was fake. Like, the banshee is fake, there is no curse, and we're not actually in the Borders.'

"*Really. . .*" Riley kept a little too quiet after that.

"Riley?"

Realization hit me as hard as that tsunami which put me in a coma.

"RILEY!"

My heartbeat thundered. "Oh my – are you serious? This all is actually *fake*. Wha –?"

My racing thoughts were interrupted by a frustrated Camilla.

She stomped angrily to the living room. Thankfully, she just huffed and sat down on the couch. Ivan rolled his eyes and sat down as far from her as possible. I quickly sat down, because the dizziness was intensifying now, and the pain was again blurring my eyesight. A ringing sound was in my ears, kind of similar to an audio feedback.

After that, I couldn't remember exactly what happened. My memory became hazy.

All I could recollect was Ivan and Camilla arguing with each other.

I got up, deciding that I couldn't take any more of this antagonism. I walked in front of the blazing furnace, but I slipped on something, and the desperate order from Josh for them to stop fighting was the last thing I heard before I fell into the roaring fire.

And no one noticed.

Chapter 29

Josh

Josh was so done with Camilla and Ivan. He had always prided himself for being patient through the most frustrating times, but these two were really testing his limits since the cavern after the tsunami.

He reached his peak when Camilla called Ivan a "monstrous clown with no hobby whatsoever".

'That's it,' he growled under his breath and stalked over to his cousin.

He pushed Camilla roughly to the couch to sit down, and turned his fiery gaze to Ivan, who wisely gulped and took a seat himself.

'You two have been pushing me since I came to Zantoris and I'm sick of it!' Josh ranted, simultaneously thinking of the worst thing to tell them. 'You know what? We're staying here, until both of you have talked it out and have become friends.'

It really was the worst thing to tell them. Protestations rose at once.

'I am *not*-'

'You can't-'

'This won't happen even in your dreams-'

'What are you even *thinking?*'

He plugged his ears to block the jumbled, disoriented complaints. 'Keep on talking, I'm just going to tune you out.'

He slumped on the couch before realizing something. *Wasn't Kendra just sitting here?*

Josh got up and looked in the bedroom, kitchen, balcony and even the bathrooms. No sign of her.

'Kendra's gone,' he announced to the sulking pair in the living room.

'What do you mean?' Camilla frowned.

'I mean she's gone,' Josh went on, trying to subdue the rising panic in his chest. 'Like, I can't find her anywhere. I've looked everywhere.'

'Did you check the bathrooms?' Camilla asked.

'*Everywhere*, Camilla.'

'She could barely walk,' Ivan said. 'She couldn't have gone far.'

Out of the blue, a buzzing noise entered Josh's head like an annoying fly.

Touch the fire.

He looked around, surprised.

'Do you guys hear it too?' Josh asked in a somewhat shaky voice.

The voice spoke again, *Everyone can hear me, Josh.*

'Who *are* you?' Camilla exclaimed.

It doesn't matter! Now, stop asking questions and touch the fire, if you want to see Kendra again.

'And we should trust you because . . .?' Ivan said.

I'm the one who directed you towards the necklace in the river. Isn't that proof enough?

'No,' Camilla said.

Okay, let me rephrase that, she sounded slightly threatening now. *Do it or Kendra—and you—will die.*

Josh sighed. 'Cam, get the ice pack ready.'

After she did, Josh gingerly brought my finger close to the fire. It already grew pretty hot.

A little closer.

He barely moved it half a millimeter.

Oh, just do it, you big baby!

With that, almost as if his finger had a mind of its own, it lurched forward and implanted his whole hand in the searing furnace.

Josh yelled and withdrew his hand, waving it around, sending sparks everywhere. When he put it still, he looked at it and realized that Kendra was actually transported to another place.

Josh knew because his hand started to fade to ash and crumble apart like brown sugar. If she fell into this fire then it would have done the same to her.

The others rushed forward and promptly touched the fire, as they crumbled to their friend's aid.

||||

Josh was shocked when he saw everything burning. When he regained consciousness, the first thing he noticed was the fire. Smoke engulfed his lungs and he started to cough uncontrollably. Tears sprang to his eyes as he forcefully stopped himself and took several breaths. He noticed Camilla's leg was way too close to the fire so he quickly pulled her away.

'Jo –?' That voice was cut off by coughing and choking.

Josh, knowing that the first two letters belonged to him, turned around and saw Kendra.

'Hey!' Josh rushed over and examined her. 'Are you okay? Are you hurt? Did you get burnt? What happened?'

Kendra wasn't able to answer any of his questions. She kept mumbling something over and over again. Her multi-colored eyes showed nothing but fear and horror.

'Kendra, what are you saying?' Josh asked. The smell of the smoke was unbearable now. 'You're going to have to speak louder.'

It took some time, but he quickly figured out what she was trying to say.

'We need to get out of here,' she whispered, her face red in the light of the fire. 'This is all a trick! I was deceived by –'

She was interrupted by the sound of coughing and choking. And then wheezing.

We turned around and saw Camilla struggling to breathe properly. She looked at us and exclaimed, only to start coughing again. She covered her nose and mouth and lumbered up to us.

'What's happening?' she wheezed.

'I don't know,' Josh weakly croaked. He was having a hard time concentrating on trying to make sense of what Kendra was saying and not fainting from the heat. 'I think we're in the middle of a wildfire. And Kendra's saying something. She says that this is all a trick.'

Camilla frowned and looked at her. 'What do you mean?'

'This is all fake,' she said in a trembling voice. Her skin was bright red. 'We're not actually at the Borders. This is an . . . an illusion. Either this whole time we were in Zantoris or we're actually on Earth.'

Camilla looked like she had been sucker punched in the face. Saying that the two cousins were shocked would be understating things immensely. In fact, they didn't even notice the impending wildfire.

Ivan woke up and that snapped them out of their shock.

Unlike the rest of them, he was quick to react on seeing flames all around him. He covered his nose and mouth with his hand and darted towards us.

'Where to?' his voice came out a little muffled.

Josh looked around. He saw a clearing that was fire-free. 'Come on, this way.'

The group grabbed their magically transported bags and ran into the path. Kendra's physical pain hadn't dissipated in any way, and she was still feeling weak, so they supported her. The fire did not hesitate to chase them and they didn't think twice to run.

'Over here!' Ivan yelled, and directed us toward a cave-like shelter made of stone. A large rolling stone lay beside it, big enough to cover the entire entrance.

They ducked in and Josh helped Camilla and Ivan drag the stone in front of the cave. Josh probably pulled a muscle trying to do that, but they managed to seal the entrance, just when the fire was zeroing in on them.

A deathly silence prevailed. You could only hear everyone panting and breathing . Camilla seemed to be hyperventilating.

It was almost impossible to see anything because it was pitch black. Josh fumbled for his bag and took out his phone. He switched on the torch and propped it against a corner. He spotted a perplexed and apprehensive Ivan. Camilla did the same, and so did Kendra.

Soon enough, there was enough light for them to see each other.

Kendra wasted zero time in asking her question. 'Listen, have you all noticed the weather pattern here? It's *nothing* like Zantoris.'

She was right. Zantoris didn't have cold gloomy weather. Why didn't they notice this before? But there was one place that was like that . . . and Josh knew it spelled trouble.

'Oh no,' Ivan whimpered, widening his eyes. 'Oh no, no, no this *cannot* be happening right now.'

'What?' I asked.

He took a deep breath. 'Good news, we're not on Earth –'

'Oh, thank God,' I heard Kendra whisper.

'–Bad news, we're in Devuniake.'

He said it. The very thing Josh was in denial of, but he said it. They were in Devuniake. *Of course.* That was why anything and everything was working against them. Josh also had this uneasy feeling that they were being watched very closely by someone . . .

'How?' Cam asked.

'Azmaveth, how else?' Kendra fumed, hatred lacing her voice. 'Also . . . Riley.'

We stared at her. 'Who?'

Then her story came pouring out. How an "inside voice" gained her trust and fed her lies about everything. Josh frowned. People posing as inside voices was a very old tactic used for warfare and espionage.

'We are in the Borders alright, just not of Zantoris,' Kendra said, before adding sorrowfully. 'I'm so sorry. It's my fault as well that we're here.'

'It's not,' Ivan said in a low voice, surprising Camilla and Josh. 'Anyone of us could have been deceived. I know I would. It's not your fault, Kendra.'

Kendra didn't look too convinced, but we had moved on to a more pressing topic. 'How did a *pixie* do all this?'

'Only a sprite had the ability to play mind games,' Ivan stated. 'But they're extinct now, so it's impossible.'

Josh's stomach churned and he shared uneasy looks with Camilla.

Meanwhile Kendra tilted her head. 'I forgot to ask earlier, but what are sprites?'

'A sprite, first of all, is not a drink you get at vending machines,' Ivan started. 'They are ethereal entities of nature, who have a different type of control. They control the body and mind, psychological things like memories and dreams, that sort of thing. The rarer ones controlled one of the four elements, fire, water, wind and earth, along with mind influence. But unfortunately, they went extinct a couple hundred years ago. You know that, right?'

'Yes, but how did sprites go extinct?'

'No one knows.'

Suddenly Camilla sprang to her feet and stared at the dark end of the tunnel.

'What was that?' she whispered.

Josh squinted at the darkness. One shadowy figure with a staff moved around. Wait, no, it was two. Hold on, it wasn't two either. Four figures moved at the end and the tallest stepped into the light. Josh's feet stuck to the ground as if coated in super glue.

No one had any trouble guessing who he was. Anyone would recognize that sinister pair of yellow eyes.

Chapter 30

Kendra

It wasn't Azmaveth who surprised me the most. Not even the fact that his wife Mallory was beside him, her position as if she was ready to fight.

No, the thing which shocked me to the core was that Griffin and another girl were standing on either side of Azmaveth. The girl was the same person whom I had seen in my dream. Thana and Griffin had Azmaveth's symbol on their forearms, just as I had on my head.

These events really lowered my trust levels in Riley. She knew this whole time that we were going on a wild goose chase. And I had an idea why she would do that. To be honest, I was now a little scared of her. I had a suspicion that she was *way* more than what she claimed to be.

Griffin stood there and stared at me, poker-faced. I couldn't seem to say a word. The others glared at him. They were suspicious of him from the start so they weren't as shocked as me.

Thana tilted her head and said in an expressionless tone, 'Hello, Kendra.'

The voice was familiar. A second later it hit me.

I surged forward, ready to clobber her, and it took both Camilla and Ivan to hold me back.

The truth was crystal clear now. Riley was actually Thana, who was posing as an inside voice. It was as if a scab had been scratched out, with the cold air coming in contact with my numb skin.

The others seemed to recognize the voice too, and Azmaveth let out a laugh.

'So, I see that is what you have named my daughter,' his English had a foreign accent I couldn't recognize. 'Riley, is it? I am not surprised. It is just like my Thana to claim she has no name. Such an honorable name, and she makes such a fool out of it.'

Azmaveth glanced at his daughter in disgust, before adding with a frown. 'Although, Riley is a good name. I approve.'

I couldn't see properly now and held the wall with one hand for support. It grew unbearably hot because of the fire, but it didn't seem to matter.

'Ah, yes the pain from Nivara,' Azmaveth remembered. He flicked his hands twice and the pain was gone completely, as if it were never there. But that did not change how I felt inside. Confusion, anger, homesickness, devastation, betrayal. Suppressing them and trying to be rational was not an easy task.

Camilla clenched her fists and stepped forward. 'What do you want, Azmaveth?'

Her snarl was so fierce that Griffin, Thana and Mallory shifted uneasily, but Azmaveth was unfazed.

'What do I want?' he mused. 'Well, that is simple. I want her.'

He pointed to me. My heart felt like it stopped beating.

'Come with us, Kendra,' he continued. 'You have no idea who you actually are, *what* you actually are. You don't know the things you are capable of.'

My heartbeat went off again and it seemed to want to make up for the time it stopped beating. What Azmaveth just said echoed in my head again and again.

No idea who I actually am.
No idea what I actually am.

No idea what I am truly capable of.

Apparently, he wasn't done. 'But, if you come with us and follow me, I can help you wield your power. Pledge your life to me, and you will get everything you ever wanted.'

'Tough,' Josh said, stepping forward. 'She's not going anywhere with you.'

'Now, now,' he tutted. 'Let *her* decide. Who are you to plan what she wants to do?'

Josh stepped back and asked, 'Kendra, do you want to go with him?'

'No,' I replied at once.

Azmaveth's smug face was replaced with a frown, like he honestly thought I was going to agree. 'What did you say?'

I looked up, hoping the tiny strip of confidence I had was visible on my face. 'I said no. I'm not going with you.'

His expression soured. 'I see. You have chosen the hard way.'

He sighed exaggeratedly as his wife, daughter and Griffin looked back and forth between me and him, horrified.

'You could have been a potential ally, Kendra Astor. You could have been wise and chosen to fight on the winning side.'

'I don't care,' I replied, my voice getting steadier. 'I'm not fighting on any side. I don't *want* to fight anyone. I don't want you to help me figure out my own power. I'll figure it out on my own. And *you*, sir, are going to keep your big, fat nose out of it.'

His nostrils flared. 'How dare you, you insolent little wretch! Looks like you're in dire need of a lesson in respect!'

He waved his hands and suddenly the body pain returned and it was worse than ever. I clung to the wall again to keep me from falling.

'In fact, if you think you are *so* strong and can handle all your power yourself, then here,' he summoned an orb. The same orb I found with Cole and Sean when they snuck into my school.

He raised it over his head, and I registered a second too late for what he was about to do.

As he threw it at me with full force, it hit my head.

Oddly, it didn't hurt one bit. It felt like having a ball of cotton being thrown at you. But the aftermath wasn't as harmless.

At first, nothing happened. The orb had vanquished into thin air. Suddenly a deep groan went up in the cave. Josh, Ivan and Camilla hastily stepped away from the entrance, keeping a good distance from Azmaveth and his minions.

Something screeched and I turned around towards the sealed entrance.

The big stone was slowly rolling itself away, and the smell of smoke reached my nostrils. I wanted to get away, but my feet refused to move.

Ivan knew why.

'Stop this,' he yelled to Azmaveth. 'Stop hexing her feet!'

Great, this guy is hexing my feet, I said to myself, my thoughts moving sluggishly.

The stone was already halfway open. I turned around my torso to look at my friends. I got the fright of my life when I saw what Azmaveth was doing. His eyes were fixed on my feet and Josh, Camilla and Ivan were being held back by Mallory, Thana and Griffin from helping me.

'Let go of me!' Josh snapped, struggling. Camilla grunted as she tried to break loose from Thana's grip. Ivan did nothing. He just stood there giving me a sad look, as if accepting the inevitable.

And finally, it was completely open. Everything outside was on fire. I struggled to move my feet but they were like stone now. I yelled in frustration, as the wave of heat hit me, and the screaming of my friends became louder. The fire spread inside, and I heard someone shouting, 'NO!'

My skin was blistered and the fire was burning me badly. I screamed as tears sprung to my eyes. I fell on my back. Smoke clouded my lungs and I was fighting a strong urge to drop unconscious. I could still hear the vague voices of Camilla, Josh and Ivan, trying to fight and call to me at the same time.

Suddenly, I heard something crack. Someone shouted in pain as Azmaveth laughed cruelly.

And that was it.

My rage exploded.

I struggled to my feet and thrust out my hands sideways. A new feeling overtook me completely.

The feeling of power. Authority.

They controlled my every move as I mentally commanded the fire to cease.

Nothing happened. But I wasn't going to let that stop me.

I sent the order one more time. "Stop!"

I thought the heat lowered slightly. Taking that as encouragement, I tried one more time.

I summoned every single bit of my willpower, as I screamed, 'STOP!'

And the flames extinguished completely.

Chapter 31

Whatever feeling controlled me, left the second the fire died out. My eyes stung and I could feel my pulse rate increase tenfold. I could move my feet again. I turned around and saw the *entire* wildfire in the forest had dissipated.

My body ached at the effort it took, and also because the pain was back.

Behind me were the unconscious bodies of Josh and Camilla. Azmaveth and his minions were nowhere to be seen, and Ivan stood between the two bodies, all the color drained from his face.

'H-how did you do that?' he whispered, trembling.

'I don't know,' I replied in an equally shaky voice. I slowly walked over to Josh and Camilla. 'Please don't tell me they're –'

'No, they're not dead,' Ivan said. 'They still have their pulses. I checked.'

I leaned against the wall and sank to the floor. 'What happened?'

'I don't know,' he replied. 'It looked like you were being burnt alive for some minutes, and then suddenly, the fire started coming towards you, and you seemed to be *absorbing* all of it. Somehow, in the process, Azmaveth and the others disappeared and Josh and Camilla fain–'

He suddenly jerked his head upright, and stared straight ahead.

'Ivan?' I called, snapping my fingers in front of his face. 'Hey, Ivan?'

He didn't move. I frowned and walked to him. I made a conscious decision not to ask Riley, or Thana, as to what was happening.

Alright, Kendra, think. What could possibly be happening?

I looked at his face again. His unblinking eyes stared straight ahead, and he didn't move a muscle. His face was pale and expressionless. This was very familiar. I think I had seen this when . . . when I had a vision.

I relaxed my shoulders. Ivan was having a vision. I decided that when he came to, I'd ask him if he was willing to tell me.

I looked around and my hands began to tremble as I slowly began to relive each second of the dreadful feeling I had a minute ago. It was interrupted when I heard a groan. I turned to where it came from and saw Camilla slowly getting up. She rubbed her eyes and looked at me. The minute she did that, she freaked out and scrambled as far away from me as possible.

'It's okay!' I told her, holding up my palms. 'I'm not going to hurt you.'

She didn't answer. She just stared at me fearfully and slowly crawled backwards.

I sighed. 'Look, I'm sorry if I scared you or anything, but I promise that I don't know what that was, and I won't do anything like that right now.'

She hesitantly relented and inched closer.

'Do we have any water?' she asked in a faint voice.

I hastily searched the bags and shook my head. We were all out of water.

'Never mind,' she croaked. Then she looked at me. 'Kendra, *what* happened? How are you alive and . . . what's wrong with him?'

She pointed to Ivan.

'I think he's having a vision,' I replied. 'And if you're asking me how I'm alive, honestly, I don't know. Ivan told me that the whole wildfire of the forest started coming to me and I seemed to be *absorbing* all of it.'

'Oh no,' Camilla moaned. 'This is bad. This is really, really bad.'

I took a deep breath. 'Camilla, I want you to give me a *clear* answer to this question. I don't care if you're not supposed to tell me, or it's too dangerous for me to know. I need to know the answer to this: what *exactly* did you find out about me in your conferences with the King and Queen?'

'Are you sure you want to know? Because –'

'Camilla!'

'Fine, fine, I'll tell you,' she sighed. 'But don't say I didn't warn you.'

Before she could continue, I heard a loud knock against the wall and a groan. Pushing away my irritation, I turned to Ivan who was slumped against the wall and clutching his head as he had just banged it against a rock.

'Hey, are you okay?' I asked. 'What happened?'

He ignored my question and picked himself up. 'We need to leave. Now.'

'And go where?' Camilla grunted. 'And how will we take Josh with us?'

'We'll manage,' Ivan snapped, obviously getting annoyed at the questions. 'Just get up and follow me. I know a place where we can stay.'

Soon, we were trudging through the forest, with Camilla lumbering behind a bit with all our backpacks and Ivan and I carrying Josh between us.

'Ivan, where are we going?' I asked several times. 'Is it something to do with the vision you had?'

He glanced back. 'How do you know I had a vision?'

I hefted Josh by the armpits. 'I know how it looks when someone is having a vision. Now where are we going?'

'You'll see,' was all he said.

We continued to walk for a long time. The air still smelt of acrid smoke and the trees were either burnt to a stump, or the branches were bare. We stepped on ash wherever we went and it was, on the whole, a gloomy scene.

After half an hour or so, when I convinced Ivan my legs were going to fall off if we walked any longer, he agreed to take a break.

'Oh, and I almost forgot,' he said. He dug through his pocket and gave me a small flask. 'Drink it.'

'I'm not going to drink it if I don't know what it is and where you got it from,' I said. 'You won't tell us where we're going, at least tell me what this is.'

'Someone gave this to me in my vision,' he explained. 'And before you ask, yes, you can communicate with people in visions. She said that if you drink this, the pain of your curse will be gone.'

'Who was the someone who gave you this?' I asked skeptically.

'Isla.'

Camilla choked on air. 'What?'

'Yep,' Ivan said. 'She told me to keep going north and we will find her house there. She said that she can tell us what to do next.'

'And you believe this lady?' I said in disbelief. I was a little skeptical of dreams and visions now than Riley–Thana told me that visions and dreams can be fake.

'She's *the* most famous queen of Zantoris, why wouldn't I believe her?' he replied. 'Now drink.'

Hesitantly, praying that the thing in the flask isn't actually poison, I took a sip of it.

It tasted like avocados. At once, the pain in my body went away completely, like a load had been taken off my shoulders. I was amazed and relieved.

'Better?' Ivan asked.

I nodded, a smile tugging at my lips. I had almost forgotten what it felt like, having a body which didn't pain at every single joint all day.

'How much farther *is* her house?' Camilla asked.

'Well, she told me to keep going north until we reach a mountain chain,' he replied. 'In the middle of that we should easily find her house.'

'So about all this being fake –' Camilla started.

'No,' Ivan interrupted. 'We will talk about that later, when Josh is here.'

That left us all in silence. I badly wanted to ask Camilla the long-standing question, but I was a little hesitant with Ivan present. He got up after two minutes and said that we had to keep moving.

'We've barely been here for five minutes,' I grumbled, getting up.

'I know, but it's getting dark,' he replied. 'We can't stay in a forest when it's dark.'

We picked up our pace. It was almost night and I thought I heard the sound of wolves howling. But, reminding myself that animals didn't exist here, I kept moving.

We stopped in a clearing with four paths leading to four different ways.

'Which one do we take?' I wondered.

Camilla looked at each of them for a few seconds and pointed to the one to my right. 'That one.'

Ivan cocked an eyebrow. 'How do you know?'

'I just do,' she replied.

'Well, that's reassuring,' he said. 'Forget it. We're not choosing a random one.'

That seemed to ruffle her feathers. 'Well –'

'Stop it!' I snapped. 'Cam, why should we take that one?'

She shrugged. 'It's a gut feeling.'

'Then we'll take that one,' I decided. 'But remember the way. In case it's not, we could come back here.'

So we went to that path. I was seriously tired. My legs were stiff and my arms felt like they were going to fall off from carrying Josh. But I didn't seem to mind as much as I usually would. I still felt free after the pain went away.

I saw a figure darting in the distance. Panicked, at first I thought it was a wolf. Then I remembered that animals don't exist outside Earth.

Then Ivan, who was in front of me, stopped so abruptly that I tripped and poor Josh's head hit the ground.

'What happened?' I asked, picking myself up.

'This is it,' Camilla said.

It was dark by now and all I could see was a light in the distance.

The light blinked a few times before a voice rang out, 'Come quick! It's not safe to be out this late around here!'

We walked over there through what felt like a great field and close up, I saw Isla's face more clearly.

In the golden light of the lamp, I could see that, despite being over five or six million years old, she had no signs of aging. The only difference I could tell between her and other pixies was that her hair was white as snow and her pupils were narrow slits, like a reptile's. This unnerved me a little, but she gently took Josh and our backpacks from us and hustled us inside.

Her living room was warm. It was pretty old-fashioned and was actually a sunken living room.

Isla gently laid Josh on a sofa and turned to us.

'Would you like anything to drink?' she asked.

'Water would be fine,' I said.

She nodded. 'Sit down.'

She scurried off to the kitchen. Camilla sat beside Josh making me and Ivan sit opposite them.

The air smelt of old books and leather and we could hear the banging of pots and pans from the kitchen. I saw a glass cupboard over the furnace where different vials were kept in orderly rows. My eyes traveled down to the crackling fire.

An overwhelming desire to touch it overtook me. I immediately looked away to control it.

Isla came back, balancing four glasses of water on a tray. She gave one to each of us and put the fourth on the table.

Isla sat down on an armchair beside the fire. In the firelight, I realized that minus the white hair and creepy pupils, she looked like one of those women in the oil paintings I found in the Fake Prince's Castle.

'I assume none of you are hurt,' she said.

Camilla shook her head. 'Not us, but my cousin –'

'Ah, yes,' she said, getting up to go to the cupboard of the vials. 'That's easily treatable.'

She took a tiny beaker filled with shimmering purple gel. She rubbed her hands with it and applied some of it on Josh's forehead.

At once, his eyes flew open and he stared at the ceiling, gasping. He groggily got up and looked straight ahead. The first face he saw was mine, and keeping in mind the previous experience which knocked him out in the first place, he was not enthralled.

He, like his cousin, yelled and scrambled as far from me as possible, climbing on to the backrest of the sofa. That led me to wonder whether I actually looked that monstrous, or being dramatic just ran in the family.

It took him a second to realize where he was. 'Where are we?'

We took five minutes to explain everything that happened, and after I apologized a few times, he sank down to the seat, seeming more relaxed.

'Thanks for taking us in,' he told Isla. 'How did you know we were around?'

'It is not the first time Azmaveth has done something like this,' Isla replied. 'He loves to pluck random pixies from Zantoris and put them on Earth. He would give them false memories and when they reach here, they either get killed by the wildfire or he kills them just for entertainment. Everyone you have met, Griffin, Trevino, Serban, they are all on his side and were in on the plan. He even sends his daughter Thana to act as an inside voice and direct them to exactly the place where he wants.'

At this she looked at me.

I buried my face in my hands. 'Look, I am so, *so* sorry and . . . why am I wasting my breath like this? I know what I will say doesn't even cover half of it.'

All of them looked unsure as to what to say.

'It's not your fault,' Ivan said gruffly.

'Any one of us could have gotten fooled. You just happened to be the chosen one,' Josh said.

'Yeah,' Camilla agreed.

I still wasn't too sure. 'But –'

'Now, that's quite enough,' Isla interrupted. 'Your friends have made it quite clear that you are forgiven and that you are not accountable for it. Let's move on. And again, I am assuming none of you are hurt.'

She looked pointedly at Camilla who sighed and rolled up jeans. 'Mallory slashed this with her dagger when I broke free and tried to run to the fire.'

I realized that that was the cracking sound I heard. As I looked at Isla treating the ugly gash, the same anger which motivated me to control the fire started building up in my chest. My hand started to grow suspiciously hot.

'Kendra . . .' I heard Ivan whisper.

I looked at him and he scooched further away, obviously startled by something. He discreetly pointed to my hands with his eyes, and I realized that my fingernails were emitting smoke. I knew that it was soon going to turn into fire if I didn't do something quick.

I took a few calming deep breaths and thought about some rapid good memories. The smoke subsided.

'Oh yes, we need to talk about that,' Isla pursed her lips. 'Would you children mind if I talk to Kendra alone? You can go upstairs and choose which rooms you want.'

There was a little uncertainty in my friends' faces, but nevertheless, they power-walked upstairs to pick the best rooms first.

Once they were out of sight and earshot, Isla looked at me sadly. 'I'm sure there is a lot going through your mind right now.'

'Understatement,' I muttered. 'I don't get it.'

'You can control fire,' she explained. 'Azmaveth threw the orb at you and that made all the wildfire in the forest come to you, like how bees go back to their hive. Your body absorbed all the fire—you're immune to them—and now you can control it with much more ease now that fire is part of you.'

'No, when I said I don't get it,' I said, 'I mean, that I'm a Terran. How can I control fire? I'm not supposed to control any part of nature. I'm supposed to have things like turning invisible or reading someone's mind. And even that is supposed to come when I'm eighteen. And when Azmaveth said that I don't know who I am . . . I have a feeling that he meant it literally, not in the philosophical way you see in movies.'

'Oh, he didn't. He definitely meant it literally. But are you *sure* about what you first said?' The way she said it made me feel uneasy.

'Am I sure about what?' I asked.

'That you're a Terran.'

'O-of course.' But I wasn't confident when I stuttered and my gut started telling me otherwise.

'Kendra, my dear,' Isla said, taking my hands and placing them in hers. 'You are not a pixie.'

My stomach began to churn and a knot in my chest tightened. 'What am I then?'

'A sprite.'

Chapter 32

My head started to spin and I was at a loss for words. 'How . . .?' something about my voice had changed. 'It can't be. It has to be a mistake. They went extinct years ago.'

'That was true,' Isla agreed, the level of calmness in her voice scaring me even more. 'Until now.'

I slowly withdrew my hands from the former queen. 'Is that why I can't teleport?'

'Yes.'

'And which is why my blood is red?'

'Yes.'

'And why I can speak Zanarian?'

'Well, yes,' Isla said. 'Sprites are usually multi-lingual, so it makes sense you can speak the language fluently.'

My mouth fell open. 'Sprites are supposed to be extinct,' I repeated, my voice quavering.

'Yes, but now they're not,' Isla said.

'*How?*'

'I don't know that,' she replied.

'Does . . .' I hesitated. 'Does this mean my mom and dad aren't my real parents? Because I thought that these Supernatural-Born-To-Human-Parents only happen with pixies.'

Isla's expression softened and she wiped a stray tear off my cheek. 'They're still trying to find out, dear.'

'Who's they?'

'I'll tell you later,' she promised. 'The only thing you need to know is that you have to start controlling your power.'

'Why?' I groaned. 'The last thing I want right now is to have anything to do with fire.'

'You have no choice,' Isla said, firmly. 'Kendra, you are one of the rare sprites who had power over an element. Don't take that for granted. You *need* to start summoning and extinguishing it on command, otherwise . . . you just need to. Now go upstairs and wash up for dinner.'

'But –'

'Go.'

I walked to the staircase. My thoughts were crashing into each other in a frenzy. I was so lost that I tripped over the step when I tried to exit the sunken living room. I muttered under my breath and went to the stairs.

I started climbing to reach the top floor. A huge window faced me and the roof was slanted. In front of the window was a sitting area, complete with four beanbags. I dumped my bag on a red one, but that color reminded me too much of fire so I transferred it to a blue one.

Only one room's door was open, so I guessed that that was meant for me. I quickly freshened up and went down. My friends were already there and a delicious aroma wafted from the kitchen. Josh was helping Isla in the kitchen while Ivan and Camilla were already sitting at the table.

'You knew?'

'This whole time,' Camilla replied. 'Alazar and Ardella warned me and Josh not to tell you, but I guess we don't have to worry about that now.'

'Why?' I was getting a little sick of saying that word over and over. 'What would have happened if you just told me about it from the beginning?'

'Honestly, I don't know,' she admitted. 'But that's what the rulers wanted, so you gotta obey it.'

'Did you know?' I said to Ivan. He just shook his head no in response.

Apparently that was it. We sat there in silence, but what was going on in my head was not even close. I still hadn't quite recovered from the fact that I am part of a species which is supposed to be extinct and that I can call upon fire. I didn't understand why I had *that* one of all things. In most of the books and movies I know, the magic always suits the personality.

Fire is just so destructive and unwelcoming. I'm not like that.

'Kendra?' someone called.

I snapped out of my daze and looked at Camilla. 'What?'

She pointed her fork at the plate which came out of nowhere. 'Aren't you going to eat your food?'

I looked down and all around the table which was laid with other foods I didn't recognize. The others were halfway through eating. 'When did all this come?'

'Five minutes ago,' Isla said. 'Now eat before it gets cold.'

I silently ate, while the others snuck concerned glances at me. Just to keep my mind off things, I started ranking all the new dishes on the table in my head.

I went up to my room, determined to get some sleep. But I just couldn't (big surprise). I realized that it was really hot in the room, but since this house was still in the olden times, I had to open the windows as a solution.

I sat on top of the warm blankets, thinking about what Isla had said. I badly wanted to know what was the vision she saw, which made it seem that I needed to learn how to control fire immediately. The silence had my ears catch vague conversation going on downstairs. I slowly moved towards the staircase for a better hearing.

'I don't believe this,' Ivan's voice came, sounding irritated. 'Why won't you just tell her? She deserves to know.'

'I understand what you're saying, young man, I really do,' Isla said, sounding earnest. 'But you do not understand. What I saw will just worry her. I don't want to do that.'

Camilla scoffed. 'Right, like she's totally relaxed right now.'

'Miss Isla, I understand your concern,' Josh piped up. 'I agree, if we tell her, it will just put a heavy burden on her. But we can't hide this forever. If we postpone it to the last minute, then it might be too late. She needs to know.'

'Fine,' she sighed. 'I will tell her tomorrow during breakfast.'

'The whole thing?'

'We'll see.'

After a minute, I heard footsteps pounding on the stairs. I slunk away to my bedroom. I would like to say that I was able to sleep well with the satisfaction of knowing that I'll be given all the information I want.

I really didn't. It was only at five am that I fell asleep. Unfortunately, all of us were supposed to be awake at six.

Breakfast was not-so-surprisingly served late. Isla didn't want any help, probably to stall the revealing of her vision.

She told me to go outside, where everybody else was.

In the light of day, I could see everything clearly now. The sky was tinted its signature gray hue and Isla's humble cottage was ringed by a long stretch of mountains surrounding the area. I was glad to smell something other than smoke. Josh saw me and waved.

I went over there and sat on the damp ground. We said nothing for a while until . . .

'You were listening last night, weren't you?' Camilla said.

I nodded. 'How do you guys know Isla's vision?'

'She told us,' she replied. 'She told us because she thought that we could keep the information safe and tell you when it was absolutely necessary. But we thought it was best if you knew now.'

'What is it then?'

'We can't say. Isla said that she'll tell you.'

This was punctuated by another string of silence.

'Kendra, there's also something else you should know,' Josh said, keeping his eyes to the ground.

My heart sank. 'And that is?'

'Almost a year has passed on Earth.'

A surge of shock overtook me, before it was replaced with frustration. I wanted to scream and uproot every single weed from the ground. Due to some miracle, I was able to hold myself back.

'How do you know?' My voice was so low and controlled that everyone seemed taken aback.

'Um, well, Camilla opened her phone, and the date was still adjusted to Earth's,' Josh explained. 'Today is 25 December.'

Looking at my disgruntled face, he added, 'I know this isn't exactly the best Christmas ever, but we gotta get used to this now, according to Isla.'

'Why?' I asked.

'She'll explain all of it to you at breakfast.'

'On the bright side,' Camilla said. 'Your birthday's coming up. We'll be able to celebrate that.'

I shook my head. 'No, it's not fair that I get to celebrate my birthday and you all miss yours.'

'Hey, it's cool,' Josh smiled.

I clicked my tongue. 'No, it's not cool. How about we smush everyone's birthday on mine? That way we can celebrate all the things we missed out on and even the New Year, while we're at it.'

'Your birthday's on New Year's?' Ivan said. 'That's cool.'

I smiled a bit. 'New Year's *Eve*, actually. I was born at exactly 11:59 p.m.'

He raised his eyebrows.

I laughed at his amazement. 'Yeah, my mom said that the firecrackers erupting outside the window at 12:00 really matched her mood.'

'But how did you cope with being around the loud noise?' Ivan said. 'You know, with a newborn's ears being sensitive and all.'

I explained to him what my mom had said the doctors had done, and that somehow led to another completely random discussion. Ivan seemed to have reverted to the guy who was somewhat friendly to us, and the way we chatted and laughed, you'd think that we didn't have a care in the world.

But Camilla and Ivan consciously ignored each other. Their feud still needed to be settled. I decided to let it go, thinking that they'll soon make up.

Chapter 33

The happy atmosphere was dampened, however, when Isla called us in, announcing that breakfast was ready. I would get the truth that would most probably ruin my life. Not that it was all sunshine and rainbows at the moment.

We ate silently for a blissful two minutes before Camilla cleared her throat. Isla picked her food before starting, 'Kendra, there is something you should know.'

I tried to act surprised. 'What is it?'

She took a bite of her food and chewed for exactly ninety-two seconds. She let a dramatic pause hang before finally speaking.

'I was visited by the current rulers of Zantoris—Alazar and Ardella in a vision. They told me to be prepared to receive you when Azmaveth brought you here. They informed me that they knew your whereabouts ever since the tsunami carried you to Florida, but they did not intervene since they had a separate plan for you.'

'Tell them we decline,' Ivan said quickly. 'You should have done that yesterday, when I told you to.'

'You don't even know what it is,' Isla said. 'Who knows, you might like it.'

'Any "separate plan" a king and queen have for you is always bad,' Ivan retorted.

'Well, it's too late now,' Isla shrugged. 'I already accepted on your part.'

Camilla raised her eyebrows. 'You did *what*?'

'It was not your place to accept for us, Isla,' Josh said, scowling.

'We *told* you we don't want to be in this.'

'Like I said it's too late,' Isla said. 'Alazar and Ardella think that you are now Insiders of Zantorian Defense, Sector 5.'

That made no sense to me, but there was an uproar among my friends.

'Are you kidding me?' Ivan shouted, while Camilla buried her face in her hands. Josh seemed torn between crying, or screaming or both.

'What's Insider of . . . of whatever you just said?' I asked.

'Sector 5 is one of the more dangerous parts of the Zantorian Defense Organization,' Isla explained. 'They have to go to dangerous territory, often fatal for pixies, all to investigate suspicions the government has. They are like the FBI. That is the investigation team on Earth, right?'

I nodded, lost in thought. 'In America, yes.'

'And now, thanks to someone, we're going to be a part of all of that,' Josh scowled at Isla, who ignored him. 'You completely left this part out yesterday!'

'You aren't going to be a *part* of it,' she said. 'You're merely people who know everything about Sector 5 and just help out.'

'Oh my God, we're not even getting paid,' Camilla grumbled.

'Just call Alazar and Ardella, and tell them that we decline,' Ivan told her. 'There is *no way* we are doing thi-'

'Your sister is a part of Sector 5,' Isla interrupted.

Ivan's face went whiter than snow. Camilla looked up. 'Skyla? I thought she was studying to be in the medical profession. Did she lie?'

'N-no,' Ivan whispered. 'Pixies can't lie.'

'What happens if they do?' I asked.

'They get marks on themselves,' Ivan replied. 'Like scars or scratches. Any more than fifteen of them, and they would get a fate so twisted . . .' Ivan's voice trailed off before finishing the last word. 'Is Skyla, you know, -'

'She's okay,' Isla assured. 'She has only lied five times in her life, and she does not seem to plan to continue that act. Your parents have also divided the burden and told everyone at once about the fabrication, so nobody would suspect anything. Members of Sector 5 have to live extremely private lives, you know. They can choose to hide any way they wish, but no unauthorized person should know of their profession.'

'How come I never saw the marks on my parents or Skyla?' Ivan asked.

Isla gave a slightly knowing look. 'Why do you think they prefer wearing full sleeved clothes?'

'We still decline,' Camilla decided. 'Isla, tell Alazar and Ardella *right now* that we aren't going.'

Isla sighed. 'I can't say this enough, but it's too late. It would be incredibly rude and embarrassing for me to tell Ardella and Alazar that you change your mind.'

Camilla opened her mouth, but Isla held up her hand, saying sternly, 'That's enough. You are going. End. Of. Discussion.'

'*Excuse* me, but since when did you get the liberty to force us?' I blustered to the adamant woman. 'I don't care *what* you've accomplished in your life, you can't do that.'

Isla huffed. 'I'm not going to waste my breath on this. Some way or the other, the king and queen are going to make you. I know this is slightly unethical, but trust me when I say that this is for the best. Ardella and Alazar have seen something in you which they think would be of great use for the defense of our country.'

I wondered what they had seen in us. All we did this whole time was panic, run, fight amongst ourselves, panic some more and trust strangers even after being taught our whole lives not to.

Isla read my mind and said, 'Of course, you're not *perfect*. No one is, but all the members of Sector 5 will help you become strong both physically and mentally, which are equally important.'

No one said anything more, which set the conclusion.

We were going to Sector 5.

Chapter 34

'But, of course, that doesn't mean *I* can't help you,' Isla continued, clearing our plates. 'Come into the kitchen, and I'll tell you about a certain natural occurrence you should be aware of.'

We followed her into the kitchen, sharing uneasy glances, and Isla announced that she would be happy to take any questions before she told us.

Camilla asked, 'Exactly, how much time has passed on Earth?'

'Almost a full year,' she replied. 'Today is 25 December.'

'So we've been reported missing?' Josh guessed.

Much to my surprise she said, 'No, you haven't. See, your known ones do not have any knowledge of pixies or anything else related to extra-terrestrial beings. So to them, you were there the whole time. A bit like false memories.'

I felt a twinge of sadness, and I could sense it in Josh and Camilla too. We had missed out on so much and everything our loved ones knew about us would be unreal.

But something crossed Ivan's mind which I didn't think of. 'Kendra . . . your brother. And his friend. *They* know about us. That means . . .'

I turned white, while Isla frowned. 'Well, that complicates things a lot.'

'You think?' Camilla said.

'I-is there any way I could contact him?' I stammered. 'My brother, I mean.'

Isla shook her head. 'No, there isn't.'

I felt like sobbing, when Ivan corrected her, saying, 'Yes, there *is*.'

Everyone looked at him questioningly and Isla demanded, 'How?'

'Don't you remember the legend of the Golden Cave in Ambrosa?' He prompted.

Isla frowned and rinsed the soap off a plate. 'That is a *very* old technique, Ivan. Who says it will work?'

He shrugged. 'No one, but we've got to try.'

We've got to try.

I was on the brink of giving up. These words sounded alien to me now, completely made up.

Isla sighed. 'Okay. Kendra, before you go to bed tonight, come to me.'

When I nodded, she continued, 'And now, this phenomenon...'

Chapter 35

'Have you ever heard of the silver lightning?' she asked. 'Yeah,' everyone except me replied in unison.

'Kendra, the silver lighting is a once in a lifetime phenomenon,' Isla explained. 'It flashes once in a millennia, and it is said that, irrespective of who or what you are, if you look directly into it with naked eyes, it's bad luck. When a silver lightning occurs in Zantoris, it means that something big—and probably life-threatening—will happen. The last time it was spotted in Zantoris, the bloodiest war ever recorded in our history commenced. That was the same war when Ciar conquered several countries of the Zantorian Empire.'

'Yikes,' I muttered. 'Yikes, yikes, yikes.'

'What happened?'

'I, uh, saw a lot of them in the visions I have been having. Also on the first day I came to Zantoris.'

'Why didn't you tell us?' Josh frowned. 'We agreed to not hide any visions we were having.'

'Which concerned the trip,' I corrected. 'These ones were so weird and made so little sense that I thought it was impossible they could be related to this. But all of them ended with a pitch black night sky with a lightning flash flaring thrice.'

'That is what I saw too, at the end of all my dreams,' Camilla murmured, sounding a little guilty.

Isla looked amused. 'How many more secrets are you all keeping from each other?'

'Just get to the point,' Ivan said, sounding mildly irritated.

'This particular lightning has meaning,' Isla said. She dried her hands on a towel and leaned against the kitchen counter. 'Especially since at least two of you have looked at it, something big is definitely coming. When you go to Sector 5, you'll find that the one thing they're working on is the meaning of this silver lightning.'

We were quiet for a while, until Ivan popped the big question, 'How is that supposed to help us?'

'You can get a head start,' Isla suggested. 'They are surely going to tell you to help with the investigation.'

'And how exactly are we going to do that?' Josh enquired. 'We don't have the necessary equipment or books.'

Isla frowned. 'I didn't think of that. That means that's all I can do to help. You're free to go now.'

I was sent outside to practice summoning fire and controlling it on command. Instead, I went to the living room. Camilla was sitting by the fire, looking pensive.

I went and sat beside her. She didn't notice me until I cleared my throat and said, 'How are you doing?'

She shrugged. 'Terrified and mad, but otherwise fine.'

'Honestly, you have to tell me how you are keeping it together,' I told her.

'That's the thing,' she chuckled. 'I'm not. I'm scared out of my mind, Kendra. The only reason I'm not screaming right now is because you guys are coming with me. So if I die in great suffering, it might as well be beside you.'

'Ditto,' Josh agreed, entering, almost tripping on the step before he took a seat opposite me. 'Only we aren't going to die. Hopefully not.'

The uncertainty was visible in his eyes. We all sat there for a while, not saying anything, but feeling a slight glimmer of safety in each other's presence.

After a few minutes, I saw Ivan hovering in the background. 'Um, do you mind if I sit with you?' he asked hesitantly. 'Isla told me to go outside, but I don't want to and there's nothing else I could do so. . .'

My eyes softened. The way he spoke with such timidness and uncertainty made my heart melt.

Josh gestured to an empty sofa with his head. 'Sure.'

So the same silence was carried out, only with another life present. I figured it was a matter of time before Isla kicked us outside, probably with a side lecture on how all this generation wants to do is stay inside.

Camilla apparently had enough of the silence and said, 'So, what do we do now?'

Josh stared at his palms. 'What she said. We need to go, find these people and help them.'

'And we're just supposed to *accept* that?' Camilla exclaimed. 'Without having any say in this matter?'

'She *did* say we have no choice,' Josh argued.

'Doesn't mean we have to just do as she says. Maybe we could just refuse to do it and force her to teleport all of us back home?'

'She's not going to do that,' I said. 'Maybe we should just do as she says. My only doubt is . . . how do we know this isn't another trick?'

'I've been wondering that too,' Ivan said, quietly.

Isla, who had been listening to our conversation suddenly broke in, 'I understand that all of you might have a hard time trusting *anything* after this. And I am not forcing you to believe in all this. But what I *have* to force you to do is to keep traveling until you reach your goal.'

'But why us?' I groaned. 'If you want to find someone to help, why can't you get more reliable people, like *adults*. We're all just twelve.'

She had a sort of a far-off look in her eyes. 'You'll know soon. I don't know myself, but I know that there is a specific reason Alazar and Ardella saw each of you as worthy people. Now, go outside and get some fresh air, and Kendra, remember what I said. Start working on your powers.'

We picked ourselves off the couch and slowly trudged outside. We sat in the same spot as we did in the morning.

I looked at my palms. Keeping in mind what Isla said, I stared intensely at my hands and told them to burst into flames.

Nothing happened.

I closed my eyes. I started thinking of things related to fire.

Fire. Flames. Light. Warm. Hot. Burn. Destroy.

I shook my head. All that was present inside me was the bitterness towards this newfound power of mine. I tried mentally commanding the fire to come, but nothing came except harmless sparks from my fingertips.

'Try again,' Josh said. He and the rest were looking on intently.

I dug my hand in my pockets, suddenly feeling self-conscious. 'Never mind.'

I looked around me. Cool wind gently caressed my skin and the magnificent mountain range seemed to glower down at us puny mortals.

The day went on. I kept trying to summon fire. I went near the fireplace to see if it would work better there, but it didn't. Others watched my pitiful tries. Ivan said that there was one way he could help me, but Isla wouldn't have it. Apparently, I had to "earn it".

At lunch, I was in a really bad mood. I wolfed down everything in two minutes and stomped up to my room without saying a word or acknowledging anyone.

I, frustrated and tired, yelled at my hands to burst into flames.

Suddenly, my palms grew hot. They kept increasing in temperature until my tiny hope was strengthened that this could be it.

But the minute I let go of my anger, the heat subsided and my hands were back to normal temperature.

I screamed and kicked things around.

Looking at my backpack at the other end of the room and my chair lying on its back, I calmed down a little.

I thought for a while.

Back in the cave, what possessed me to control the fire was anger. I thought that Azmaveth had hurt Camilla and I was furious that he had the nerve to do that. So that means that the only way I can summon my power is if I was angry.

What Isla expected me to do was summon and control it irrespective of my mood.

I sighed. Who was I kidding? That's impossible.

My ears picked up sounds of muffled conversation, and from the sound of it, not a friendly one.

Knowing well who it could be, I followed the voices to see what was happening.

It was coming from Camilla's room. As guessed, it was about Ivan. Although, this time, he didn't seem interested in picking a fight.

In fact, both of them were having the most civil conversation in all their five years of knowing each other.

Chapter 36

'I really *am* sorry, Camilla,' Ivan insisted. 'You're not *really* sorry, Ivan,' Camilla said. 'Stop lying to yourself. You only *wish* you were sorry, but you're not. And . . . neither am I, to be honest.'

He sighed. 'Look, I'm not expecting you to forgive me. But we need to try and be more agreeable. We can't have a repeat of what happened at the hotel.'

'I know,' Camilla said, softening her tone slightly. She sighed. 'God I feel so bad. Kendra's an angel, being so nice to us. I know *I* would be mad if someone screamed over my head and just *let* me fall into a fire.'

Ivan agreed. Since there was nothing to fill the conversation but awkward silence, Ivan came out and Camilla shut the door from inside a little too aggressively. He didn't seem that surprised to see me. He just nodded and went outside.

I followed him. 'Hey, everything okay?'

He turned to me with a tired smile. 'You heard the whole thing, what do you think?'

'Don't worry,' I assured him. 'She'll forgive you, eventually.'

'Will she?'

'Okay, fine, she probably won't,' I admitted. 'To be fair, you *were* really mean to us at school.'

'I know,' he said, his head lowered to the ground. It was late afternoon and the gleaming sun made his blond hair sparkle brightly. 'But for what it's worth, I'm sorry. I was a jerk.'

I opened my mouth to say it was okay, but no words came out.

It wasn't the fact that all three of them were screaming over my head when I was in immense pain. It was what they said got to me. I still cared for them all, but it would be a while before I remembered the incident without blood rushing to my cheeks.

'You don't have to say it's okay,' Ivan said, almost as if reading my mind.

'Look, just . . . hang in there,' I said, not knowing what else to say.

'Thanks,' he replied.

I turned on my heel to leave when I thought of asking something. There was a ninety per cent chance Ivan was going to tell me to mind my own business. But my curiosity got the better of me.

'Why did you hate us?'

Ivan looked up, baffled. 'Um, what?'

'Like, was there a, uh, specific reason you didn't like us?' I asked, hastily adding, 'If you don't want to tell me you don't need to. I know it's not because we're Terrans.'

He shrugged. 'It's not. This anti-terran was only a pretense.'

Apparently, that was it. I turned to leave, when he said, 'You know, Kendra, you're lucky to have two friends like Josh and Camilla.'

That made me think. At first, I only considered those two classmates, nothing else. But after all this time, after everything they had done for me, it was tough for me to think of them as anything other than friends.

'Don't take them for granted,' Ivan continued. 'At school . . . you know how it was for me. Everyone wanted to be around me because of my parents. You three are the only ones who have done something for me out of genuine feelings. Even if it was insulting me. Thank you.'

I studied his face. It held a sort of uneasy expression, telling me he wasn't used to doling out apologies or words of gratitude. Especially to his ex-nemesis. But if we were to get through the crazy journey ahead of us, we needed to become respectful acquaintances if not friends. And I was proud of him for having the courage to take the first step, something neither of us did.

I must have been smiling wider than intended because Ivan looked slightly weirded out but smiled back with a closed mouth.

At tea, the first thing Isla asked was, 'Any luck, Kendra?'

I shook my head.

'Well, try to do it quicker,' she told me as gently as possible. 'You will need to resume your journey soon.'

'When, exactly?' Josh inquired.

'I was thinking maybe on New Year's Day?' she suggested.

All of them slowly nodded one after the other.

'Isla can you please help me a *little*?' I pleaded. 'I can't control this fire on my own, I really can't.'

'You can do it,' she assured me.

So helpful. My eye roll indicated I was not going to hesitate to show my irritation.

After tea, I went to my bedroom and continued my attempts which got me nowhere. Now that I had established that it only properly works whenever I'm angry, my brain conveniently refused to get angry.

I couldn't even scream into my pillow. Even if I had the tiniest ounce of frustration, I had to try and channel that to anger and summon fire.

Isla refused to help me, and prevented anyone else from doing so. I was starting to resent her a bit. I didn't care that she was one of the most prominent personalities to break the glass ceiling, this lady was starting to annoy me a *lot*.

Wait...

I closed my eyes and concentrated on the frustration I had towards every single person who had ever irritated me in my life.

It took a lot to convert frustration to anger, but fortunately, a lot of people drove me up the wall.

Isla, Thana, Griffin, Mallory, The Obnoxious Ivan from School, my brothers whenever they were annoying, all the people who were mean to me in my human school, Miss Harold and more.

Slowly, so much exasperation gathered in one place, anger started to build up.

And then the whole room caught fire.

Chapter 37

It happened very slowly at first. My hands felt like they were being pressed against a hot iron, but this time, I made a conscious effort to push aside any sort of hope, excitement and or thought of anything positive.

My hands grew unbearably hot, but it didn't bother me. The heat increased every second, until I sort of zoned out for a minute.

Then I noticed that it wasn't increasing any further. I opened my eyes to see tiny flames dancing on my palms, like a lit gas stove.

I broke out into a huge grin, but I quickly killed it when the fire dwindled a bit. I was about to walk downstairs with my hands alight, when I tripped on my backpack which I had earlier kicked. Unthinkingly, I put my hand on the wall to stop myself from meeting the ground and the curtain caught fire.

I watched, stunned. My hands were still on fire and I told it to stop, desperately, as I watched the other curtain set ablaze. My mood was anything but positive. I considered going to the bathroom and using water, but a chair was in front of the door, and it was on fire. (By now, everything was on fire.)

I did the only sensible thing in my brain. I kicked my backpack out of the room so it wouldn't get burnt and yelled at the top of my voice, 'ISLA! ISLA, COME HERE!'

Doors swung open and I heard someone exclaim, ironically, 'Holy smokes!' at the smoke billowing out of my room. Two people started coughing, and a hazy figure appeared in my doorway, with their nose and mouth covered with a hand.

'Kendra!' Josh called. 'Get out of there!'

'I can't!' I replied. 'My hands are on fire and if I come out, I might set something else up!'

Suddenly a jet of water came my way and it drenched me from top to bottom. The entrance was free, and my hands were out.

Camilla stood there with a garden hose (heaven knows where she got that from) and holding out one hand, she urged, 'Come on!'

Long story short, I emerged from the room, but my tension levels caused fire to rekindle, almost destroying the whole staircase. But Ivan put all of it out and I had to submerge my hands in a bowl of cold water to cool down.

Dinner was awkward. I was prepared for a lecture or scolding, but Isla called it "progress" and didn't even seem to acknowledge that I had destroyed an entire room.

Before I went to sleep (on the couch, that is), I went to her, as instructed in the morning.

I found her brewing some frothy, light orange elixir which smelt of burning cookies.

She looked up gravely as I entered. The only light which came was from the gas stove. Her stark white hair was now red and her slit pupils looked even more unnerving than a snake's.

She took a glass beaker and scooped the liquid from the pot.

'Drink,' she instructed.

'What is this?' I asked.

'Drink,' she repeated.

I took it from her. Despite being on the stove, the liquid was oddly stone cold, and it tasted the same way it smelled.

I drained the glass to its last drop and gave it back to her. 'Now what?'

'Before you close your eyes to go to sleep, say your brother's full name five times,' Isla said. 'And throughout, keep his picture *very* clear in your mind. This drink is powerful, so you will fall asleep the second you close your eyes.'

'And I will see him?' I said, hopefully.

'Yes,' she replied, with a small smile. 'Now, go to sleep. I've already put a pillow and a blanket on the couch.'

I was already jogging to the living room before she could finish. I propped the pillow the way I liked it and threw off the blanket as it was a warm night.

'Cole Astor,' I mumbled under my breath five times. In my head, I pictured his face the best I could remember. His black-as-darkness hair, electric blue eyes and that weird scar on his chin David gave him with a fork when we were kids.

I lay down and closed my eyes. I started feeling drowsier than I actually felt before. I felt like I was drowning in murky waters where neither the surface nor the bottom was visible to me. Like I was being hypnotized.

Then, in the blink of an eye, I found myself in an empty room. No furniture or windows. Everything was white, even the floor. It was so white I wasn't even sure whether I was standing in a room, or in a place of nothingness.

On the far end, I saw a figure lying on the ground. It got up with a jerk, as it took in its surroundings with confusion.

Cole had *definitely* changed since the last I saw him. His hair had grown so long, it reached his collarbone and his dark circles were so deeply accentuated, it creeped me out. When he finally saw me, he just kept staring, which made it even harder.

I decided to start the conversation. 'Hi.'

His face hosted a buffet of emotions. The ones I managed to recognize were shock and disbelief.

'I can't believe it,' he mumbled, his voice sounding far off and muffled.

Eyes red, he scrambled to his feet and ran to me. He stopped at an arm's distance, studying my face cautiously and hesitating to come forward.

I held my hands out in a calming gesture. 'It's me.'

The minute I said that, he tackled me with a hug. 'Oh my God, I can't believe this.'

He sounded more emotional and so *vulnerable* than I had ever heard him. I realized that the last time his guard had been down completely was when we were kids and everything seemed to be perfect.

As for me, it took a lot of strength to not burst into tears. After everything that had happened, and what I had to do now, a hug made me feel like brown sugar in the middle of a tornado.

We pulled away, and then Cole pushed me roughly. 'Do you have *any* idea what you have put me through? These seven months have been literally driving me *insane!* Mom and Dad are considering sending me to a psychiatrist!'

I bit my lip. 'What happened?'

'*You're* asking me that?' he scoffed. 'No. You will answer that first to me.'

'All this is fake. We were never at the Borders of Zantoris. Azmaveth tricked us into coming to the Borders of Devuniake. You know Azmaveth, right? You saw him with the banshee, which by the way . . .'

Cole was a good listener. He heard everything from start to end. I told him about Azmaveth, Thana posing as an inside voice, me being a sprite and having fire powers and what we had to do now.

His face was more focused and calmed down now, despite all the things I told him.

'Now you tell me,' I said. 'What happened at home?'

He took a deep breath and explained. 'When all four of you disappeared, I expected you to come after a second or something, since you said that that would happen. And it did, only . . . it wasn't you who came back. It was like some robots replaced you. They looked exactly like all four of you, but they acted so monotonous and so *automated*, it was scary. Like AI robots replaced you. I knew that this wasn't you at all. No one else batted an eye, except Sean. We avoided those creepy dolls and acted so weird around them, that the others started feeling scared of us.'

Cole sighed as the unpleasant memories came flowing back to him. 'We kept searching for you in the middle of the night and for the rest of our trip. It was not easy. When I got home, Mom and Dad noticed my behavior and started speaking to a psychologist. Couldn't blame them, though. Looking back, we did act really weird. And seven months of living with those talking mannequins and not knowing where you were was just . . . hard.'

I was stunned. 'I'm sorry, I really am.'

He pulled me in for a hug once again, mumbling, 'You're actually here.'

I grinned, sniffling a bit. 'Anyway, how are Mom and Dad doing? And David? And Cottonball?'

'All of them are doing fine,' Cole replied, a soft smile on his face. 'We're actually renovating the attic, you know. Like, it's so big that Mom and Dad decided we can use it as an extra recreational room.'

'Really?' And like that, we launched into a discussion on all the new things which took place on Earth. Apparently, some sort of an epidemic had set off in China. But aside from that, the days looked pretty promising.

Suddenly, my whole vision turned hazy and unfocused. 'Woah, what's happening?'

'I think that means our time is up,' he guessed, his voice sounding downhearted. 'I *will* see you again, right?'

'I don't know,' I said. 'I'll ask Isla for a bottle of this thing I just drank but beyond that . . . ' I trailed off and it was all I could do to keep myself from sobbing.

'Well then, bye. See you soon.' He gave me a quick side hug, before we could fade out completely. 'Stay safe. Please.'

I was only given the chance to smile back, before I woke up, the sun rays from the window casting their light on my face, and soft wind tickling my cheeks. I also found myself on the floor. I figured I must have fallen off in the middle of the night.

At breakfast, my spirits were lifted a lot.

I was even inclined to give my fire thing another try, and yesterday, I had been more than willing to give up.

After breakfast, everyone relaxed outside in our usual spot.

'So, Isla agreed to make us a cake for 31st December,' Camilla told us. 'She just needs to know if there are any allergies among us. And yes, Kendra, I told her about your deal with cinnamon.'

Ivan frowned, but then his brow cleared. 'Oh, yeah. I keep forgetting you're a sprite.'

'What does being a sprite have to do with that?' I asked.

'Sprites are allergic to cinnamon. Which is unfortunate, because plants similar to cinnamon grow like weeds in Zantoris. You will have the same reaction against these plants.'

I wrinkled my nose slightly.

'Anyway, anything else?' Camilla said.

There wasn't, so Camilla rushed inside the house to tell Isla.

When she came back, she had another piece of news. 'Isla wants to take us somewhere after the celebration on New Years' Eve.'

'Where?' I asked.

She shrugged. 'Some old rival of hers. He insists that there is something he has which can help us.'

'Two questions,' Ivan said. 'How does this guy know about us, and what is *he* doing in Devuniake?'

'How am I supposed to know?' Camilla snapped, before relenting a little. 'I don't know. I'll ask Isla.'

I took a deep breath, making sure to inhale every bit of the sweet morning air, and looked up at the sky.

I wasn't sure if it was my imagination or not, but I swear I saw, in the middle of the day, a single strip of bright lighting flashing in the sky thrice.

And I had looked directly into it.

Chapter 38

The day progressed forward. I still wasn't able to accomplish Mission Fire.

I tried repeatedly and failed just as many times. And before I knew it, five days had passed.

I felt disheartened that our day of departure had almost arrived and I had accomplished nothing. Still, I had cake and my birthday to look forward to. Sorry, *our* birthday.

The celebration was pretty low-key. Since it was my real birthday, everyone insisted that I cut the first piece of cake. We stuffed our faces with food, smiling as though we did not have the fate of the world balancing on our heads, while Isla stood in the background with a tight expression.

Eventually, she did break it to us that we needed to go see her old rival, Caelus.

'Already?' I said, as I climbed off the chair and picked up my bag. We had packed everything the day before.

'Yes,' Isla said, firmly. 'Your ride is waiting outside.'

'You mean, you aren't coming with us?'

'No,' she replied. 'I must remain here, in case more unfortunate souls like you four get abducted by Azmaveth. And I also swore to myself that I would *never* see Caelus again as long as I live.'

The fierceness in her voice assured us that it would be pointless to try and convince her otherwise. We walked outside to find the strangest chariot we had ever seen.

It was fully transparent. Wispy mist made its shape and outline, while the two horses looked like they were made of wind, with bolts of lightning arching through their entire body in the most terrifying and dramatic way.

While I was preoccupied with the safety of that thing, Ivan, Josh and Camilla disappeared back into the house to fetch our bags, leaving me with the Elder.

I took a deep breath. 'Isla, can I ask you something?'

'Of course, dear,' she replied.

'Do you know who Aithne Einar is?' I asked. This was the question I had forgotten to ask, and I seized the chance the moment I remembered.

Isla tensed and her eyes turned steely. 'Where did you learn that name?'

'I -'

'Kendra,' Isla grabbed me by the shoulders and looked into my eyes. 'DO NOT enquire about this lady anywhere in Devuniake. Not even to the others. Not until you find Sector 5. Promise me that.'

Startled and dazed, I quickly promised and she let go of me just as the others came back.

Isla turned to all of us and said, 'Well, this is it. Be safe, and do well. Good luck.'

We thanked her and boarded the chariot.

Ivan didn't seem very fazed by the abnormality of the chariot and casually climbed up and sat on the seat. It looked pretty fragile and transparent, but it sounded like he was walking on solid wood. Camilla strode on it confidently and so did Josh.

Trying my best to hide my nervousness, I climbed in and sat beside Ivan.

I hadn't even sat down properly before the vehicle zoomed away at full speed.

I screamed at full volume, and Ivan looked like he wanted to jump off to get away from me. The thing had started without any warning, and I clung to the sides to prevent myself from falling off.

I was left breathless as everything around us zoomed past and I wanted to faint when I realized that we were high up in the sky.

'Calm down,' Josh said, in such a low and soothing voice. My vision cleared and I realized that we were actually moving pretty slowly. It was like looking outside a window on an airplane, only you get a full 360 degree view.

I sat down on my "seat" properly, which felt as good as any chair, and my feet felt as if they were on a glass base.

I looked at my friends. I was expecting amused smirks - it was very much there, but I also saw a twinge of nostalgia.

'I remember the first time I climbed onto these wind chariots,' Josh recalled. 'I screamed even louder than you.'

Ivan chuckled. 'Impossible.'

I tried not to look embarrassed. 'What about you two? How was your first time experiencing these?'

Ivan sighed. 'I hated it. I was never comfortable flying, and I'm still not.'

'Me too,' Camilla said, with a small smile, looking at him. Ivan seemed surprised that Camilla acknowledged his existence after ignoring him for six days, and so were we. But he initiated the conversation with her. 'Really?'

'Yes,' she replied. 'I always got sick in airplanes when I was younger. Especially in turbulence, they were the death of me. Even now, I'm feeling a little dizzy, you know. So, I feel your pain.'

'Great,' Ivan said. 'I mean, not great . . . because you feel dizzy right now, and all. Um, do you want some cinnamon crystals? Isla said that something inside those can help with vertigo and nausea.'

'Sure,' Cam accepted. 'Do you mind, Kendra?'

'Go ahead,' I told her.

I looked down. We were *way* up. We were now above the clouds, which covered every square inch of the sky below us, and the evening sky gave each of them a golden tinge.

I observed the horses, to kill some time. They ran at what seemed like full speed to them, but everything seemed to go past slower than a tortoise. It was a little comical, seeing them flail their hooves like that midair.

After forty-five minutes, we reached. I knew when the whole thing shuddered, giving me a start, as it felt like we were falling, seeing as we were on a see-through vehicle.

The horses—whom I named Timmy and Billy in my head, to keep things simple—slowly descended. Their hooves touched the tip of a cloud, and we slowly dived down.

The clouds were *extremely* thick. We went down, and after five minutes, I realized we were still smothered with the mist-like fluff.

'How much longer?' Josh asked, in a muffled voice.

Timmy neighed which could have been, *'Be patient!'*

I tried to be. But after ten minutes, we still could not see the ground.

'Wait, these are not clouds,' Josh realized. 'It's fog.'

Just then, we could finally see something, but we couldn't catch it. The road was literally two inches below us. Timmy and Billy touched down, and that was when I realized how fast we were actually going.

I was left breathless as we started moving at top speed. Everything was a blur of white and dark green. I looked up and saw the sky was still its depressing gray and most of it was hidden by heavy fog.

Billy neighed something to his friend, and they both slowed down a bit.

I could see everything much more clearly now. We were going

through dense woods, very much like the one we were stuck in during the wildfire. Sharp, cold wind whipped against our faces, and I finally understood why Isla insisted that we wear sweaters and jackets.

It was colder than a winter in Antarctica. Probably, the only reason why we were not dying of frostbite was because we weren't regular humans. Snow lay thick as far as the eye can see and a few feet above the ground was fog. We couldn't see any tree or *anything* unless we were two meters away from it.

It was miserable, yes, but also fascinating. I had always wanted to see snow. A different occasion and slightly less fog, and this would have been *perfect*.

Timmy and Billy hovered above the snow, leading me to believe it must have been pretty deep.

'W-why is it so cold?' Camilla chattered. 'It wasn't like this in Isla's place.'

'That place was in the south,' Josh explained. He was the one who didn't seem to mind it at all. 'I think we've traveled more up north.'

'It's s-so cold,' Ivan said, looking like a blithering mess. His lips were chapped and were turning to a slight blue color. Icicles hung from his hair, which was almost white now.

'Kendra, can you light a fire for us or something?'

I shook my head.

So we spent the rest of the ride freezing our hinges off. Then Billy neighed to us as if to say *we're here*.

I looked ahead to see that we had come to the end of the woods. Leaving the trees and the mist behind, we came face-to-face with lofty, snow-capped mountains, similar to the chain we saw back at the border. But instead of rolling fields, lying at the foot of the range was a calm lake, sporting its beautiful navy waters as it lazily flowed towards east.

Despite the cold and the gray skies, the view was breathtaking.

Suddenly, the ground opened and we tumbled down, screaming. The chariot and horses were nowhere to be seen and we were free-falling to our deaths. The hole above us clammed shut leaving us in darkness.

Then we found ourselves in the middle of a warm cozy living room, with a huge fire. My mind was spinning. I didn't understand how we came here, without even feeling any impact.

I was standing in the middle of the room, perfectly unharmed. Josh and Ivan both plopped down on couches, while Camilla wasn't so lucky. She was lying on her back near the fire. She didn't realize until she noticed her hair was slowly getting singed.

'Gah!' she yelled, as she scrambled back. Then she took in her surroundings. 'Where are we?'

Then out of nowhere, a hearty voice cried out, 'Ah, welcome! I've been expecting you!'

Chapter 39

We turned to see a man, dressed in formal, all-black clothes advancing towards us. His dark eyes glinted, and shining silver hair reached his collarbone. He wore a smile which was lost somewhere between an amused smirk and a goofy grin. He looked so polished and handsome that one could mistake him for a celebrity.

But he reminded me of someone so much that the answer clicked within a second.

'You look like Griffin.'

Why, oh why, did I say that out loud?

But it was true. Minus the friendly expression, he looked painfully like Griffin. The others realized it too and their mouths hung open like goldfish.

Caelus's smile wavered. 'Yes, that would be about right that I do. After all, he is my son.'

'You're Griffin's father?' Josh exclaimed. 'Like –'

'Alright, house rules!' Caelus suddenly interrupted. 'Number one, *no* mention of that scoundrel I am fated to call my son. My life is better off without remembering that traitor. And no shoes inside the house, so if you could remove them and keep them in that corner, that would be great.'

We did as he said, and then sat down on one couch. There were other seats, but we still weren't sure whether Caelus actually disliked Griffin or was just putting up an act. Also, Griffin must be *way* older than we estimated, since he is the son of an Elder.

'Anyway, let's start over,' Caelus smiled. 'I am Caelus,

dominator of the wind. I am sure you guessed that with one look at the chariot. And what are *your* names?'

We introduced ourselves. Caelus explained that when he found out we were there, he wasted no time in contacting Isla and pleading with her to let us meet him.

After all the explanations were done, I asked, 'Sir, what was the thing you wanted to tell us?'

His eyes dropped, looking solemn, as if attending someone's funeral. 'Now, I assume you know that you will be required to travel through Devuniake, right? For that, there will have to be some *major* changes.'

'Um, can you elaborate please?' I asked.

He looked directly at me as if just realizing something. 'You're not a pixie, are you?'

'Is that relevant to my question?'

'Yes.'

'Then you're right. I'm not a pixie.'

He didn't ask me what I was, though. I was secretly relieved, because I was still feeling self-conscious about that.

'All pixies know of Devuniake's oppression of certain classes. Vampires and leprechauns laugh it off as a silly tradition. Dwarves aren't even *aware* of this fact. Neither were sprites, when they were still alive. You're a dwarf, right?'

'Of course.'

'Anyway, all pixies are divided into two classes,' Caelus told us. 'The topmost is "Zantorian" which will be you, Ivan. You can use that to your advantage at all times. Alas, Camilla and Josh, "Terran" is the lowest, so you must be mentally prepared for what you are about to face.'

Camilla and Josh didn't look too pleased. But they nodded understandingly.

'What about me?' I asked.

'You will be a special case,' Caelus told me. 'Your life will be very tough. You will be isolated and forbidden from having any interaction with the outside world.'

I shrugged. 'I think I'll be able to handle that.'

Caelus smirked. 'If you say so. General rule for Terrans, you are to bow or curtsy to any Zantorian you meet. And for all of you, don't talk to each other at all if there are pixies around. Mingling outside your coterie is prohibited. And music and dancing are frowned upon, so avoid doing either if possible.'

I wrinkled my nose as if I smelled something bad. If I couldn't even have music, goodness knows how I will keep my sanity. Ivan crossed his arms and looked disinterested, Camilla was lost in thought while Josh dutifully took down notes in the notebook he borrowed from me.

'Now we come to dressing habits,' Caelus said. 'Girls, go into that room and you will find my wife. She will explain everything to you. Boys, follow me.'

Caelus' wife, Fairleigh, was a sweet-natured pixie who seemed to be quite astonished to learn that I was a dwarf.

'You don't look like one,' she remarked, folding some clothes. 'No offense, though. I certainly have no right to judge.'

She then opened a suitcase from under the bed, and out tumbled a cascade of clothes, limited to only colors of black, gray and brown.

'In Devuniake, we wear dark colors so we remain warm at all times,' Fairleigh explained. 'Quick, try these on. They should be the right size for you.'

She handed me a bundle of clothes and turned to Camilla. 'I might need to look somewhere else for you, you're rather tall for your age.'

Fairleigh scampered out of the room, and I ducked behind an opaque screen. When I came out, no one was in the room, leaving me to gaze at myself in the mirror.

I had donned a metallic blue silk shirt and a black skirt which made me look older than I actually was. I had thin stockings and black sandals to complete the look. I let down my dark tresses, something which I rarely did, and raised my eyebrows at how good I looked.

'Admiring yourself?' Camilla called, as she walked in, wearing similar clothes.

I smiled. 'I can get used to these clothes.'

'Yes you can,' Camilla replied. 'But as you get older, you will get more uncomfortable clothes. We will then transition to gowns and hooped skirts and darker clothing—the whole Victorian package.'

I bit my lip and sat on the bed. Sighing, I said, 'I still can't believe we're doing this.'

'Neither can I,' Camilla said, taking her place next to me. She didn't seem to find anything else to say. Fairleigh popped her head in the room and told us that we had to eat.

None of us could eat much, but Caelus insisted that we have some light snacks. There were cinnamon crystals and lemon shards. Naturally, I went for the second one, but Caelus stopped me at once.

'Lemon is lethal for dwarves,' he explained. 'I apologize for bringing them out in the first place. I should not have done that. Have the Crystals, instead.'

Lesson for today: Lying is *always* going to backfire.

Trying to keep a straight face and with horrified pairs of eyes ogling, I choked it down.

Nothing happened in front of the Elders, but that night, I threw up a lot. My friends were up all night, as they hopped about, helping me clean up, or holding my hair. Camilla's room was farthest away, so she didn't hear anything, but at one point she came into my room to see if I was doing okay after the whole cinnamon fiasco.

I seemed to be fine after some time, but they stayed with me to make sure. I curled up on the bed, Camilla found solace in the open closet, Josh and Ivan were on the floor leaning back to the walls.

'I've been thinking,' I started. Everyone looked up. 'All of you saw that sphere-like thing Azmaveth threw at me, right?'

Josh nodded. 'It seems that that contained your powers or something. And after he threw it at you, all the fires wanted to come towards you, like moths to a flame.'

I hesitated. 'Yeah well . . . I never told this to anyone, but on the day I came to Zantoris, before hearing the explosions and all, I saw Cole and Sean at Aheart.'

Camilla frowned. 'What were *they* doing there?'

'They had the sphere with them,' I recalled. 'They looked as if they were trying to hide it, and when I walked into them, they seemed very protective of it. Do you think that is the same one Azmaveth had?'

'It has to be,' Camilla said. 'That sphere contained your power, so it has to be the same one. But why did Cole and Sean have it? Did they even know what it was? Kendra, did you ask Cole when you saw him in your dream?'

I bit my lip. 'I forgot.'

'Never mind, ask him when you see him the next time,' Josh sighed.

Everyone stayed awake till five in the morning. After that we all fell asleep for two hours. Caelus and Fairleigh were puzzled to find everyone having a sleepover at my room but didn't question us.

'The chariot will be coming in a few minutes,' Fairleigh informed us. 'Till then, eat some breakfast.'

We munched on food half-heartedly, as Caelus told us some last minute rules: Do not speak in English or any language which belonged to Earth, keep the bags and any human stuff hidden and don't talk to sketchy people.

We were all dressed in traditional Devun attire. The boys wore black tweed pants, tucking in their white shirts, over which they wore a tie and a black waistcoat. A dark coat and black loafers completed their look. Josh looked polished and immaculate, like a model student, eager to learn. Ivan managed to keep his superior air, but he had refused to wear a tie and the waistcoat, and kept his top button open.

Either way, Camilla and I cracked up when we saw them - and vice versa.

Caelus nodded. 'Well, it looks like you have to go now. The chariot waiting outside.'

We put on our jackets and sweaters over the native clothes, and pulled on our shoes. When we got outside, I saw that it was still dark as midnight, despite it being seven in the morning.

We took our seats on the chariot and there were two lanterns set ablaze by fire for us to see.

'Well, this is it,' Caelus said. 'Good luck, you four. Stay safe, and return victorious.'

We said our goodbyes and the chariot took off. Timmy and Billy took to the skies, and rose above the clouds.

It was still very cold, and everyone was shivering so badly, I felt guilty that I couldn't provide the fire.

Ivan studied my face for a while, before saying, 'You know, Isla isn't here. So maybe I could help you with your powers.'

My hopes were lifted. 'Really?'

'Yes,' he replied. 'Water and fire are two completely different things, no questions asked. But my coach had some hand and mind exercises which he says helps with the technique.'

'Oh,' I lowered my head. 'Actually, mine has nothing to do with technique. See, I can only summon fire when I'm angry.'

Ivan frowned. 'I see.'

We were quiet for a while, before he asked me a question. 'Kendra, what do you feel about your powers?'

I thought for a while. 'To be honest, I kind of hate them. Ever since I got them.'

'Why?'

'What is there to like about fire?' I exclaimed. 'It hurts so many people.'

'Maybe you need to concentrate on the good side,' Ivan suggested. 'Fire also gives light, like it is giving us right now. It also provides some warmth in the cold, like right now. Just focus on the purpose. Here.'

He snuffed out the flames from one lantern. 'Light this back up. Concentrate on how you're feeling about lighting it.'

I took the lantern in my arms. I opened the top, and placed my hand on the coal inside. It was hot but all I was concentrating on was lighting it. I didn't feel angry, just . . . calm.

I tried multiplying it. I relaxed my tense shoulders and exhaled, imagining all my fear and confusion inside me escaping through my nostrils.

My hand grew warm, and I didn't stop mastering my inner peace. The smell of smoke reached my nose, and I heard Ivan whisper encouragingly, 'Keep going. You're doing great.'

My fingernails started emitting smoke in slightly bigger amounts, and I decided to close my eyes and think of a calming memory.

I was back home.

A normal Saturday morning, where I was staring at the ceiling, feeling all snuggly and comfortable under the blankets.

Cottonball meows and walks up to me, and rests on my stomach. Her way of saying *Good Morning*. From downstairs, I smell fried eggs and waffles, while David and Cole bicker over any random petty thing they happen to disagree on. Mom is on a call from work, and Dad complains that the boys are too noisy as he vacuums. Sleep washes over me again as I doze off contentedly.

The sound of a snap opened my eyes to my present reality.

The coal was set ablaze, with the brightest fire we had ever seen.

www.ingramcontent.com/pod-product-compliance
Lightning Source LLC
LaVergne TN
LVHW061609070526
838199LV00078B/7224